"So our marriage wouldn't be permanent then?"

"No."

This was beginning to sound much more favourable. "And we wouldn't be sleeping together?"

The corner of Alex's lip curved up, yet his eyes darkened. "This isn't make-believe, Olivia. It would be a real marriage."

Her stomach flipped at the thought of them in bed together.

Making love.

"I swore I'd never marry again."

His eyes took on a softer look. "This wouldn't be for love, Olivia. You wouldn't have to worry about me hurting you."

She wasn't so sure about that.

The Throw-Away Bride
by Ann Major

Leo's arm came around her possessively, and he grinned, showing off his perfect, white teeth.

"Good. You're still here," he said.

"It's my bed. My house," Abby said. "Where would I go?"

"So – are you going to marry me?"

"There are a million logical reasons why that's a very bad idea."

"You're pregnant. If we're unhappy, we'll get a divorce. Big deal."

Big deal? To Abby, it was a *very* big deal.

Available in November 2009 from Mills & Boon® Desire™

THE CEO TAKES A WIFE

BY
MAXINE SULLIVAN

THE THROW-AWAY BRIDE

BY
ANN MAJOR

🌀™ MILLS & BOON®

First published in Great Britain 2009
Harlequin Mills & Boon Limited,
Eton House, 18-24 Paradise Road, Richmond, Surrey TW9 1SR

The publisher acknowledges the copyright holders of the
individual works as follows:

The CEO Takes a Wife © Maxine Sullivan 2008
The Throw-Away Bride © Ann Major 2008

ISBN: 978 0 263 87118 0

51-1109

Harlequin Mills & Boon policy is to use papers that are natural, renewable and recyclable products and made from wood grown in sustainable forests. The logging and manufacturing processes conform to the legal environmental regulations of the country of origin.

Printed and bound in Spain
by Litografia Rosés S.A., Barcelona

THE CEO TAKES A WIFE

BY
MAXINE SULLIVAN

Maxine Sullivan credits her mother for her lifelong love of romance novels, so it was a natural extension for Maxine to want to write her own romances. She thinks there's nothing better than being a writer and is thrilled to be one of the few Australians to write for the Desire™ line.

Maxine lives in Melbourne, Australia, but over the years has travelled to New Zealand, the UK and the USA. In her own backyard, her husband's job ensured they saw the diversity of the countryside, from the tropics to the outback, country towns to the cities. She is married to Geoff, who has proven his hero status many times over the years. They have two handsome sons and an assortment of much-loved, previously abandoned animals.

Maxine would love to hear from you and can be contacted through her website at http://www.maxinesullivan.com.

Dear Reader,

I must admit that when I read about those high-profile couples who marry, I sometimes wonder if it's for love or convenience. And if it's for convenience, what goes on behind the scenes? Why do you marry someone you don't know or don't love? *How* do you? You'd surely have to feel some sort of attraction for the other person to make it a real marriage.

This is the case between Olivia Cannington and Alex Valente, the heroine and hero in my book. Born with silver spoons in their mouths, they have the responsibility of having to marry for a year for reasons other than themselves. Neither has any intention of getting emotionally involved, but in the end it's their attraction for each other that sabotages them, and they eventually find their sacrifice hasn't been the sacrifice they thought it was. They fall in love.

Sometimes it takes a while for some people to realise it, but whether rich or poor, if you have true love you have it all.

Happy reading!

Maxine

To all my workmates at my day job.
Thanks for all your support and enthusiasm.

One

"I presume you asked me in here for a reason, Dad?" Alex Valente said, his tone cool and collected as he sat in front of his father's desk in the opulent tenth-floor office overlooking Sydney Harbour.

There was a moment's pause. "Yes, there's a reason," Cesare Valente replied, leaning back in his leather chair.

Alex ignored the mixture of pride and regret in his father's eyes. They'd never been close, despite working together all these years. Cesare Valente had come to Australia as a child and was the founder of

the House of Valente. Alex was its CEO. The two of
them had taken the Australian perfume dynasty and
turned it into a national success.

But it wasn't enough. It had never been enough—
for either of them. There were more successes out there,
more opportunities to seize, including their upcoming
launch in the States of their newest and finest perfume
yet—Valente's Woman. Alex knew his father admired
that same drive to conquer in himself. It was part of the
reason he'd been tasked with the USA launch.

"And that is…" Alex prompted, leaving the
sentence hanging.

"I've come to a decision…" Cesare's pause was
surely for effect. "You're thirty-five years old. It's
time you married and produced an heir."

Alex felt a brief moment of shock, then his eyes
narrowed and his lips twisted. "I'll take your wishes
into consideration *if* I ever decide to marry."

"You're not taking me seriously, *figlio mio,*"
Cesare said, lapsing into Italian to say *son of mine.*

Alex made a sound of derision. "There's a reason
for that." He was a Valente, and Valentes didn't like
being ordered about. His father knew that.

"I'm very serious about this," Cesare said quietly
and firmly. "I'm getting older and I've recently had
a…health scare."

Something jolted inside Alex's chest. "You didn't tell me about that."

"No, I didn't." Just for a moment Cesare's eyes clouded over, then cleared. "I was having chest pains. They thought it was a heart attack, but I'm thankful it wasn't. *This* time. It's stress. I have to slow down, but I'm not going to hand over the reins of the business to you until I see you married with an heir on the way."

Alex shot him a withering look. "You're not asking much."

"I'm not asking, Alex. I'm telling. You've got six months in which to find yourself a wife and start a family or…"

Alex's brow winged upward in challenge. "Or?"

"I sell the House of Valente to one of our competitors and give the money to charity. And I promise neither you nor your two brothers will see a cent."

Alex's jaw clenched. "I could always declare you insane."

Cesare gave a small smile. "You could *try* but I don't think any judge will give you power of attorney. I'm as sane as you are and I intend to do what I like with my own company."

Alex swore then pushed to his feet. "I don't need

your money, Dad, nor do I need to be CEO. I'll survive without you."

"But will your brothers?"

Alex's shoulders stiffened. He took his status as eldest brother seriously. His own mother had died when he was three years old and Cesare had married again soon afterward. That marriage had lasted all of a year, just enough time for Nick to be born. Then his father had married Isabel, and had stayed married ever since. Matt at least had both his parents around.

"If you don't do as I ask, then I'll sell tomorrow. You and your brothers will be out on your own."

Alex glared down at him. "We're grown men. We'll survive."

"Oh, I have no doubt about that. But do you think it's fair for them to lose their inheritance like this?"

"Don't manipulate me," Alex growled.

"This isn't manipulation. It's a guarantee," Cesare said with quiet emphasis. "Alex, this is too important to me. It's my legacy to my sons. One day you'll realize this when you have a child of your own."

"Go to hell." Alex strode to the door and closed it behind him with controlled anger. He always wore his detachment like a second skin, but right now he was in danger of losing even that.

One week later

"And now," a woman's well-spoken voice said, "here is Anastasia stepping out for an evening of glamour in a beautiful gown that is sure to make a statement. The plunging neckline…"

Alex heard the female voice through the microphone as he strode along the corridor toward the hotel ballroom. Her tone intrigued him even before he saw the woman, her accent Australian with an American twist, its slightly husky quality entrancing him beyond the beat of the music.

"…and doesn't this set a new style? The classic black is…"

His steps lengthened. He had to see this woman. Had to know if she looked as good as she sounded. He pushed open the door and stepped inside the room, the muted lighting allowing him full view down the well-lit center aisle to the tall, graceful blonde at the podium.

She'd been worth the rush.

Definitely.

Strikingly beautiful, with golden-blond hair pulled back in a sophisticated chignon, she carried an elegance that was as natural as breathing.

There was a round of applause as the model on the runway walked off, and he noticed his stepmother wave to him from the front row. He realized she must have been keeping an eye out for him. He hadn't exactly been enamored of attending a fashion show, but his father had cried off sick at the last minute and Isabel had been persuasive.

He was never more glad he'd agreed to come, he mused, making his way around the edge of the room toward Isabel…toward this beauty on the stage who could have been one of the models herself.

"For our next outfit, Crystal is wearing a jewel of a gown that…"

Just as he reached his stepmother, he looked up at the podium and his eyes locked with those of the blonde. It was a moment out of time.

"Er…" She faltered just that little bit. "…this accents her perfect figure…"

Alex watched her recover and carry on with the commentary, vaguely aware of Isabel's whisper chiding him for being late.

The blonde glanced at him again and he caught a flicker of disconcertion in her eyes before she angled her chin and looked away to continue talking.

But it was too late.

He'd seen her reaction. She'd definitely felt something between them, and if that was panic he'd just seen on her face, then she was panicked by her own emotions.

Good. He wanted this woman, and what he wanted he usually got. Until now he'd been a man who only slept with a woman after he'd gotten to know her, but he'd rethink that tonight. The draw of this woman was too strong.

"And now, one of the highlights of the Cannington Collection is this delightful garment showcasing…"

Alex frowned when he heard the Cannington name but before he could think further, Isabel leaned toward him and whispered, "She's beautiful, isn't she?"

He pretended not to know who she was talking about. "The model?"

Isabel tutted softly. "No, the presenter. She's a famous fashion designer in the States and this is her fashion show. She grew up here and now she's come back to live in Australia. Her mother's Felicia Cannington, you know. The movie star."

Alex let that sink in. Most people knew Felicia Cannington was an Australian who'd made it big in Hollywood over three decades ago. She was a much-loved favorite of the big screen.

He glanced again at the beautiful blonde. "And that's her daughter up there?"

Isabel nodded. "Yes, that's Olivia Cannington."

His business brain kicked into gear and he knew he'd just been handed the perfect solution to his problems. For the last week he'd been thinking about nothing but his father's ultimatum. He'd hoped by now Cesare would admit he'd been totally unreasonable because of his health scare, but the wily old bastard hadn't backed down. When Cesare Valente wanted something he usually got it.

Not that he'd said anything to his father about it. At first he'd been determined not to give in to Cesare's demand and planned on ignoring it as long as he could.

But the guilt had been getting to him. How could he let the family business be handed over to a bunch of strangers? More importantly, how could he let Nick and Matt lose their rightful inheritance?

Now he didn't have to, he decided. He'd grant part of his father's wish *only* because he'd found a suitable woman.

As for producing a child… Cesare could whistle in the dark over that. His father would be retiring within the next couple of months anyway and wouldn't be able to maintain his control over the business. No, a child wouldn't be a part of the bargain.

It would be just him and the blonde. If she was as captivating as she looked, and if she was available, then he'd found the woman to marry.

Olivia Cannington.

* * *

"Good evening, Mr. Valente," Olivia replied with as much cool politeness as she could. She'd recognized Alex Valente's name as soon as her business partner had introduced them. The House of Valente was well-known throughout Australia for its excellence in perfume design and production.

"Alex," he invited, his slate-gray eyes sweeping over her with a burning intensity that made her heart bump against her ribs.

Holding on to her composure, she inclined her head. "Alex." She ignored the meaningful look Lianne gave her before the other woman excused herself and took off across the room to see to their other guests.

Instead, she let a moment pass as she took a sip of her champagne and tried not to show how much this handsome man affected her.

Darn him. The party after the show was usually a lighthearted affair, with everyone relaxed and ready to enjoy themselves after all the hard work they'd put in to make the collection a success.

But Alex Valente had spoiled the whole thing for her tonight. From the moment he'd stepped into the ballroom he'd caught her attention. It was an attention she didn't welcome or need, but he'd been staring at her so hard during the show she'd lost her focus. It had unnerved her, making her stumble over her words. That had never happened to her before.

So she wasn't particularly happy about meeting him now. "Did you enjoy the show?" For all his sophistication, she suspected he was more at home working in his office than attending a fashion show.

"It was…fascinating."

"Do you often go to fashion shows?" she asked, making small talk, passing the time, hearing the chatter going on around them, the music getting louder.

A wry smile entered his eyes. "No. I only came to accompany my stepmother."

Olivia remembered seeing the elegant woman sitting next to him. "I see. Did she stay for the party? Is she here now?" Perhaps he'd go find her and not come back. She silently sighed. That was about as likely as the moon turning to cheese.

"No, my father wasn't feeling well tonight so she decided to go home."

"I hope he's okay."

Alex's mouth tightened. "He is."

She considered his words. "You sound certain about that."

"My father's very good at getting his own way," he said brusquely.

"I have a mother who's the same," she joked in a

moment of empathy, then regretted allowing any correlation between her and Alex.

He didn't smile.

There was a tiny pause. Then, "God, you're beautiful."

She blinked, hardening her heart as it bounced inside her chest. "Oh, puh-lease."

His jaw clenched. "Don't prejudge me, Olivia. I don't need to flatter to get my way. If I like something, I say so. If I want something, I ask."

"Or take," she said, her lip curling, instinctively knowing what sort of man he was. Yes, he was a taker. One who'd take a woman to the heights, then down to the very depths of her being.

"See," he mocked. "You know me already."

She drew her shoulders back. "Mr. Valente—"

"Alex."

"Alex, look. I don't mean to be rude, but—"

"I have a proposition for you."

Shocked, she still managed to shoot him a withering look. "That figures."

An icy glint appeared in his eyes. "That's quite an attitude you've got there."

She suddenly felt defensive. "It's justified."

A moment crept by. "So every person you meet is judged by one criterion, are they?"

His question made her angry. He must be intelligent enough to know that all her life people had used her to get to her mother. And now they used her in her own right. Not that it got them very far these days.

Not after Eric.

What a fool she'd been for marrying such a liar and a cheat. Five years ago she'd been twenty-two and unprepared for his lesson in deception. Little had she known he'd wanted her for her money, until he'd found another woman with even more money and had run off with her.

Her chin lifted. "Mr. Valente, if all this is leading somewhere, please tell me where."

"Dinner."

Her heart thudded once. "What about it?"

"Have dinner with me tomorrow night."

Her heart thudded twice. "I can't."

He met her gaze for long seconds. "You have another engagement?"

"No."

There was a slight lifting of his brow. "Then why not have dinner with me?"

She hated this interrogation. "How do you know I'm not involved with someone?"

"If you are, I feel sorry for him. I wouldn't like it

if *my* woman was attracted to another man the way you are to me."

She sucked in a lungful of air. "Don't be ridiculous. I'm not attracted to you."

He raised his brows.

"Look, I'm sure any other woman would be only too glad to go out with you." She drew herself up taller. "Please excuse me, now." With that, she walked away with her back straight and her head held high and let herself be swallowed up in the crowd.

She half expected him to follow her, but after that he seemed to have disappeared. She was glad, she told herself. She already had a headache from the music that was getting progressively louder.

Going out for dinner with a man like Alex Valente would not be prudent, she knew. She already had enough disasters to deal with—she wouldn't add possible heartache to the list.

Two

The next day Olivia was in her office when a courier delivered a letter for her marked Personal.

There was just something about that strong handwriting that put her on alert. She gazed down at the white envelope in her hand, noting the way her name had been written in bold strokes. Her heart skipped a beat. Was she being silly to think this was from Alex Valente?

It was.

It read, *Dinner tonight. Seven-thirty. Sylvester's Restaurant.*

She stared at the note, her blood pressure beginning to rise. The sheer arrogance of the man! He sure didn't take no for an answer.

Heavens, just the thought of spending an evening with Alex Valente was enough to give her a serious case of goose bumps. She couldn't deny she was deeply attracted to him. There was a strength about him that appealed to her.

Of course that was probably because the men in her life had always been weak in some way or other. Her parents had divorced when she was two, and her father had ignored her for most of her life. Her successive two stepfathers had both been kind but self-centered. And her ex-husband had only been interested in himself. They hadn't been good examples of the male species.

So why did she think Alex Valente *was?*

By six that evening she knew she would meet him. She had too much to worry about these days and wondering what Alex wanted from her did not need to be added to her list.

At least the restaurant was neutral ground, she told herself, showering then dressing in one of her own classic designs. The cream-colored pantsuit flattered her tall slim figure. Matching leather pumps completed a sophisticated but businesslike effect.

She might as well have worn nothing, she mused

an hour later. Alex had watched her entrance into the restaurant with a masculine appreciation that sent a tingle of anticipation along her spine.

"Glad you could make it," he said, his voice low and throaty as she reached the corner table.

"*I'm* not," she said, then quickly cleared the huskiness from her throat.

A knowing look entered his eyes. "So why did you come?"

She angled her chin at him. "To tell you that I found your note arrogant and to make it clear I want nothing to do with you."

"You could have just phoned and said the same thing."

"But would you have given up?"

He arched a brow. "Do I look like a man who gives up?"

"No."

"Then you have your answer." He held out her chair for her. "Let's eat first."

She swallowed. First? She didn't much feel like eating, but the waiter was hovering, so she went through the motions and ordered a glass of mineral water, then glanced at the menu and ordered veal.

"You've obviously done some checking to find me," she said, once they were alone.

"I needed to get the note to you," he dismissed, as if checking up on people was what he did every day.

Well, she'd done some checking herself this afternoon, but she wasn't about to tell him that. She'd heard of the House of Valente—who hadn't? But until now she'd never been interested in reading the odd gossip column about the love exploits of the three Valente brothers.

"Alex, I—"

"I love your name," he cut across her, his voice suddenly deepening to a murmur. *"Olivia."*

Her heart fluttered at the sound of her name on his lips. He made it sound so sexy…so downright delicious…so….

All at once she realized what he was doing and her mouth tightened. He obviously liked to interrupt her with a personal comment just to throw her off-balance.

"I was named after Larry," she told him, hiding a smirk.

His brow arched. "Larry?"

"Sir Laurence Olivier. You know, the actor."

His hard, sensual mouth visibly relaxed. "Oh. I know who he is. Or was."

She emphasized a sigh. "Alas, he died before I was born, but he was like a favorite uncle to my mother."

Alex's eyes held amusement. "I can see you're trying to put me in my place."

An odd exhilaration filled her. "Did it work?"

"No. But then, I have friends in high places, too. And they're all still alive." One corner of his mouth twisted upward. "I'd say you've tried that little trick before."

"Not since I was a teenager. I've grown up since then."

"And very nicely, too," he drawled.

While the waiter was placing their drinks on the table, Olivia couldn't help but take a proper look at Alex from beneath her lashes. Lord. The man was handsome to a fault, his dark looks a lethal combination of virility and commanding self-confidence, the superbly tailored suit he wore merely an excuse to take a second look at him.

Then she noticed he'd seen her assessing him. Her cheeks warmed as her heart tried to settle. She was grateful when he started to discuss less personal things and Olivia felt herself relax as the conversation stayed on general topics.

"Are you close to your mother, Olivia?" he said, just after the waiter took away their empty plates.

Uneasiness sliced through her. "Why do you ask?"

"You were raised by your grandmother here in

Australia, weren't you? Your mother lived in Los Angeles." He made it sound as if her mother had deserted her.

"It wasn't like that," she said, defensively. "My mother's work was in Los Angeles. She thought I'd have a better upbringing with my grandmother and I did. Nanna and I loved each other." Her heart squeezed at the thought of her grandmother's passing seven years ago.

All at once she realized she was justifying her family. "Look, why did you invite me here, Alex?"

"Because you need me."

She almost choked. "Excuse me?"

He sent her a mocking look. "Let me put it another way. You need my money."

She suddenly felt a chill. Could he know about her mother's debts? It had to be the best-kept secret in LA, but only because she worked hard to earn the money to keep up her mother's normally elaborate lifestyle.

Oh God. Could Alex actually know something about her mother? If he did, would he use that knowledge? If rumors started that her mother was in debt up to her neck, her mother's career, already on a downhill slide, could be all but over.

Her mother would never survive the humiliation.

She needed to play this cool. "I don't know what you mean. Why would *I* need your money?"

"Your business is floundering, Olivia. You and your partner overextended by opening boutiques in Sydney, Brisbane and Melbourne and now you're in debt. You should have just started with the Sydney one."

She let out a slow breath of relief. So, he didn't know about her mother at all. Thank heavens!

And funny, but she was pleased to hear his opinion. It had been her intention to open one boutique at a time but Lianne had persuaded her otherwise, her partner thinking it was a great idea to go for three at once.

And it would have been if all their clients had paid them the money they owed.

Naturally the fashion show had put them further in the red. As had another of her mother's lavish parties put together as a means to help her get a part in a movie that now wasn't even getting made.

"You need cash to get your business out of trouble," Alex continued, bringing her mind back to their conversation.

She shrugged. "It's a temporary cash flow problem, that's all."

"You're an exceptional fashion designer, Olivia,

but that won't save your business. You need money and you need it quickly."

"I can get the money if I want. I have connections." And the minute she used them, her boutiques would no longer be her own.

"So why haven't you used those connections before now? You're leaving it a bit late."

She picked up her glass of mineral water and took a sip, giving herself time to reply. "Pride, I guess. I don't like owing anything to anyone. But if it comes to the crunch, I'll swallow my pride if I have to."

A long moment crept by, then, "Marry me, Olivia, and I promise you won't owe a thing."

She gave herself a mental shake. "Excuse me?"

"Marry me."

She laughed as she put down her glass. "You're delusional."

Challenge flared in his eyes. "Far from it."

This was absolutely crazy. She'd only just met the man. Did he even know the type of person she was? Did he care?

"I'm attracted to you," he said, his gaze dropping to her mouth as if he was tempted to kiss her. "And you're attracted to me. You felt it as soon as we first saw each other."

"The only thing I'm feeling is disbelief. And anger." A woman would have to be desperate to marry a stranger, much less marry a man like Alex Valente. He had to be kidding.

A look of implacable determination crossed his face. "What's that perfume you're wearing?"

She stared at him, baffled at the change in subject. "You must know what it is. It's Valente's Woman."

"So you like it then?" He didn't give her time to answer. "Or did you wear it just for me tonight?" he asked, his voice taking on a husky quality that shivered through her.

She ignored that shiver. "No, I didn't wear it just for you tonight. It happens to be a gorgeous scent and I love it. I wear it all the time." And that was the truth.

He inclined his head, his eyes turning business-like. "And so do most women in Australia."

"I'm sure you're right." This particular perfume called to something inside her. It possessed a fascinating quality and retained a sensual edge that, to her mind, made it the perfect perfume. She rather thought she'd like to wear it for the rest of her life.

"We're about to launch it in the States in a big way," he said, drawing her from her thoughts. "And I've come to a decision. We can use all the publicity we can get, but I can't think of any better publicity than the CEO of the House of Valente marrying someone with the famous Cannington name."

She was so shocked at his reasoning, it took her a moment to think past what he was saying.

And then a derisive sound escaped her mouth. "Let me get this right. You'll pay me to marry you for the sake of a *perfume?*"

"Why not? I've heard of worse reasons. And while it's too late for the launch right now, we could eventually promote the perfume along with your line of fashion." He leaned back comfortably in his chair and took another sip of his Scotch. "Marry me and I'll pay all your debts."

Pay her debts? Plus the chance to combine the Valente perfume and her fashion designs? The thought of it intrigued her.

Then she realized she was actually thinking about it. Good grief! There was no way she was going to consider marrying a man for money. No way at all.

Her hand tightened around her glass. "As delightful as your offer sounds," she said with sarcasm, "I really can't accept it."

His gaze penetrated to the bone. "You're between a rock and a hard place. How else will you get the money?"

"Perhaps I'll go to the newspapers and sell them a story. I'm sure they'd be *very* interested in your offer."

His look was of faint amusement. "But then I'd have to tell them about your financial crisis. And I'm sure they'd be equally as interested in that, if not more."

Damn him. She had to protect her mother, especially now, when Felicia badly needed to get her career back on track. After all, the one time she'd really needed her mother, Felicia had been there for her, helping her through the divorce. Not to mention, her mother had given her money to help start up her fashion design business in the first place.

But as Olivia looked at Alex, her brow crinkled in a frown. What was this actually about? What was his reasoning behind it all? A man like Valente didn't need to marry *her*. His own family had plenty of wealth and privilege. She couldn't see how Valente's Woman could possibly fail in America. Not with Alex Valente running the show.

She tilted her head and considered him. "There's more to your offer than you're saying."

Wary surprise flickered in his eyes. He took a sip of his Scotch before answering. "That's very perceptive of you. You're a sharp lady."

Her heart gave a little flutter at the compliment. "This isn't about me," she reminded him.

Sudden tension tautened the hard line of his shoulders. "My father thinks it's time I married. He says he'll sell the business and give the proceeds all away to charity if I don't, and neither of my two brothers nor myself will get a cent."

She blinked in shock. This man would hate to be told what to do. "That seems rather drastic."

"My father never does anything in half measures," he said, somewhat cynically. "He's being forced to retire for health reasons, and he's tasked me with the American launch. I expect he'll want me to take over as head of the company, only he won't do that until I'm settled."

"So you're after your father's approval then?" she said, somewhat surprised by the thought. Not that there was anything wrong with wanting a parent's approval. It was just that Alex seemed too independent, too remote to worry about what anyone else thought.

Not a flicker of emotion crossed his face. "No, I couldn't care less about his approval," he said, confirming her intuition. "This is for the sake of the company and for my two younger brothers."

She frowned. "It's a big request."

His mouth set in a stubborn line. "I've decided to play along for a year."

"So our marriage wouldn't be permanent then?"

"No."

This was beginning to sound much more favorable. "And we wouldn't be sleeping together?"

The corner of his lips curved up, yet his eyes darkened. "This isn't make-believe, Olivia. It would be a real marriage."

Her stomach flipped at the thought of them in bed together.

Making love together.

Feeling flushed, she had to drag her eyes away from him…then back. "If the Cannington name is all you want, you could always marry my mother," she joked, but instantly regretted it. Her mother was still a beautiful woman. And she'd been married three times already.

His gaze strayed over her. "No. You're the one I want."

His comment snatched her breath away. With a supreme effort, she mentally fought to put up a wall. "I've been married before, you know."

His eyes narrowed. "I know."

Panic rose in her throat. She couldn't do it. No, not for the business. Not for her mother. Not even for a year. The heartache had been too much last time.

Somehow she managed to get a grip. "But I'm divorced. Doesn't that make me less than perfect?"

she said, giving him an out, putting a stop to all this craziness. She had to.

Someone had to.

A frown creased the skin between his brows. "No, it doesn't."

A warm feeling bounced inside her chest, but she tried to stay strong. "I swore I'd never marry again."

His eyes took on a softer look. "This wouldn't be for love, Olivia. You wouldn't have to worry about me hurting you."

She wasn't so sure about that. Heartache and marriage usually went together. It had happened in her mother's three marriages, and in her own one.

Alex placed his half-empty glass on the table. "I'll give you twenty-four hours to think things over."

"How generous," she quipped. Somehow she didn't think a lifetime was enough to think things over with this man.

"Be home tomorrow night. I'll drop by your apartment."

"Or you could just phone me," she mocked, using the same comment he'd used when she'd first arrived.

"No chance. I'm not letting you escape."

Her chin lifted. "You may not have a choice."

"You may not either."

Just then the waiter returned and she bit her lip to
stop from making a remark. Fine. She'd allow him
the last word.

This time.

Olivia spent a restless night thinking over Alex's
offer, trying to decide whether she needed to take the
drastic action of marrying a man for money. One
minute she convinced herself she could do it, then she
couldn't. She would, then she wouldn't.

Heavens, if it'd just been for the business's sake
she'd dismiss it out of hand and take her chances with
a bank. But the opportunity to earn some money
without needing to pay it back, and without needing
to explain why half of that money needed to go to her
mother, was sobering.

Yet marriage?

She couldn't.

And then she reminded herself how her mother
had helped her through the divorce. Shattered by
Eric's betrayal, the last thing Olivia had expected
was that her mother would bring her back home to
Australia for a few months to recover. Olivia
wouldn't forget her mother being there for her.

But marriage to Alex? Dear Lord, she wasn't sure
she could ever learn to trust another man.

She froze. Or did she really need to worry about trust? Alex *had* said it wasn't a love match, so at least he was being upfront about it.

The next evening she opened her apartment door to him with a noncommittal expression, but her pulse had quickened. There was no doubt he affected her. Everything about him suggested an intense and indelible masculinity that made her tingle.

This isn't make-believe, Olivia. It would be a real marriage.

She swallowed hard and closed the door behind him. "Would you like a drink?"

He stood a few feet away in the open-plan living room. "What do you have?"

She pasted on a false smile. "Prune juice?"

He gave a husky chuckle. "Coffee if you have it."

"I do." She went to turn toward the kitchen.

"Remember those words."

She stopped with a frown. "What do you—" She realized what he meant. "Oh."

"They sound perfect for a wedding ceremony, don't you think?" His eyes were watchful.

But she wasn't about to give him the satisfaction of telling him her decision yet. Let him wait. He had to learn he couldn't always get his own way. Or control people. Not *her* anyway.

She turned and walked into the kitchen, then glanced up to see him following her. Ignoring him, she reached for the coffeepot but could feel his eyes looking around the apartment then on her, no doubt comparing her modest surroundings to a Hollywood lifestyle.

Only she couldn't explain that she lived modestly for a reason. That she'd been paying her mother's debts off these past few years. Anyway, this was no hardship. She'd been mostly raised by her grand-mother here in Sydney in a comfortable suburban house, far from the excesses of LA.

"You enjoy being a fashion designer?"

She poured the coffee into two mugs. "Yes. I wouldn't do it otherwise."

"You never wanted to be a movie star like your mother?"

She passed him a mug. "I can't act."

He casually leaned against the door frame. "So it doesn't run in the blood then?"

"I'm a simple girl at heart," she half joked, then rested against the kitchen counter and looked at him over the top of her mug. "If you're expecting more then you're going to be disappointed."

His gaze lingered on her. "No, I don't think I will be," he murmured, making the breath hitch in her throat.

"I—" She wasn't even sure what she was going to say. Something…anything…to stop the overwhelming need to step into his arms. "This is crazy," she said.

"No, it isn't."

Realizing she was giving away too much of what she was feeling, she swung around and placed her coffee mug in the sink. Taking a calming breath, she turned back to meet his eyes. "Alex, look—"

"What's your decision, Olivia?"

"I'll marry you," she said, seeing his eyes flare with satisfaction—mixed with something else. "On one condition. You give me half the money now."

Whatever that something else was that she'd seen lurking in his eyes disappeared. He gave a hard laugh as he put his mug down on the table. "I'm a businessman, Olivia. I'm not about to give you any money before you marry me."

She felt a spurt of anger. "My word isn't good enough?"

Irritation swept over his face. "Look, this isn't about your word. It's not personal. This is a business decision."

"Not personal? You want me to marry you and share your bed and you say it's not personal?" Her brow arched. "Just when *does* it get personal, Alex?"

His jaw set but he acknowledged her words with a nod. "Okay, I concede the point."

Olivia met his gaze levelly. "Then we have an agreement?"

A brief hesitation as he scrutinized her, then, "Yes."

Relief swept through her. Relief she would get the money, not relief she was marrying him, she told herself. "Good."

For a moment she wondered if she should tell him about her mother's money problems. Could she trust him? No. She didn't know him at all. Besides, it was her mother's secret.

As for her own secret, she'd never tell him about that. She wouldn't *have* to tell him about it, considering the briefness of their upcoming marriage.

Suddenly he was all business. "Can you be ready in two weeks' time?"

Her mouth dropped open. "*Two* weeks?"

"We have to do this as soon as possible. I've already booked the Sydney Opera House for the ceremony."

She swallowed, ignoring for the moment that the Opera House was one of the most beautiful venues in the world. "You were *that* certain of me?"

"Yes."

"You're an arrogant bastard."

"I believe you've mentioned that already," he drawled.

"I can't possibly be ready in two weeks' time. I'm off to LA in a couple of days. I promised my mother I would visit with her. She hasn't been feeling very well lately."

And that was an understatement. Her mother knew she couldn't continue with her lavish parties and her high maintenance. She knew it was coming to an end unless she found herself a major role.

All at once Alex looked thoughtful. "You know something. This could play in our favor. If you keep a low profile while you're over there, it will add to the mystique of our wedding."

Our wedding.

She sent him a cynical look. "Yes, and we definitely want mystique for those perfume sales, don't we?"

He glanced at her oddly, as if it was a given. "It'll help your sales as well."

Okay, so he was right. But getting her mother to keep a low profile when the media were bound to be knocking at their door? Impossible! Of course, using Alex's "mystique" angle might be the way to go. Felicia loved "mystique." She knew the value of it.

"What about your father?" Alex asked, drawing her from her thoughts. "Do you want him at the wedding?"

An old heartache jarred but she quickly stomped

on it. "No. He lives in Vancouver with his family and I have little to do with him."

He nodded with a grimace. "Some men don't know when they've got a good thing."

She shrugged. "Owen Cannington was a B-grade actor who gave it all up years ago. He divorced my mother when I was two."

"She kept his name," he pointed out.

"Only because she was becoming well-known as Felicia Cannington." Her lips twisted. "Mum said she may as well make some use of him."

"Sounds like the divorce was amicable," he mocked.

She couldn't help herself. She had to smile, if only the tiniest one she could find.

Taking her by surprise, Alex was suddenly in front of her, putting his hand under her chin. She started to speak, but his mouth closed over hers, holding her there beneath him, taking without asking, as if it was his right.

And then his tongue dipped inside her mouth and did a sweep, exploring her, getting to know her, until she shuddered from a flood of sensation that shook her world.

He eased back, his eyes dark with a passion that didn't surprise her at all. "There," he murmured huskily. "At least that's one thing we've got out of the way."

She swallowed hard. "Um…I didn't know it was *in* the way."

He arched a mocking brow before leaving. They both knew she was lying, if even to herself.

Three

A|lex watched Olivia walk toward him in her wedding gown. The white, off-the-shoulder, satin dress was slim and elegant, and it looked absolutely stunning on her. How had he not known she existed before this? he wondered, filled with a deep satisfaction that he'd found the woman he'd wanted for his temporary wife.

God, she was beautiful.

Beautiful and lovely and so very picture-perfect.

Surprisingly he'd missed her these last two weeks and had actually been pleased to see her when she'd arrived back in the country only forty-eight hours ago.

There'd been a hell of a lot to do with a high-profile wedding such as theirs, the time having gone fast, though not fast enough for his peace of mind. He'd wanted this marriage signed and sealed and he wanted Olivia Cannington in his bed. Just the thought of making her *his* sent the blood rushing through him.

Right then she reached him and their eyes met for one long moment before they turned toward the female marriage celebrant.

The ceremony began, and through the huge window in front of them, they could see the sun shine on the spectacular backdrop of the famous Sydney Harbour Bridge suspended over vibrant blue water dotted with sails.

They exchanged traditional wedding vows, and Alex felt a twinge of guilt when he promised "to cherish her until death do us part." He would have liked to change the vows to "to have and to hold for as long as they both stayed married." Only he didn't want to think about divorce on their wedding day.

Then suddenly their marriage was a fact and he was told he could kiss the bride.

With pleasure.

Soft pink colored Olivia's cheeks as he leaned toward her. Seeing her eyes drop to his mouth sent something powerful flaring inside him. He placed his lips against hers for a long moment that wasn't wholly for the benefit of their guests.

Tonight there would be no audience….

Soon they stood on the steps of the Opera House, where it seemed the world's media wanted to take their picture.

Not that he minded, usually. He'd grown up in the Australian spotlight, but this was different. One part of him felt a wedding day should be private, yet another part was gratified he'd done the right thing in using this avenue to highlight Valente's Woman.

"Can we have a photograph of you and Olivia looking deep into each other's eyes?"

He glanced at Olivia with a sideways smile. "Can we do that?"

She gave a tight smile. "Yes, I think we can," she said, but only he could see her eyes were guarded as he turned to stare into them.

"You're doing fine," he murmured, noticing the flecks of different shades of blue that sparkled in her eyes.

She winced a little. "This is hard work."

"Just pretend you love me," he drawled, attempting to put her at ease.

A genuine smile tilted the corners of her mouth. "It would be easier if I didn't hate you so much."

He chuckled and cameras snapped all around them, and he realized being joined in holy matrimony with Olivia was going to be more than interesting. She was a challenge. And he liked challenges.

"Can we have a picture of you both with the bride's mother?"

Alex felt Olivia stiffen beside him and that reminded him of last night's dinner. She'd seemed edgy around Felicia, as though she expected her mother to take center stage all the time.

And of course "the star" had done exactly that, he remembered with mild amusement. The older woman was elegant and charming, and he could easily see where Olivia got those same qualities from.

Yet he sensed Felicia had an emotional fragility about her that Olivia didn't. Perhaps that's what made Felicia such a good actress, he mused, as she came forward and smiled at the cameras like the pro she was.

"Felicia, how does it feel to be the mother of the bride?" one of the journalists called out.

"Old," she said with a pout.

Everyone chuckled. "You're not so old, Felicia," the journalist said.

Felicia sent him a stunning movie-star smile.

"Darling, I love you." She winked. "Come and see me after the reception."

"I'll hold you to that," the reporter quipped with a huge grin.

Felicia chuckled, stepping between Olivia and Alex and linking her arms through theirs. "Let's smile for the cameras, darlings."

A few minutes later, they were *still* snapping pictures. Alex looked across at Olivia and could see how much of a strain it was becoming. He felt the same. On the other hand, Felicia seemed as though she would go on forever, cornering the attention and loving it all. It's what she did best.

He stepped away from the women. "Right, that's enough," he all but growled. They still had a reception to get through.

Felicia darted a look at him and seemed to realize the moment was over. She turned back to the cameras and clapped her hands. "Right, fellas. That's a wrap. This is my daughter's day and I want to go play mother of the bride."

Alex looked beyond the words and realized something. He had no doubt Felicia loved her daughter, but he had to wonder if Felicia didn't love Felicia just that little bit more. He suddenly had a new appreciation of what it must be like to live with a superstar.

And he had a new appreciation of Olivia as her own person. For Olivia to get out from under her mother's shadow, to make a name for herself as she'd done, showed her depth of character. He'd chosen well in his bride.

Hell, and he'd just gotten married!

His sacrifice had been worth it.

Then he looked at his new wife and all at once it didn't seem like such a sacrifice. There would be benefits.

Very nice benefits.

Not the least of which would be making love to a flawless beauty who put up walls he now intended to pull down.

Olivia was glad when they moved back inside the Opera House to the waiting reception. Not that she had escaped the prying eyes. There were at least three hundred guests here today and the haste of their marriage had most of them looking at her and Alex with suspicion.

Was she or wasn't she?

It was a thought she tried to put to the side and not think about. It had been the same last night at a Valente family dinner in her honor. She couldn't help but note the question in everyone's eyes.

Everyone's except Cesare Valente's.

He knew why Alex was marrying her so hastily.

Surprisingly, Olivia hadn't expected to like Alex's father, but she did. And his stepmother, Isabel, was a doll. Both his parents hit it off really well with Felicia, and Isabel had even promised to keep an eye on Felicia until her mother returned to the States in a week's time. Her mother was such a good actress that a week of being charming to people who were charmed by her shouldn't be so difficult.

As for herself, she hadn't realized how much of an actress she was until today. As she danced with Alex, she tried not to let everyone see how much he affected her. And *he* knew it, too. That confident, arrogant gleam in his eyes told her how *much* he knew it with every step they took.

"You look beautiful in that wedding dress," he murmured, sending her heart pounding like a hammer.

"Thank you."

"Was it something you just threw together?" he teased.

Her lips twitched. "Actually I designed it for the daughter of a billionaire, but the wedding was called off at the last minute so I got to keep the dress."

"I hope they paid you for it."

She glanced away then back again. "We're still

working on that." The father was being obstructive, which no doubt accounted for his billions.

Alex frowned. "Let me know if you need any help."

Olivia couldn't help it. She chuckled. "What are you going to do? Set the dogs on him?"

He grinned. "I could rough him up a little for you."

She laughed again and his grin widened. Maybe it was from being whirled around the dance floor, but all at once she felt giddy—giddy with the pleasure of looking at him. Seconds ticked by, and the gleam in his eyes told her he felt something, too.

The music ended, giving her the chance to move out of his arms. Soon they stood talking to his two brothers and Olivia tried to look calm.

"How's it feel to be an old married man now, Alex?" Nick Valente teased, his lips curved in a confident smile that must be a family trait.

Alex slid his arm around Olivia, pulling her close to smile down at her. "Can you blame me for wanting to tie the knot with this beauty?"

She felt herself flush, but drew her gaze away from Alex and found both Nick and Matt considering her with piercing eyes.

"No," Matt drawled. "I can't say I blame you at all."

Olivia stared at all three men. *Handsome* was too tame a word for them. Yet it was more than just looks. It was an innate quality. They were men who knew who they were and what they wanted. Nothing would stop them.

She wondered if they suspected the sacrifice their older brother had made for them. Alex had told her they didn't know about his father's demand, but she wasn't so sure they didn't suspect something. It was there in the way both men looked at her, as if they didn't trust any woman or her motives, and especially when that woman had hooked one of them in marriage.

Thankfully, Isabel came up to them with Cesare, sniffing back tears in an elegant manner. "Cesare, I can't believe our eldest boy is now married."

Olivia knew that Isabel was Alex's stepmother, not his real mother, who had died when he was small, but by all accounts he considered Isabel his "true" mother.

Cesare glanced at Alex then away again. "Izzie, he's a grown man, not a boy," he said, a hint of gruffness in his voice that made Olivia look at him and wonder if he regretted forcing his son into this marriage. A moment later she came up against a new, determined look in the older man's eyes that said his moment of regret had passed.

"Oh, Cesare," Isabel lightly scolded. "I'm allowed to be sentimental today. I'm the mother of the groom." She hugged Olivia. "And I have a beautiful daughter now, too," she said, sending a warmth through Olivia that made her suddenly want to cry.

"Pity I didn't see her first," Nick joked, giving Olivia a slow wink.

"It wouldn't have mattered," Alex said, pulling her in even closer against his hip, his voice totally serious. "She was mine from the moment I saw her."

She gasped, even as Nick stared at Alex and held his gaze. Then whatever he saw had the middle brother nodding in agreement. "I believe you're right."

Olivia's moment of warmth disappeared but before she could take them to task for their comment, Isabel said, "Stop it, you two. You're embarrassing Olivia."

But Olivia wasn't embarrassed.

She was angry.

It was bad enough knowing she'd walked into this marriage with her eyes open, but making her sound as if she was something to be tossed back and forth between the brothers didn't make her feel exactly civil toward them.

As if Isabel knew, she clicked her tongue and slipped her arm through Olivia's, drawing her away from Alex. "Come on, sweetie. Let's go see your mother. She'll be missing you."

Olivia gladly let herself be taken away, but a few steps on, Isabel squeezed her arm. "Take no notice of them, Olivia. They're fine men who get a bit carried away with their own self-importance at times." She laughed lightly. "Their father's the same."

Olivia found herself smiling back. It was good to know Isabel understood. This Valente woman knew how to keep her man in line.

Then she realized *she* was one of the Valente women now. Would she be able to keep Alex in line? Unlikely. She'd probably go mad in the attempt.

Hours later Olivia had changed out of her wedding finery into a soft-pink suit. Alex had also changed out of his tuxedo into dark trousers and a sports jacket. Then they said their goodbyes, hopped in a limousine and headed for the airport, where a private jet would fly them up along the coast far north of Sydney to the Valente holiday home near Ballina.

"So," Alex said, once they were in the air and comfortable on the luxurious leather chairs opposite each other. "You enjoyed our wedding?"

She gave a polite smile. "The venue was perfect. Thank you."

"You were wrong about not being able to act. You did well."

Her smile widened with self-derision. "Perhaps I should become an actress after all?"

His face closed up, his jaw clenching. "*After* our marriage is over. Not before."

"I'm not sure your brothers were fooled."

"Even if they suspected something, I won't be telling." Tension suddenly filled the air. "I suggest you stay away from them as much as possible."

If they'd been a normal married couple she'd think he was a little jealous of her spending time with his brothers. As it was, it sounded as if he was just being possessive of her. She was *his* now.

Her lips tightened. "I don't plan on spending any more time with your brothers than necessary."

"Good."

Their gazes held for a brief moment before she turned to look out the window. All at once she felt tired. The last thing she remembered was how exhausted she felt by everything.

She woke to find Alex leaning forward, his warm hand clasping her knee, gently shaking her awake. "We're almost there," he murmured, his eyes a dark smoky gray, his touch a caress that radiated upward along her thigh.

Quickly she pretended he wasn't having an effect on her, but that was like pretending he didn't exist. He *did* exist, and so did his touch. And knowing he'd been watching her sleep...

She shifted and he dropped his hand. "I hope I wasn't sleeping with my mouth open," she said, trying to keep things light.

He leaned back in his chair with a masculine smile that smoldered with awareness. "I'll let you know tomorrow if you snore," he drawled, his gaze dropping to the white camisole she wore beneath her jacket.

She could feel her nipples tighten and her cheeks heat up. "I've been told I don't." There!

His smile disappeared. His eyes flicked out the plane's window then back. "We'll be landing soon. Do you want to freshen up? There's bound to be a photographer or two at the airport." He sounded detached now.

She groaned inwardly, not wanting to be on show anymore today. "Didn't they get enough pictures at the wedding?"

He shrugged.

She gave a nod of acceptance then stood, unnecessarily smoothing her skirt. "I'd better go make myself presentable."

"You're more than presentable," he said, a throaty quality to his voice that made her want to break into a run.

Make that a sprint, she decided, ignoring Alex's gaze down the length of her back as she calmly made her way to the bathroom. Once inside she collapsed back against the door. Whoever said love made the world go round hadn't got it right. It was more sexual attraction that did that.

The sunset was beautiful as they departed the jet, but Olivia barely had time to notice as they walked through some camera flashes to another waiting limousine. She usually wasn't unnerved by the media, but right now she was. At the wedding it had been different.

Less personal.

Now she suddenly felt off-balance and—dare she think it—out of her depth with everything. It was bad enough that Alex probably guessed how she was feeling, but she didn't want the world to know it, too.

Twenty minutes later they drove along a winding road to a floodlit mansion. Set in a lush sub-tropical garden, the two-story house had wide verandas surrounding both top and bottom levels. Palms swayed in the light breeze off the crystal waters and tapped against the louvered-glass windows that covered most of the house.

An older Australian couple greeted them at the door to welcome them to Villa Valente and then Alex suggested she retire to the main suite where they would eat a late dinner.

"I have a couple of calls to make first. I'll join you in about half an hour."

She nodded with relief, looking forward to having some time alone as she followed Harriet up the stairs. They had a minor discussion about the wedding, and the older woman, who seemed very nice, showed her around the deluxe suite, which included a small intimate table set for two in the corner.

There was a pale-blue silk gown and matching robe draped on the king-size bed. "Is this from Alex?" Olivia asked, carefully keeping her voice blank, not sure if she liked him buying her clothes. It smacked too much of proprietorship.

"No. It's a wedding gift from Martin and me." Harriet's face softened. "I know you're a wonderful fashion designer, Mrs. Valente, but I thought you might like this as a personal gift from us. You don't have to wear it tonight if you don't want to."

Olivia relaxed with a smile. "It's lovely, thank you. And yes, I *will* wear it tonight."

"It's our pleasure." Harriet walked to the door. "Let me know if you need anything else."

Olivia nodded, but as the door closed she looked down at the bridal lingerie that was even more glamorous than that she'd planned on wearing for Alex, the outfit he would take off her slowly and seductively, or perhaps in a hurry. She trembled with fear—not of him physically hurting her—but of him physically *knowing* her body.

But, she reminded herself, she'd married Alex today. She'd made a promise to be his wife.

When she came out of the bathroom after showering, the man himself was standing near the table. He'd obviously showered in another bathroom then changed into gray trousers and a black polo shirt that made him look drop-dead handsome.

Heat flared in his eyes. "I didn't think you could get more beautiful," he rasped. "But you are."

Giving an inner moan at the way she dissolved at his words, she shrugged. "Harriet and Martin bought it for me," she said quickly, not wanting him to think she'd dressed like this totally for *him*. "I couldn't *not* wear it."

He held her gaze a moment more. "They have good taste."

She stepped forward, looking at the table. "Speaking of taste, this all looks very delicious."

He waited until she was closer then held out a chair for her. "Yes, it does. Nothing but the best for—"

"A Valente?" she quipped, taking a seat.

"I was going to say for *you*," he murmured near her ear.

"Oh." He was close behind her. She expected his hands to slide over her shoulders and she tensed, preparing for it, almost *wanting* it. But that was only because she *wanted* to get this out of the way, she told herself when he sat down opposite and passed her a glass of wine.

His glass clinked intimately against hers. "To us."

She held his gaze, feeling herself flush. "To us."

They both took a sip from their drinks, then Alex placed his glass on the table. "Now, what would you like to try first?" he drawled, a roguish glint entering his eyes.

She swallowed hard and tried to act sophisticated. Was he suggesting she try him?

Heavens, if he expected her to take the lead then he was in for a shock. There wasn't a woman alive who wouldn't like to make love to him, including herself, but tonight she couldn't quite bring herself to make the first move. She just wasn't sexually experienced enough to be blasé about all this.

She swallowed past her dry throat. "The seafood salad looks nice."

He shot her a knowing look. "Yes," was all he said, then gestured for them to start helping themselves.

After that they ate and made idle conversation about the house, the weather, the food. It wasn't a getting-to-know-you time but more a staving off of the inevitable—at least, for Olivia.

And then Alex took a slip of paper out of his pocket and pushed it across the table toward her. "Here's a check for the rest of the money. I want you to have it now and not after we make love."

His face was unreadable but something softened inside her, despite her pulse leaping all over the place. It was nice to know he was sensitive about her feelings.

"Thank you," she whispered, leaving the check where it was for the moment. She'd paid half of his other generous check into her business account and half into her mother's account in LA. It had held both banks at bay until she could cash this latest check.

As for Alex, any man who put his family first had to have some sort of sensitivity about him, she admitted, liking that he was doing this for his brothers, just as she was doing this partly for her mother. They at least had this in common.

And that reminded her.

She tilted her head at him. "Alex, I like your father. I think his heart's in the right place."

In a split second Alex's jaw hardened. "You've known him five minutes and you figured that out, did you?"

Oh damn. She regretted saying anything now. Their moment of bonding had disappeared.

"Sometimes you don't need to know a person long to know what they're like," she pointed out coolly. "*You* certainly made up your mind about me quickly enough."

A heartbeat passed, then his hard mouth visibly relaxed and the sexy look in his eyes told her seduction was now on his mind. "Yes, I did, didn't I?" Without warning, he reached across and lifted her hand in his, tugging her gently to her feet.

The breath stalled in her throat. Oh heavens. What had she started? "Alex, I—"

"And that's because I know when something feels right," he cut across her, pulling her the few steps toward him around the table, making her tremble, his intention obvious.

"Alex—"

"And you feel right to me, Olivia Valente," he murmured, pulling her onto his lap, his intense gaze holding hers still, just like his warm hand was holding her waist still. "Very, very right."

She licked her lips. "Alex, can we please—"

"Yes, we can," he muttered, and lowered his head.

Four

Alex's mouth covered hers and the room grew silent as he held her, absorbing the texture of her soft skin against his own. He'd only kissed her twice before, so he wanted to stay like this for a while and appreciate every inch of her mouth.

He did for several heartbeats.

But soon he couldn't ignore his need to explore farther. He needed to delve into her luscious mouth, then uncover her bit by bit. He wanted to know the excitement, feel the intensity, learn the mystery of her body.

And he wanted it *now.*

He parted her lips with his own, and her sweet breath slid straight into him. He groaned and took a moment to savor it, before letting his tongue do a silent sweep.

He moved his mouth over hers slowly. And then she started to kiss him back, learning *his* taste, feeling *his* excitement as pleasure surged through him.

When he finally began to ease away, he scraped his teeth lightly across her bottom lip. "Third time's the charm," he murmured, noting the way her pupils had dilated.

She blinked. "Um…third time?"

"This is our third kiss." He bent his head again. "And this…" he needed more "…is our fourth."

He kissed her deeply again before drawing back to place kisses along her smooth jawline. His lips brushed against her earlobe and he lingered there, breathing in the light floral scent of her hair.

After taking his fill, he leaned back and ran a finger along the underside of her chin. Then he followed the column of her throat to where her quickened pulse drummed at its base, down to the first dainty button of her blue robe resting on her cleavage.

His libido climbed.

"Undo it for me," he commanded.

She gasped, her blue eyes widening. "The button?"

"Yes." He only had one hand free, the other was holding her by the waist. "Then undo the rest of them."

Her eyes were hesitant beneath her long eye-lashes, but after a moment she lifted her hands and began to do as he asked. The silk parted as button after button broke free, leaving behind the blue silk gown made to capture a man's attention.

It did.

And there was nothing pure about the thoughts running through his mind. "You dazzle me," he rasped, seeing the outline of two dark nipples peeking through the shiny material.

He felt her quiver as his thumb ran over the tip of one bud. He did it again, then held the nipple between his finger and thumb, squeezing lightly. Her quiver turned to a shudder.

Relishing the feel of her coming alive under his hands, he bent his head to that breast and began sucking through the material, flicking her with his tongue.

She gave a whimper and her head arced back against his shoulder. One of her arms came around his neck and she held on to him, burying her face in his nape and breathing deeply. Just as quickly, she pulled back, as if caught doing something she shouldn't.

He felt heat explode inside him. "Do that again," he muttered against her breast.

She froze for a split second, hesitated before she did it again, making him groan. They stayed like that for a short time, then finally he lifted his head and she moved her face back.

He looked into her eyes. "A man could lose himself in you and never want to be found," he rasped.

Her eyes darkened. "Oh, Alex."

His gaze slowly slid down her body to where the material pooled at the apex of her thighs. He looked up. "You don't like me saying that?"

"Yes." She swallowed. "I do."

His palm slid downward, over her abdomen and her soft mound before resting between her legs. She gasped as he stroked her with his finger through the gown. "You don't like me touching you?" he teased huskily.

"Yes..." her throat convulsed "...I do."

He had to feel her naked body. He had to see all her creamy smooth skin. He pushed to his feet, with her in his arms, and stood her in front of him. Then he eased the silky robe off her shoulders, letting it drop to the floor. The matching nightgown was next and he shuddered when he saw how perfect she was.

Their eyes locked.

"Alex," she murmured, her eyes darkening, her cheeks coloring, though she made no attempt to cover herself.

Lifting her, he carried her to the bed. After laying her down he began stripping off his clothes.

Their eyes locked again before her gaze ran down his body and she gave a soft gasp. He knew if he didn't touch her…didn't taste her…wasn't inside her soon…he'd explode.

He joined her on the bed and this time her mouth parted even before their lips touched. He gave a low sound of approval, and she answered his kiss, her hands coming up to cling to his shoulders. Willingly, he let her pull him closer, until his bare flesh was pressed against her soft skin, savoring the aching anticipation.

Breaking away, he heard her moan as he got to his knees and launched a trail of kisses over every inch of her body, marking her as his own. She was smooth all over, but never more velvety than between her thighs. He parted her with his tongue and loved her until she arched under him, her hands threading through his hair wildly until she trembled, then shook, then was hit by a shockwave that went on and on.

He reveled in her release but when her climax

ebbed, he could wait no longer. He rose up over her and reached for a condom in the bedside drawer. There was no question on his part as to whether he would use one. And she didn't ask.

With precision, he rolled it on himself while she lay watching. He was aware of nothing around them. He was tuned in solely to her.

And she was glorious.

He entered her slowly, sensation heightening as he sank deep into her warmth. Her gasp reverberated around the room and he took a moment to let her get used to him.

And then he began to move, to thrust in and out to the rhythm of their bodies. But, before too long, the rhythm wasn't enough. Nothing was enough.

Until she clenched around him and like a flash of white heat he exploded with pleasure.

Olivia woke to find herself curled up against Alex. Her husband.

Her *temporary* husband, she reminded herself as her eyes flew open, knowing there was nothing temporary about the two of them right now. Her body seemed permanently attached to his, her mind now burned by memories of his lovemaking.

There was no escaping how Alex had made her

feel last night. He'd been considerate, yet his need for her had surprised her. It had been so intense, so breathtaking.

It had taken a certain kind of man to do that, keeping it physical, but allowing her some sort of emotional connection that had nothing to do with love.

Her throat went dry. Why was she thinking about love just because she was in a man's arms? Love belonged to other couples. Love was not part of her agreement with Alex, she reminded herself, as she tried to ease away from him and slide out of bed.

"Don't move," he murmured.

She froze.

He rolled to face her, and for a long moment his slate-gray eyes lingered on her face. "Where do you think you're going?" His voice thickened, the heat of his arousal filling the space between them.

She tried to think. "Er…it's time to get up," she said, then immediately felt her cheeks warm.

His lips quirked with male humor. "Are you asking me or telling me?"

She resisted the urge to tease him back. "Telling you."

He gave her a knowing look. "You were fantastic," he said softly.

She blinked at him, her heart sinking. "I was?"

His gaze dropped to her naked breasts. "It's been a while, hasn't it?" he said in a husky tone.

She didn't answer. She couldn't. His words reminded her of Eric, who'd thought nothing of praising her just to take the suspicion away from his affairs.

"Don't be embarrassed because you don't sleep around," Alex continued, his palm sliding over her hip. "I actually like that you don't."

"Double standards, Alex?"

His hand stilled, his gaze sharpened. "Not at all. I've never been one to sleep around." He must have seen the disbelief in her eyes because he stiffened. "And I definitely won't sleep around on my wife."

An odd thrill raced through her, but she still couldn't let her anxiety go. "Yes, but women must throw themselves at you all the time."

His brows drew together, then understanding dawned. "I'm not like your ex-husband, Olivia. Just because women offer doesn't mean I accept."

Still, she couldn't let it be. "Yes, but you must have accepted sometimes."

Suddenly his eyes hardened. "There's only room in this bed for two people. You and me. Not your ex. Whatever happened between you two shouldn't be brought here."

His words were the mental slap she needed. "Yes, you're right."

He held her gaze for a few heartbeats, then his eyes softened. "Let him go, Olivia. Don't let him spoil what we have."

Her stomach quivered. "I don't know that we have anything."

"You don't?" He gave a throaty chuckle and the sound slithered down her spine like warm silk. "Maybe I need to refresh your memory."

Without giving her a chance to argue he slid her across the sheet and pulled her under him. Their bodies touched and that's all it took for flames to spark between them.

And then he took her higher and higher, out of control, until she went up in smoke, leaving an after-burn that continued to glow long after he'd brought her to fulfillment.

When she next awoke she found herself alone amongst the sheets, all that was left of their night together. Then she moved her legs and winced a little.

All?

No, there was *this* reminder, she thought, thankful Alex wasn't there to see her blush. Her body was so pleasurably sore, so very conscious of their lovemaking. She'd used muscles she hadn't used for years.

Remembering, she threw back the sheet and hurried to the bathroom. If she stayed in bed she'd be thinking about last night, and right now she didn't need that. Alex might have made her forget all about Eric during their lovemaking, and he might have made her forget *herself,* but now it was time to keep moving. Otherwise she could be tempted to lie in bed and wait for Alex to come back and join her.

And if he saw her like this then he'd think he held her in the palm of his hands.

No way.

She'd given him a year of her life. She wasn't giving him her soul, too.

After showering, she went downstairs and found her way to a huge sunroom which ran the full length of one side of the house. A table was set for a late breakfast, but there was still no sign of Alex.

Then Harriet appeared, clicking her tongue. "He's in the study catching up on some paperwork, though what paperwork there is to do on the first day of his honeymoon is beyond me." She showed Olivia her seat then started fussing around the table.

As a businesswoman herself, Olivia knew the paperwork never ended, honeymoon or not. And she was rather grateful that Alex was busy, even if she couldn't say that to the other woman. She was supposed to be a blushing bride, after all.

Oh heck. She *was* a blushing bride. She just wasn't a blushing bride *in love* with her husband.

"That's okay, Harriet. I'm not feeling neglected." She gave a smile. "Not with all the attention I'm getting from you."

Harriet stopped her fussing and smiled at Olivia. "We're so happy that you married Alex. He needs someone of his own."

This was news to Olivia. Alex had family—a father, a mother, two brothers. He must have plenty of friends.

Of his own.

Yes, there *was* a difference, she silently admitted. Apart from her mother she had no one of *her* own. Oh, she'd thought she'd found that special person when she'd married Eric, and for a short while she'd believed it. She sighed. Ignorance was sometimes bliss.

Of course, she wasn't ignorant about this marriage. This time she had gone into it with eyes wide open. This was a marriage of convenience. Their work came first and rightly so.

The housekeeper offered to cook up some eggs but Olivia declined and said that cereal was fine. Harriet nodded and left the room.

For the first time Olivia got to look at her surroundings. The room was decorated in soft yellows, pale greens and creamy whites. A fountain stood in one corner, close to wicker chairs and a sofa—a place to sit and relax. Potted plants and paintings filled the room. The large glass dining table she was sitting at was no doubt where Alex had enjoyed many a meal. The view of the ocean from here was unsurpassed.

Just as she finished eating and was drinking her coffee, Alex appeared. She ignored the fact that his sheer presence took her breath away as he walked straight over to her, cradled her face in his hands and brought his lips down to hers.

What a kiss!

Then he eased away, the look in his eyes filled with complete satisfaction before he walked around the other side of the table and sat down.

"Sorry I'm late," he said casually, as if he hadn't just made her tremble. "I got caught up on a telephone call."

His casualness made her elation disappear. No doubt he was used to women being accommodating—to both his kisses and his work demands.

Couldn't he be a little considerate of her sensibilities? What if she had really been in love with him? His treatment would crush her. It was just as well she was a working woman, and could give as good as she got.

She placed her napkin on the table and stood. "That's okay, Alex. I've got a couple of business calls to make myself." She started to leave the room.

"Olivia?"

She stopped to look at him. "Yes?"

"The study's the fourth door on the right."

Was that a gleam of humor in his eyes? Had his mouth just twitched? She inclined her head. "I'll find it."

Once in the study she sat down at the desk, feeling quite proud of herself. Even if he *had* found her little protest silently amusing, she'd still scored a point.

Then she picked up the telephone, but felt rather silly when she realized she had no one to call. Having cleared the decks at work for the week, and with Lianne insisting she only call under dire circumstances, who else was there to phone?

Her mother.

Felicia wouldn't think it strange for her daughter to call and see how she was. Only, when she called the Valente estate in Sydney, the housekeeper said her mother had gone out for the day with Alex's parents.

Sigh. There was no one else she dared call. She knew a lot of people in the States, but they'd think her mad checking in on the day after her marriage.

"Finished your calls yet?"

She looked up to see Alex standing in the study doorway. For a moment she suspected he was being sarcastic, but then she saw that he was serious.

Okay, so he may well have been amused by her antics when she'd left him in the sunroom, but he hadn't actually been disparaging of her work ethic.

"Yes, I have."

"Then let's go for a walk down to the beach."

All at once she realized he'd changed from trousers and a polo shirt into something much more informal. Her eyes slowly slid down the length of his lean body, now clothed in a white T-shirt and tan-colored board shorts, with leather sandals on his feet. He looked like a sun-worshipping surfer ready to tackle the waves.

"Where's your surfboard?" she quipped, not really meaning to be funny.

He grinned. "It dumped me years ago."

Olivia couldn't help but chuckle even as she gathered her breath. Lord, that grin made him look young and carefree, and she had trouble associating this man with the same CEO she'd married.

Quickly, for something to do, she glanced down at the slacks she was wearing. "Give me five minutes to change into something more casual."

"Like some help?"

Her heart bumped against her ribs. "No, thanks. I've been dressing myself a long time now," she said, walking toward the door, trying to appear nonchalant.

"It was the undressing I was more interested in," he teased, moving aside from the doorway, allowing her to pass him.

She hid a smile, otherwise he might think she was encouraging him to come up to the bedroom and make love to her.

She wasn't.

No, definitely not.

"I'll meet you on the front veranda in five minutes," she heard him say as she headed for the stairs.

"Fine."

Olivia deliberately took ten minutes to change into Bermuda shorts and a sleeveless top. Then she applied sunscreen to her exposed areas, and grabbed her sunglasses from her purse and put them on.

"That was a long five minutes," Alex said, his own sunglasses not hiding his scowl as she pushed open the front screen door and stepped out onto the veranda.

"I didn't know we were clock-watching."

"We're not." He glanced at his Rolex, then grimaced. "Habit." Taking off the watch, he placed it on the table behind him. "Now, let's go get some fresh air." He held out his hand.

For some reason she found herself hesitating.

"Harriet's watching from the window," he drawled.

"She is?" She went to turn around but didn't get a chance to look before he stepped forward and slipped his hand around hers, tugging her down the front steps and through the short grass to the side of the house. Hand in hand they started walking along a dirt path leading to the beach.

He slanted her a mocking smile. "See, we actually look like lovers now."

"Oh, but—"

"What? We're not lovers?" He stopped and faced her. "Then who was that gorgeous woman in my arms last night?" Suddenly his smile disappeared, his dark glasses hiding his eyes but not the huskiness in his voice.

She could feel her cheeks warm. "Maybe she was a dream?"

"Oh yeah," he murmured. "She was that."

Her heart flipped over. "Alex, I—" All at once the ocean breeze picked up and swirled around them like a small whirlwind, snapping her out of the moment. "Um…that breeze is pretty strong," she said quickly, then turned and continued to walk, surprised when he let her drop her hand from his. She half expected he would tug her back around to face him, pull her up close and…

He fell into step beside her, not touching her now. "Yes, that breeze is good for clearing out the cobwebs," was all he said.

She ignored a stab of disappointment, but it was her own fault. She could have chosen to stay where she was and let him kiss her. Yet she knew why she hadn't. Despite them being lovers, she wasn't in love with him. For her to initiate making love with him would be the equivalent of walking down the main street of Sydney naked. She'd feel totally exposed.

Ahead, the path looped over a small sand dune and down to a sun-kissed beach, scattered with couples lying on towels or parents playing in the shallows with their children. An older man jogged along the water's edge. A couple of surfboard riders bobbed out in the sea, their wait for larger waves appearing to be in vain today.

She sighed in appreciation. "It's beautiful."

"Yes."

She kicked off her sandals, enjoying the feel of

soft sand trickling through her toes. "It's been ages since I walked along a beach."

He stepped out of his own sandals. "Then what are we waiting for?" When she went to pick up her sandals, he instructed, "Leave them. We'll get them on our way back."

She blinked in surprise. "But won't someone steal them?"

He gave a dismissive shrug. "If they're that desperate then they're welcome to them."

"Oh." She shrugged. "Well, I guess a man like you doesn't need to worry about the cost of things."

A muscle tightened at the edge of his jaw. "A man like me?"

She hesitated, realizing she'd said the wrong thing. "It's just that I noticed you left your Rolex back on the veranda."

"So?"

No getting around it now. "Admit it, Alex. You were born with a silver spoon in your mouth. You take some things for granted."

"I seem to remember you've got one of those silver spoons, too."

"Yes," she admitted slowly, "but I was raised frugally by my grandmother." And while Olivia wouldn't call herself in the least frugal, she still couldn't be so cavalier about things like leaving expensive watches out in the open, or even sandals on the beach.

A mask came down over his face. "I keep what's important."

Five

Olivia stood and watched Alex turn and walk along the sand. His words had been steely and totally no-nonsense—the tough CEO coming to the fore. The hard-hitting man was such a part of him. A woman would be incredibly lucky to have him love her. To be so fiercely protected by him. And he *would* be fiercely protective. She knew that instinctively.

He turned back to her. "Coming?"

His words jarred her from her thoughts and she fell into step beside him. She didn't want to think about Alex and another woman, so she changed the subject to try to break any tension between them. "Do you come here often?"

A moment crept by before he glanced at her from behind his sunglasses. "I usually make it for Christmas with the family. It's good to get away from the city and the December heat."

She nodded. "Sounds wonderful." Oh, how she remembered those long, hot summer Christmases. Her mother had always come home to spend the holidays with her and Nanna and they'd had a great time as a family. Then Nanna had died and the last few years she and Felicia had spent Christmas in LA, and nothing had been quite the same. She supposed that was all a part of growing older.

"You'll get to find out yourself this year, Olivia. Christmas is only a couple of months away."

His words startled her. "But I usually spend Christmas with my mother."

"We'll invite her here then." It was more an order than a suggestion.

"But—"

"It would look odd if you take off for the States and leave your new husband here during the festive season," he pointed out.

"You could always come to LA," she said, not even sure she wanted him there, though she knew it would seem strange without him. Good Lord, and she'd only been married a day.

"No." His voice was firm, his chin stubborn. "My parents will be here and my two brothers. I won't break family tradition."

Something in his tone roused her curiosity. This man was deeper than she'd first thought. And much more family-oriented than he let on. No wonder his father had been able to blackmail his son into getting married.

Marriage to a man like this would have been a dream come true for her if it had been a real marriage. A permanent marriage. She sighed. It was just as well it wasn't a real marriage because then he'd want a real family with her and—

Suddenly he stopped, put his hand on her arm and spun her toward him. She was in his arms before she knew it, his lips against hers, taking her by surprise with a kiss that made her forget they were on a beach for all to see. All that mattered was his kiss. And the next.

He eventually pulled back, but she was unable to read his eyes. And that was the trouble with sunglasses. They hid his eyes as well as her own.

She cleared her throat. "Um…what was that for?"

"Someone's taking pictures of us. I wanted to give him something worthwhile to report."

Her heart thudded to a stop. "How nice."

"I thought so," he said, not seeming to notice her sarcasm as he picked up her hand in a possessive manner and began walking her along the shore, as though she was his girl and he was showing the world exactly that.

She hid her disappointment. "Are we still being followed?" she asked for something to say, trying to find her mental balance, pretending she didn't care about being used for publicity purposes while on their honeymoon.

Then she winced inwardly. What was the matter with her? Their whole marriage was going to be one big publicity event. Could she really blame Alex for taking advantage of that right now?

"No, I can't see him. Anyway, forget it for now. He's going to take our picture whether we want him to or not."

He was right and after another hundred yards she began to relax again. The sound of the water lapping against the shore and the feel of the breeze skimming her cheeks eased her concerns considerably. How could she not relax? This was a perfect setting; it would help even the most stressed person to unwind.

Just then the sun went behind a frothy white cloud, and for a few seconds the world was darkened then just as quickly thrown back into a shower of sunlight. Wanting to capture the scene in her mind, she stopped and whipped off her sunglasses to better appreciate the brighter sunshine and rich colors.

Her fingers itched. "Ooh, the light and colors are just marvelous. I'll have to bring my sketchbook down here and capture it all in a design."

He took off his own dark glasses, his gaze sweeping the beach in front of them, as if looking at it through her eyes. Then he looked at her. "I'd like to watch you design something."

She blushed with pleasure. "I've had an idea for some time to put an Australian mark on an international design. This may be just what I've been looking for."

"You're quite a talent, aren't you?" he said, his eyes full of admiration.

Her heart skipped a beat but she managed a short chuckle. "I haven't designed it yet."

"I have every confidence it will be a winner."

She quickly placed her sunglasses back on to hide her eyes, not wanting him to see she was almost made shy by his praise. "Thank you," she murmured.

Heavens, she was used to being held in high regard by the rich and powerful. She'd designed clothes for some of the most famous people in the world. Yet this man—her husband—made her self-conscious when he praised her talents?

Crazy.

He put his sunglasses on. "Are you ready to go back? I need to get some more work done, I'm afraid."

She nodded. "Okay, but I think I'll grab a sketch-book and come back down while you're working."

"No."

She blinked at his unmistakable air of command. Was she hearing right? "Pardon?"

"I don't want you coming down here by yourself. You could get harassed and I won't be around to help."

"The media are not out in force, Alex. There's only the one guy who—" Suddenly she caught a movement out of the corner of her eye and she spun toward it. Just as quickly she twisted back toward Alex. "That's not a reporter," she hissed of the photographer a couple of yards away. "He's only a kid."

"He's a teenager and now he's just run off, no doubt looking to sell the photographs to the highest bidder." Alex's mouth flattened. "I meant what I said, Olivia. Don't come down here by yourself."

She lifted her chin. "You're blowing things out of proportion."

"Humor me."

"I'd rather strangle you."

He arched a brow but his lips quirked. "That's a bit drastic, don't you think?"

"Look, I'm not used to sitting around all day doing nothing."

"Then it's about time you did. We have a swimming pool up at the house. Why not laze around it for a couple of hours? And I'll take you into town for dinner tonight."

Her pulse leaped at the thought of dinner with him, despite herself. "I'm not a child to be rewarded for keeping out of your way while you're working." Her chin set stubbornly. "As a matter of fact I still have some work to do of my own," she fibbed. "I wasn't going to work on our honeymoon but…" she paused deliberately "…if you're working then I may as well, too."

He tensed, a muscle starting to tick in his jaw. "Sorry about that. My father has been easing off on the work lately and that's put more pressure on me."

"Oh." Something about his words clutched at her heart. Perhaps it was the rough edge of emotion in his voice that made her soften toward him. "Alex, I understand." She still didn't like being told what to do, but she'd cut him a break this time.

He inclined his head, his mouth not as tight as before, his shoulders not as tense. "Good."

Then he cupped her elbow and they walked back up the beach. Surprisingly their sandals were still where they'd left them, but she didn't look at Alex nor did she say a word as they stepped into them and made their way up to the house.

Once there, he took off for the study, reading through a handful of phone messages, already forgetting that she even existed. Olivia watched him go, a silly sense of loneliness filling her. She was never lonely.

It must be because she felt suddenly tired, she decided, and went up to the bedroom to take a shower to wash off the sand.

When she came out, dressed in her silk bathrobe, the bed looked so very inviting. Perhaps if she lay down for just a few minutes....

She woke to find herself covered with a light blanket, the bedside clock showing midafternoon. Feeling guilty, she threw back the blanket, got dressed in white capri pants and a cherry-red top and hurried downstairs. Alex was still in the study, but he put his pen down when he saw her in the doorway.

"I'm sorry," she said. "I didn't mean to fall asleep for so long. It was supposed to be a quick nap."

"No need to apologize. You must have needed it." His gaze traveled down her body, his eyes darkening at every lowering inch. "I was tempted to join you," he murmured, his raspy voice sending a frisson of excitement racing through her.

She moistened her lips. "I thought Harriet might have covered me up."

She hoped.

She prayed.

A faint smile curved the edges of his mouth. "No, it was me."

She gave an inner gasp. Her bathrobe would have covered her, but the fabric was thin....

"By the way, Olivia, you don't snore," he said, his voice silky smooth.

She felt the flush of heat enter her cheeks. "That's good to know." It was time to get out of here. "Um, I missed lunch so I might go get a snack." She half expected he'd want to join her.

But his eyes turned businesslike. "Don't forget I'm taking you to dinner in town. Let's make it seven."

"I'll be ready."

He nodded and picked up his pen. "You'd better go get something to eat."

Before she'd even stepped away to head toward the kitchen, Olivia heard the preoccupation in his voice and knew it wasn't with *her.*

She sighed as that strange sense of loneliness filled her again, but she quickly pushed it aside. She had too much time on her hands right now, that's all. It wasn't that she was feeling like a neglected bride.

Not at all.

Alex sat back in his chair after Olivia left and tried to focus on his work again, but she unsettled him and he wasn't sure he liked being unsettled. Never before had he ever let a woman distract him from his work. He was usually able to keep the two things separate. He liked it that way.

Of course, he'd never been married before.

Never had a woman living with him.

Never had a woman on his family turf.

The family's Christmases had always been here at Villa Valente with his parents and his two brothers and sometimes various relatives, but neither he nor his brothers had brought their girlfriends here. None of them would ever give a woman that false sense of power over them.

Yet having Olivia here now wasn't about giving her the wrong impression. Olivia already knew the score. This year they would be together, and next year they wouldn't be, and that was the way they both liked it.

And the way they both wanted it.

It had to be that way.

For now he'd enjoy the benefits of having a beautiful woman in his life—and in his bed. Making love to Olivia last night for the first time had been amazing. She'd been married before so he hadn't expected to be her teacher, yet there had been an innocence about her, as though he was the first lover to give her more than he took.

And in the giving he'd been given back far more than he'd ever expected. She'd turned into a more than willing pupil. He hadn't been joking when he'd said she'd been a dream to make love to.

And this afternoon when she'd been sleeping…if he hadn't known she was so exhausted he'd have woken her up with a kiss to that gorgeous mouth of hers. And then he'd have kissed her all over before making her his again.

Hell, just thinking about it sent the blood pounding to his groin but he told himself that waiting would make it all the sweeter. Later this evening he would wine and dine her, then make love to her over and over.

But that was easier said than done when he saw her later coming down the stairs dressed in a short brandy-colored dress that showed off her gorgeous curves and long slim legs. Its off-the-shoulder design highlighted a tanned collarbone that deserved to be kissed.

She was exquisite.

He wished now that he'd stayed in their bedroom and watched her dress, smoothing silk stockings up along her legs. Of course if he'd stayed they'd still be in the bedroom.

In bed.

And he'd be inside her.

"I'm going to make love to you later," he said huskily as she approached him. "You know that, don't you?"

A becoming flush stained her cheeks. "So you're not sick of me yet?" she joked.

He frowned. Where had that come from? Her ex?

"No way, sweetheart," he growled, then put his hand under her chin and gave her a hard kiss, more than satisfied by the hint of pleasure he saw in her eyes when he pulled back. "Come on. Let's get out of here." He cupped her elbow and led her out to one of his father's Mercedes. If they didn't go to dinner soon, they'd never get there.

Fifteen minutes later, they were sitting in an intimate corner of the best restaurant in town and Alex was studying the blond beauty in front of him. He could have been sitting amongst the Miss World contestants and none of them would hold a candle to Olivia.

Her eyelids flickered. "Stop staring, Alex," she said in a throaty voice.

"Why?"

She shot him a wry look. "Okay, let's change the subject. Tell me about your Italian background."

"Why?"

Her gorgeous lips curved upward. "Because I've just realized I've never asked you before. I mean, I know what I've read in the papers and that you're Australian-born, but that's about all I know about you."

He leaned back in his chair, pleased she was interested enough to ask. "What do you want to know?"

"Can you speak Italian, for one thing? You never do."

"My grandparents came out from Italy after the war and they taught me when I was growing up, but I prefer to speak Australian." He'd loved his grandparents but they were gone now and he had no interest in speaking Italian with his father.

"And your father?" she said, honing in like a dentist's drill on a sore tooth. "He speaks fluent Italian, doesn't he? Was he born in Italy?"

Alex's brows drew together. "I thought this was about me, not my father."

She cooled a little. "I'm only trying to understand the man I married."

"Don't," he snapped, then grimaced at the withdrawal on her face. He sighed. "Look, my father was twelve when he came here. Eventually he made his millions and later married my mother when he was around thirty. She was Australian and she died when I was little. That's it."

Her eyes softened and filled with sympathy. "I'm sorry."

His stomach knotted. "Yeah, so am I."

The only vague memory he had of his mother was of sitting on her knee. He also had a couple of old photographs. She'd been raised by an elderly aunt so he hadn't even been able to ask her family about her. Cesare Valente certainly hadn't wanted to talk about her.

The only reason he'd known why he was called Alexander and not the Italian form, Alessandro, was because Isabel had told him his own mother had insisted on it. Surprisingly, Cesare had kept that pattern when Nick and Matt were born. In some corner of Alex's heart, he liked to think his father had done it out of respect for his first wife. On the other hand, perhaps that was just foolish thinking.

"What about your grandparents, Alex?" Olivia asked, drawing him from his thoughts. "They're not still alive, are they? I didn't see them at the wedding, but no one has mentioned them."

"They died years ago after a long and happy

marriage." He gave a harsh laugh. "I can't say the same for my father," he said, thinking about his father's three marriages.

She tilted her head. "But Cesare has been married to Isabel for a long time now. They seem very happy."

He scowled. "They are," he grudgingly admitted. "I guess I have to give him credit for that."

She nodded. "It's probably part of the reason he wanted to see you married." Then she hesitated, as if she wasn't sure whether to say something or not. "He cares for you, Alex. You may not be able to see it, but I can."

"Perhaps." He wondered what she'd think if he told her his father wanted him to have an heir, too. But why mention something that wasn't necessary? In six months time Cesare would be on his way to retirement, if not before. He wouldn't be able to dictate to any of his sons after that.

The arrival of the waiter to deliver their drinks gave Alex the chance to end the discussion, but as he watched Olivia smile her thanks at the young man, he felt a jolt inside his chest. If he had to have someone have his child, she would be the perfect choice.

He pushed that thought aside. "Now it's your turn. Tell me about your ex-husband," he said, watching her stiffen. He knew what the papers had said about the other man, but he wanted to hear Olivia's version of it all.

She held his gaze. "I met Eric when I was just starting out as a designer. I was working in Paris and he was this really handsome, debonair Englishman. I'd never met anyone like him before." A derisive sound emerged from her throat. "I don't want to meet anyone like him again."

"He cheated on you." It was a statement, not a question.

Her expression clouded. "Yes. He thought I had a personal fortune because of my mother. When he discovered that she wasn't supporting me as much as he thought, he dumped me for a woman who had more money."

Anger rippled through Alex. "The bastard."

She inclined her head. "Thanks. I know it sounds horrible, but by that stage I was glad to get rid of him."

"No, what sounds horrible is him using you the way he did."

"Thank you," she whispered. She looked hesitant, then said, "He's the main reason I have trouble trusting people these days."

Alex knew that took a lot to admit. "Yet, as a stranger, you trusted me enough to marry me."

Her tight expression relaxed into a smile. "Yeah, go figure."

Something warmed inside him, but before he could savor the moment, their meal arrived. The food was superb and afterward they strolled along the promenade. He couldn't wait to get her home and make love to her.

And when they finally made it to their bedroom and he pulled her into his arms, he felt her tremble from head to toe in a way that none of his other lovers ever had. It made him feel special, as though he was the only man on earth who could fulfill her needs.

And that affected him more than anything.

<u>Six</u>

The next morning, Olivia couldn't settle. She and Alex rose late then had breakfast together in the sunroom, but he was preoccupied and soon afterwards went to the study to work. She knew he had a lot to prepare with the launch of the perfume in a few weeks' time, but she still had to fight that feeling of neglect again. So she made calls to Lianne and her mother, only to find they were still getting along just fine without her.

Everyone seemed to be busy except her.

She needed to throw herself into work.

Without warning a vision came to her for her next

design and she remembered the colors of the light-blue sky blending with the dark-blue ocean spilling white froth along the golden sand. The effect was eye-catching and perfect for her next designs.

She would call it the Valente Collection, she decided. After all, she was a Valente now, if only temporarily. And Alex had said they could eventually combine her designs with Valente's Woman perfume.

She hurried to find her sketchbook and pencils, intending to sit on the balcony and draw with the full view of the ocean before her. Only, this far away the vibe wasn't quite the same. She needed to get up closer and steep herself in the colors and textures of the scene. It was important that she connect with her surroundings.

Alex need never know, she decided as she left the house. Heck, she wasn't going to be told what to do anyway. If she wanted to go down to the beach, she would. This was her work, and she wasn't going to miss out on an opportunity just to appease a husband who was busy with his own work anyway.

Of course, walking along the dirt path to the beach hadn't seemed scary when she was with Alex, but now she could hear all sorts of noises in the grass that reminded her of snakes.

She picked up a long stick just in case, and made sure her footsteps trod heavily, hoping any slithery surprises would hear her coming and disappear into the longer grass.

It was a relief when she reached the beach, but she didn't want to think about the walk back to the house so she put it out of her mind. In next to no time, she'd made herself comfortable on the sand, with a small grassy dune at her back as she reached for her pencils, blocked out the world and began to let the magic take over.

She had no idea how long she stayed there, but it wasn't until a shadow fell across her that she realized it must have been a while, perhaps even a couple of hours. She looked up and angled her chin, expecting it to be Alex. Only the man standing there didn't resemble her husband at all.

In his fifties, he leaned forward and looked at the design on the paper. "Is that going to be in your next collection?"

A reporter.

Ignoring him, she quickly closed her sketchbook and got to her feet. In her haste, she dropped the book and gasped when he scooped it up before she could.

She held out her hand. "That belongs to me. If you don't return it I'll call the police."

"Little lady, I intend to return it," he said with a smirk. "After you answer a few questions for me."

An interview.

"Look, you obviously know who I am. You must also know that I'm on my honeymoon." She wanted to snatch the book out of his hand, but she made herself stay calm.

"Speaking of honeymoons, I'm surprised your husband lets you out of his sight."

She knew that whatever she said could be miscon-strued. If she said Alex was working, this man would make something of it and report that their marriage was already on the rocks. If she said Alex was napping, the papers would report him ill, or worse, on his deathbed.

"He'll be along shortly," she said, hoping to give herself time to reason with this man.

He snorted.

And then, miracle of miracles, she saw Alex striding toward them, a thunderous expression on his face that she knew was for her. "See, I told you," she told the older man and was pleased to see him blanch. Good. He was nothing but a bully.

"What's going on here?" Alex demanded, step-ping close, putting himself between her and the other man in a protective fashion.

She could afford to relax a little now. "Alex, no need to worry. I dropped my sketchbook and this, er…man was just giving it back." She held out her hand. "I'll take that now, thank you."

The reporter looked at Alex then at her, then finally gave it back. "Here we are, little lady."

Olivia took it, pretending she didn't want to snatch it to her breast. And if he called her "little lady" again she'd probably hit him with it.

Alex turned to Olivia. "Right. Lunch is ready," he said, then taking her by the elbow he shot the other man a hard look and led her away, a bit like a hardened criminal on the run. Any moment now, she expected him to bring out the handcuffs.

Once out of earshot and on the dirt path back to the house, he growled, "What the hell were you thinking, coming down here by yourself?"

She shrugged, hoping to dislodge his hand, but his grip was firm. "I needed to do my designs and the best place for that was down here at the beach."

"I told you I would bring you down here myself."

"You were working. I didn't want to disturb you."

"I *prefer* that you disturb me." He shot her a searing sideways gaze. "See what can happen when you don't listen?"

She frowned. "Don't you think you're overreacting a little?"

His jaw clenched. "No."

"But—"

"No buts. The guy was a reporter who would have stolen your designs if I hadn't turned up. And there wouldn't have been a bloody thing you could have done about it."

"I'd have charged him with theft," she said with more bravado than she felt.

He flashed her a look of disdain. "So you know his name then? You know where he lives? And you have proof he stole your designs?"

She grimaced. Put like that…

"It's as well you came along then," she conceded, glad to see they were coming up to the house. Anger radiated from him in waves, and this would be a good time to escape to the bedroom.

Without warning he halted, a pulse beating in his cheekbone. "You just don't get it, do you? You don't know what could have happened. You don't know—" He stopped, let go of her elbow before he expelled a breath, then stormed off with a snarled, "Forget it."

She stared after him in surprise, his back ramrod straight as he strode past the front steps and down the side of the house to the rear. What on earth was his problem? This was definitely over the top.

Then she realized Harriet was standing on the

veranda watering some potted plants, her face full of concern.

Olivia let out a slow breath and continued walking to the house, then up the steps. She wasn't sure how much she should say, if anything, but Harriet was no fool.

"He found you then?" the older woman said, putting the small watering can down on the table.

Olivia nodded. "Yes."

Harriet sighed. "He was concerned when he couldn't find you. He seemed to know you'd gone down to the beach."

Olivia gave a defensive shrug, still stinging from Alex's reaction. "I decided to do some drawings, that's all. I'm not sure why that's a problem."

The other woman's eyes softened. "Olivia, don't be too hard on him. He has his reasons for getting upset. *All* the Valente men do."

Olivia's forehead creased. "Why? What do you mean?"

"His mother, Isabel, was attacked on that beach twenty years ago," Harriet said, making Olivia gasp. "It was late afternoon and they'd all gone down there for a swim. Afterward they were coming back here when Isabel realized she'd left a beach towel behind and she went back to get it." She winced. "No one thought anything of it."

"And?"

"For some reason, Alex decided to go back and check on her while the others continued walking home. When he got there, the beach was deserted except for some drunk who was trying to force her to the ground. Alex was only fifteen but he got the man away from her. Then Nick appeared and the police were called and the man was charged with assault, but everyone was horrified at what could have happened."

"Oh my God," Olivia murmured, picturing it all. No wonder Alex had been adamant she not go down there alone. To find his stepmother being attacked must have been terrible.

"No one ever talks about it," Harriet continued, "but it's always at the back of our minds. Alex would have been worried something might happen to you."

Olivia shivered in the heat of the day. "Thank you for telling me, Harriet. At least I understand now."

"And that's half the battle," Harriet said, smiling in sympathy.

Olivia gave a small smile in return. "Yes."

But she had to wonder what the other half of the battle would be.

Olivia stayed out of Alex's way for the rest of the day, while he stayed in the study working. She felt bad now for giving him such a fright. If only he'd told her what had happened with Isabel at the beach, she'd have understood and tried not to worry him.

Poor Isabel. It must have been a terrible experience for her.

And poor Alex. He'd be the first to save anyone from being hurt, not just a loved one.

Not that *she* was a loved one. Not in that sense. No, being Alex's wife didn't mean anything more than that he would protect her if she needed it.

So why did she feel strangely disappointed it wasn't more than that?

Pushing that thought aside, and as a peace offering, she decided to have a candlelit dinner for the two of them. She put her head together with Harriet and they came up with a rack of lamb with roast pumpkin salad, followed by a berry ice cream log.

Then Olivia lazed by the pool for the rest of the afternoon, working on her designs until just before six. She was glad that Alex didn't seek her out, and suspected he was still in the study.

He was.

He put down his pen and leaned back in the leather chair, when she entered the room. She told him Harriet was preparing a special dinner for them.

"What time?" he said, distractedly.

"Seven-thirty."

He looked at his watch, then back at her. "I'll be there."

She frowned. "You shouldn't be working so hard, Alex."

A shadow of irritation crossed his face. "It has to be done."

"Harriet won't forgive you if you fall asleep in her dinner."

He held her eyes for a moment, then straightened and picked up his pen. "I'll be fine."

She paused. "You won't forget, will you?"

"I'll be there," he said without looking up.

Aware she was being dismissed, she went up to the bedroom and took her time dressing in one of her own designs that was casual yet dressy enough for dinner. She was just putting the finishing touches to her makeup when she heard the splash of someone diving into the swimming pool outside.

Going to the side window, she looked down and saw Alex doing laps of the pool. He was magnificent as he sliced through the water, his broad shoulders tanned and toned, no doubt getting rid of pent-up energy.

And that was a good thing, she thought, tempted to stay and watch some more, but forcing herself to go down to the kitchen to check that everything was set with Harriet.

She was in the dining room, unnecessarily straightening the settings on the table, when Alex came into the room right on seven-thirty. Dressed in beige cargo pants and a blue shirt, he looked fresh and vital and more handsome than ten men put together.

His gaze slid over her white sleeveless dress flaring gently to her calves, a gold belt looping her waist. A glint of approval in his eyes made her stomach dip before he transferred his gaze to the flickering candelabra.

There was a slight lift of his brow. "Candles? It's not even dark yet."

She ignored his lack of romanticism. "I know, but it adds a nice touch, don't you think?" She gestured with her hand. "Here. Sit down. The food's all ready to be served from this trolley here." It had hot and cold compartments.

"Harriet isn't serving us?" he asked, coming forward and holding out a chair for her first, then sitting opposite her.

"No. She and Martin have gone into town to watch a movie."

His lips twisted as he looked over the table. "At least we've convinced Harriet this is a real marriage."

She blinked. "This wasn't Harriet's idea. It was mine."

His glance sharpened. "I see."

She squared her shoulders. "I wanted to apologize, Alex. For this morning. I didn't know about Isabel being attacked."

His eyes shuttered even more than usual. "I see Harriet's been talking too much."

She tilted her head. "That's why you didn't care about leaving the sandals on the beach. It reminds you of Isabel going back for the towel, doesn't it?"

The line of his mouth tightened and his shoulders stiffened, but a second later he reached over and lifted the wine bottle out of the ice bucket. "I don't like to analyze things," he said in a nonchalant fashion that didn't fool her one bit.

No, he wouldn't, she thought, watching him as he poured her a glass of wine, then one for himself. "I'm surprised your father didn't sell up after that."

A muscle jerked in his jaw. "No, we love it here," he said brusquely.

She nodded. This would be the one place they must all feel like a family, despite him not getting on with his father over the years. And for that reason it must be very special to Alex.

She took a sip of wine before saying, "Why didn't

you explain it to me? I would have understood. I wouldn't have gone down there alone if I'd known."

His gaze speared hers. "You trusted me enough to marry me, but perhaps you've got to learn to trust me in other ways."

She winced, his remark taking the wind out of her sails. Placing her trust in someone wasn't exactly the easiest thing for her to do. It was the hardest. She knew he understood where she was coming from but—

"Yes, I suppose that's the next step," she quietly agreed.

Just then the evening sun shone through the windows of the sunroom and caught the angles of Alex's face, throwing part of it in shadow.

She realized something then. For all his talk about trust, he was the one keeping something of himself in the shadows. *He* hadn't explained why he hadn't told her about Isabel in the first place.

Trust worked both ways, didn't it?

She opened her mouth to say all this to him, but another thought hit her. Or was this about something rather than trust? Was this more about him not sharing his emotions with her? His fears?

Yes, it was.

And as much as she hated to admit it, Alex's attitude was a refreshing change when all the men in her life—her stepfathers, even Eric to a deceptive degree—had been the first to share their fears with her.

Everything, actually.

They'd nearly driven her mad with their confidences. If she had to choose, she'd prefer a man who didn't need to share too many of his feelings. There was a time and a place for talking but she definitely liked the strong, silent type.

Alex was one of those.

Something softened inside her. "Alex, do you think our dinner will spoil if we leave it for a while?"

He scowled. "I shouldn't think so. Why?"

She got to her feet and held out her hand. "I want to make love to you, Alex," she said huskily. "Do you mind?"

He looked shocked but recovered quickly. "I'd be a fool if I did." He got to his feet and put his hand in hers. "And I'm no fool."

Seven

At the end of the week they returned to Sydney and moved straight into Alex's luxurious apartment at Woolloomooloo, with its spectacular city, park and harbor views and just a short stroll from the center of the city itself.

Now that Alex was back at work and she had a lot of time to herself, Olivia banked the other check that he'd given her the night of their wedding.

Her mother had excitedly returned to the States on the Valentes' private jet, having been called back for a second audition in the movie she'd been coveting. Olivia prayed her mother would win the part.

As for herself, she was excited about the designs she'd created while at Villa Valente, and during the following week she settled into working on them at her Sydney boutique while helping Lianne arrange a fashion show soon to be held in Melbourne.

And then, one evening the following week, Alex said during dinner, "We'll be going to the States on Friday."

Olivia's fork of salmon stopped in midair. "We're going in two days?"

He nodded. "The launch is set for the twentieth, but they need us there a couple of days earlier for some other publicity."

She took a deep breath and placed her fork back down on her plate. "You didn't tell me it was going to be so soon."

"You didn't ask."

"But that's the day of my fashion show in Melbourne. Lianne arranged it months ago. I have to be there."

His eyes hardened. "No. You *have* to be at the perfume launch with me. Let Lianne handle the fashion show by herself. She has staff to help her."

She didn't like the way he was dismissing her

commitments. "It's *my* name on the collection and it's *my* show, Alex. I need to be there. Lianne's gone to a lot of trouble to get this all up and running."

"And I've gone to a lot of trouble to get the launch up and running," he said, totally uncompromising.

"But I need all the business I can get." She'd paid off most of her debts but there were still ongoing ones, not the least her mother if she didn't get that part in the movie.

"Olivia, you made a deal with me."

He was right but still, his arrogance was showing again. "So this is what the next year is going to be like, is it? I'm to drop everything to fit in with your plans?"

"Yes." There was no hesitation.

She shot him a withering look. "I'm not some housewife from the fifties, you know. I have a job outside the home. I have responsibilities to others."

"No, you have a responsibility to me. It was the reason I married you, remember?" he said with cutting emphasis. "If you renege on the deal then it's all been for nothing."

Hearing him say it like that made her feel less than worthless. She had been a commodity, that's all. After the past two weeks she'd thought their lovemaking had brought them closer together. She'd thought that their getting to know each other a little might have counted.

Obviously it hadn't.

Her throat tightened. "I'll see what I can do."

"Good." His eyes said he expected it all to be sorted to his satisfaction, and no doubt every woman he had ever known had done exactly that. How she wished her hands weren't tied over this.

When Olivia went to the boutique the next morning and told Lianne of her dilemma, the other woman was as dismayed as she was about the situation, but then she became philosophical about it all. Knowing that her partner was able to handle the upcoming show without her made Olivia feel better.

Amazingly, in late afternoon, Lianne came into Olivia's office to tell her the venue for the show had been cancelled.

"You don't think—" Lianne began, then stopped.

"What?"

She shrugged. "No, nothing."

Olivia had a suspicious gnawing in her stomach. "Do you think Alex arranged this?"

Lianne looked uncomfortable. "It occurred to me just for a moment, Olivia, but Alex is an aboveboard kind of guy," she rushed to assure her. "He wouldn't do anything underhanded."

Olivia wasn't so sure, but she couldn't say that. She wanted no one to know that she didn't have complete faith in her husband.

"No, he wouldn't do anything underhanded," she agreed, despair ripping at her insides.

She'd already been through one husband who had cheated on her, so that she had married another man who cheated her in another way was easier to believe. And if she didn't believe that, what other explanation could there be for the cancellation? No, it was too much of a coincidence.

By the time she arrived home she had worked herself into a bit of a tizz. It was bad enough that *she* suspected Alex of manipulating the situation, but knowing that Lianne suspected it as well embarrassed and humiliated her.

She found him shaving at the bathroom sink, a towel around his lean hips, his broad back tanned, muscular and crying out for a woman's touch.

Pain instantly twisted inside her. Oh God, shades of Eric?

"Going out somewhere, Alex?" she snapped.

He didn't appear surprised by her presence, so must have heard her coming through the apartment. "I have a business dinner to attend," he said, smoothing the razor along his jawline. "At the Teppanyaki."

She remembered now. A few days ago he'd told her about the invitation for the men-only dinner with a Japanese billionaire.

Fine. So he wasn't meeting another woman. One thing had nothing to do with the other anyway, she thought, swallowing a silly sense of relief that he wasn't seeing someone else.

She stepped into the large marble bathroom and went up to him. "You got them to cancel the venue, didn't you?"

He looked blank. "I don't know what you mean."

"The venue for my fashion show in Melbourne has fallen through. They said there's a problem with the wiring. How convenient," she sneered.

His blank look disappeared and his mouth clamped into a thin line beneath the remaining shaving cream. "And you think I arranged it?"

"Yes."

For a moment everything went still. Something hard flared in his eyes, then cleared, and just as quickly he turned back to the sink, obviously ignoring her. Without thinking, she reached out to stop him, but instead her hand slipped along his damp skin and accidentally knocked the towel away.

Time stopped.

Even her gasp seemed to be made in slow motion.

Then she felt drawn to look downward. He was fully aroused. Heat washed over her and slowly she raised her gaze to his.

His eyes held an odd glitter. "Touch me," he rasped.

She hesitated, unable to move.

"Touch me," he repeated.

The command excited her, and she moistened her lips, seeing him tense at the action. Suddenly she wanted to see how much further she could arouse him.

Almost in a trance she reached out…and slowly…deliciously…wrapped her palm around him, gripping him fully. He felt so smooth, so firm, so incredibly male. A woman could do much to torment a man like this.

Her fingertips moved to do just that.

Instantly he put his hand over hers, stilling her. Anticipation leaped inside her, making her wonder what he would—

"You trust my body, Olivia," he muttered. "So why can you still not trust *me?*"

His words were like a slap in the face. She swallowed hard and tried to pull her thoughts together. She dropped her hand away from him. "I—"

"Think about it," he said coolly, and turned back to the sink to complete his shave, not bothering to cover himself with the towel on the floor.

For a moment more she stood there, warring emotions running through her. Then she spun away, needing time to be alone.

"Olivia?"

She stopped but didn't look back.

"We'll finish this later tonight."

She didn't reply, her heart jumping in her throat. What exactly did he want to finish? Their discussion? Or their marriage?

Olivia was in the kitchen making a cup of coffee when she heard the apartment door close. Her chest ached with a growing pain. Alex had left without saying goodbye.

Well, she wouldn't let thinking about Alex overwhelm her. She would have dinner, do some paperwork, then go to bed, just as she did every night.

Only, the massive bed seemed so empty without Alex. She tossed and turned, remembering the scene in the bathroom, her heart skipping a beat at how blatantly aroused he'd been for her.

And then her heart sank just as quickly when she remembered how fast he'd turned away. Angry, she got out of bed and made for the spare bedroom, where she tossed and turned some more. She must have fallen asleep eventually, for she awoke as the bedside lamp was turned on.

She groaned and pulled the blanket up over her head. "Turn the light off, Alex."

He didn't answer.

Suddenly the blankets were thrown back and she was being scooped up in his arms. Her eyes flew open. "Alex?"

A pulse leaped along the hard line of his jaw. "You're my wife. You sleep beside me."

A thrill zipped through her, but she lifted her chin in the air. "I'm only a temporary wife, Alex."

"Then you'll sleep with me temporarily." He walked into their bedroom, placed her on the bed and stood looking over her. "Now, do you really believe that I cancelled the venue?"

Her gaze became trapped in his, and realization clutched at her heart. His stance was defiantly male, trying to show her he didn't care if she didn't trust him.

But she suddenly knew beyond doubt that he did care.

And she suddenly knew he'd had nothing to do with the venue cancellation for the fashion show. She'd just been letting her fears and prejudices get the better of her.

"No, Alex," she whispered. "I don't believe you did that at all now."

His expression shifted with the barest hint of relief, but his shoulders gave him away. The tension seemed to ease out of him before he turned the light out and she heard him shedding his clothes.

Then the bed moved as he slid into it and pulled her up close against his chest. "Now, where were we…" he said, his voice thickening.

The next day they headed to the States in the Valentes' private jet. Alex had a heavy schedule on arrival in Los Angeles so he had to get some paper-work out of the way first. Eventually he was able to sit back, relax and enjoy the breather.

And enjoy the beautiful woman opposite him in the lounge area of the aircraft.

Even when she made him mad.

For a while there last evening, he'd been so angry with her he'd barely been able to eat dinner. How the hell could she think he'd had something to do with the cancellation of the venue? He'd never do some-thing like that.

Okay, he'd been determined she would accom-pany him to the States today, but everything he did was direct and upfront. No deceitfulness for him, and especially not when it came to family.

And right now, Olivia was family.

His immediate family.

His.

Watching her, something began to unfurl deep inside him. It just seemed so damn right having her here with him. All at once he wasn't so sure he wanted to let her go when the year was up.

And if that were the case, would she be amenable to staying? Perhaps to stretching it out for a few more years after that? Perhaps he could even fulfill *all* of his father's ultimatum?

It was crazy, but he now felt an odd lump in his throat at the thought of being a father. It was something he'd never cared about before, but with Olivia here beside him it didn't seem so unimportant.

They were halfway over the Pacific Ocean when he said, "How would you feel about having my child?"

Her head snapped up from reading a book. "Wh-what?"

If it hadn't been so serious he would have felt amused at her reaction. "I'd like to father a child and I'd like to have that child with you, Olivia. Do you have any objections?"

She was still gaping in shock. Her mouth opened and closed, then she swallowed hard. "Plenty," she croaked.

His brows drew together. "I think we'd make good parents."

She took a deep breath. "I have no doubt about that, Alex, but that's not the problem."

"Then what is?"

Her expression clouded as she placed her book on the coffee table between them. "You never said anything about children before."

A cold knot began to form in his stomach. "I know, but I've been thinking—"

"Don't." She winced. "I mean, why would you ask me this now? It's so out of the blue."

Hell. He suddenly didn't want her thinking he had growing feelings for her. Her reaction was enough to know they wouldn't be welcome. Not at all. He had to make her believe this was all about his father.

"Olivia, I didn't tell you everything about my father's ultimatum. There was more he wanted than just that I get married." He let a moment slide by. "My wife has to conceive an heir within twelve months or I still risk losing the inheritance."

The blood drained from her face. "Oh God."

Apprehension rolled through Alex at her reaction. He wasn't sure why.

She drew a breath. "Why didn't you tell me about this before?"

"Ours was…is…" he emphasized, "only a temporary marriage. I didn't see it as an issue at the time."

She frowned. "I don't understand, Alex. What's changed?"

The plane started to bounce around as they hit a patch of turbulence and Alex was grateful for the distraction.

"I've decided I'd like to stay married to you for a few more years. And if we could produce a child in that time, even better."

She sucked in a sharp breath. "No," she murmured, looking horrified.

Mixed feelings surged through him. On the one hand he understood her being taken by surprise, on the other, was it so horrible that he wanted his wife to have his child?

"I thought if we both felt the same way," he began. "We could—"

"This is so not fair, Alex," she cut across him.

"But—"

"No, I'm sorry." A look of resolve grew in her eyes. "I can't help you with this."

Anger sparked inside him. She hadn't even given it any thought. "Can't or won't?"

Before she could answer, the plane bounced even more roughly and he saw the flare of fear in her eyes. He suddenly didn't feel too at ease himself.

All at once the moment was more important than their future. "Make sure you're strapped in," he warned as he reached for the phone flashing a red light beside him.

"You, too," she murmured, a look in her eyes that said she was just as worried about him as for herself. And that made him realize that she cared about him.

How much, he wasn't sure.

As much as she was scared about the turbulence, Olivia was thankful for the interruption. Being bounced around inside an aircraft and fearing for her life was a good companion to the turmoil inside her. How could Alex have thrown her for a loop like this? Why would he want her to have his child?

The child she could never have.

Dear Lord, this was one of the reasons she had agreed to a temporary marriage in the first place. She'd thought she had no need to worry about giving Alex children and that he need never know that she really *was* less than perfect.

Her heart squeezed at the thought of her baby, lost to an ectopic pregnancy. And at the loss of any future babies she should've had. Oh, how she wished she was capable of having a baby.

Alex's baby.

Yet how could she tell him? She had to. And she would, once they were back on terra firma and in the privacy of their hotel suite with time to talk properly.

Only, after they landed—the turbulence having finally ended—they were surprised by an invitation to a luncheon with one of the most powerful men in California. It was impossible to refuse, despite being jetlagged, so they quickly dressed at their hotel and then were whisked away to his mansion in Bel-Air.

So it was early evening before they returned to their hotel suite. Olivia wanted to get what she had to say out of the way, but decided a while longer wouldn't matter. They both needed to shower and have a light dinner and unwind before she dropped her bombshell.

Unwind?

Yeah, right.

That wasn't possible, she decided as she went to return a call from her mother while Alex showered and changed.

Felicia was excited about having been offered a part in a television series, so she didn't notice that her daughter wasn't quite herself. Her mother now had the dilemma of whether to accept the part or wait to hear if she would get the role in the movie, and she asked Olivia to convey her regrets to Alex that she now wasn't able to come to the perfume launch in New York as she'd planned.

"I didn't know she *was* coming," Olivia said to Alex over dinner, after she told him the rest of her mother's news. As a fashion designer she'd thought *she* would be enough, along with the Cannington name of course. It wasn't that she minded, but she did mind Alex not telling her he'd invited her mother in the first place.

Alex shrugged. "She mentioned it at our wedding, but I thought no more of it."

She frowned, accepting what he said but more interested in his attitude to her at this very moment. He'd played the perfect husband this afternoon when they'd been in the company of others, but now, in private, he was withdrawn and cool.

"Why not?" she said to be contrary. "My mother would have been a good asset to have there with us."

"Frankly, I like Felicia but she's not the type in whose promises I would put any store." There was a tiny pause. "Not like you."

She should take offence at what he'd said about her mother but she was more concerned with what he was implying about *her*.

Her chin angled. "I didn't promise to have your baby, Alex."

A muscle tensed at the edge of his jaw. "I know."

"So don't accuse me of something I haven't done."

For a moment he looked as if he would argue, then remorse flashed across his face and he expelled a deep breath. "Yes, you're right. You made no such promise." He pushed back his chair and stood.

She reached out and put her hand over his. "Alex, please don't go. I mean, we really do need to talk about…" she hesitated "…about what you mentioned on the plane."

He stilled, then gave a jerky nod of his head and sat back in his chair. "Go ahead."

Her stomach was churning, but she had to proceed. "Alex, I need to say this. I have to make it clear to you that…" She swallowed. "*Why* I can't have your child."

"So you don't like children then? Is that the problem?"

"I love children," she said in a ragged whisper, pain and despair wrapping around her heart. "Alex, I want children more than anything and if I could, I would love to have your child."

A lump rose in her throat. She had to say it, had to put an end to his hopes. "Only I…can't. I'm infertile. I've been told I'll never have a child."

Eight

Alex felt the bottom fall out of his world. Up until this moment he had had no doubt Olivia would come around and have his baby.

She was staring at him with pain-filled eyes.

He was shaken to the core by that look, by her words. "Tell me."

She swallowed hard. "I had an ectopic pregnancy when I was married to Eric," she began, and something turned inside Alex at the thought of Olivia pregnant to another man. Something fierce and primal rose in his throat. Something he firmly pushed aside.

"My tubes were damaged…irreparably." She took a deep breath. "So it's not that I won't have your child, Alex. It's that I can't."

He heard every word she said, but he still had to ask, "You're sure there's nothing to be done?"

She frowned. "The doctor did say it was highly unlikely rather than never." She gave a dismissive shake of her head. "But he was just being kind. He meant never. I know he did."

Alex's heart started to race. "Was he a specialist?"

"No."

"So there's still some chance?"

She swallowed. "Not really. I was told at the hospital that the damage was too extensive. I have no need to question that."

He wasn't so sure. Doctors weren't infallible. Hospitals made mistakes. But he'd let that be for now.

"Does your mother know all this?"

Her eyes softened. "Yes, and she was a great help when I needed her. She surprised me."

"I'm glad." His estimation of Felicia rose. Thank God Olivia had had someone to help her through it all.

Her lips gave a wry twist. "Unfortunately, Mum thinks it's like in the movies and that it's all going to magically right itself."

His brow furrowed. "Does she give you a hard time about it?"

"Not at all. We usually don't mention it. But I know she still hopes to be a grandmother one day." Her eyes moistened and she blinked rapidly. "I wish I could give her that grandchild but I can't."

Emotion swelled inside him and he wanted to pull Olivia into his arms and comfort her, but suddenly he needed to get out or risk being the one who needed comfort. His chest felt tight with a strange anguish.

He quickly got up from the table. "Thank you for telling me, Olivia. I have to go out now." He needed thinking time.

Alone.

"Yes," she said, as if she understood.

He strode to the door and quietly left the suite, not knowing where he was going until he walked into the bar downstairs. He wanted to get blind drunk and forget the pain rioting through him.

Dammit, he wasn't used to feeling so much, so deeply. Usually he managed to keep everything under control but that was difficult when it was in his face like this. He didn't like feeling so vulnerable where Olivia was concerned, so weak and so bloody powerless.

And he wasn't just thinking about himself either. He was thinking of Olivia. And, hell, he hadn't even begun to think about the problem of an heir and his inheritance.

Okay, so he'd decided from the start that he wasn't letting his father force him into producing a child. Yet all at once he felt guilty on his brothers' behalf. And that was crazy. Why feel bad when he'd had no intention of fulfilling the second part of the ultimatum anyway? His brothers hadn't known about any of it, but they wouldn't have expected him to sacrifice himself for them on the marriage altar, let alone add a baby to the mix.

Bloody hell. This was worse than worse.

A couple of hours later, Alex returned to their hotel room, not drunk but wishing he was. It would be such a welcome state to be in right now.

All was quiet as he slipped quietly into the darkened bedroom and started to strip off his clothes. He could see Olivia's shape beneath the blankets and didn't want to wake her. Perhaps the jetlag had caught up with her. He wanted her to get as much sleep as she could.

"You don't have to sleep with me, Alex," she said in the hushed stillness. "I'll understand if you want to go to the other room."

He swore softly and slid into bed naked. "I'm your husband. I intend to sleep beside my wife."

"Temporary wife," she pointed out, but he could hear an odd catch of pleasure in her throat.

He pulled her up close against him and let his lips brush her temple. "I'll arrange for you to see a specialist. We need a second opinion."

"But, Alex, what's the use?"

His arms tightened around her. "We need to do this. Just to be sure, okay?"

"I guess so."

"Now shh," he murmured, then kissed her cheek before hovering over her mouth. He wanted to ease her pain and the only way he knew how was for them to find release in each other.

He began to make long, slow love to her. She was soft and warm, and her welcoming body certainly made him forget everything but the moment.

But when he reached for a condom, she put her hand out and stopped him. "No need for that, Alex," she murmured. "Not anymore."

He swallowed hard. "No?"

She shook her head and a lump rose in his throat. She was showing him that even though they might see a specialist for a second opinion, she would have been willing to have his child if it had been at all possible.

He brought her to orgasm, letting himself fall into the same climax with her, joining with her. It was the most incredible experience. And the most moving.

Olivia was glad when a couple of public relations staff members joined them on their private jet to New York the next day. It gave her the chance to avoid any further intimate conversations with Alex.

Heaven knows, they'd been intimate enough last night. It had been wonderful to feel Alex inside her without the use of a condom. Up until now she hadn't been able to suggest he not use one or he'd have had to ask why.

Now he knew.

But today there was just something in his eyes that made her anxious. She didn't want him getting his hopes up about having a baby. It had taken her quite a while to come to terms with it herself. The last thing she wanted was to see him going through the same thing.

He probably just wanted to make sure for his father's sake. Oh, she knew Alex would see the game through now that he had made a commitment to her. He wouldn't go back on his word, not until the year was over anyway. But once her time was up, he'd have to ditch her and find another wife. It was the way it had to be, she told herself, her chest tightening at the thought of him with another woman.

Of another woman having his baby.

Oh God. Somehow she had to refuse to get upset over that. This had been a business deal and it wasn't as if she had really meant anything to him, despite them sharing these weeks together. It was just the way it was. Yes, it was personal but it wasn't as though they were in love with each other and needed a baby to seal their love.

No, they were lovers.

And sometimes friends, that's all.

The plane landed and the next week went blessedly fast in such a whirlwind of functions and appearances that neither of them had time to think.

The launch of Valente's Woman was a huge success. In some stores the crowds were lined up out the doors to be able to buy their bottle of the expensive perfume. It helped that her mother—bless her—had asked her celebrity friends to drop in at some of the stores and that in turn created a buzz that set the customers clamoring for more.

Everyone was pleased.

Of the specialist appointment, Alex said nothing.

On their last day in New York, one of her ex-stepfathers suddenly appeared at a cocktail party.

"Olivia, darling," Randall Markham said, coming up to give her a kiss on the cheek.

Olivia looked at the man in stunned surprise. Randall had been her favorite of her two stepfathers. And he was the only one who'd remained good friends with her mother.

"Randall! What are you doing here?" she said, giving him a hug.

"Spying on you, of course, darling," he joked, keeping an old joke between them alive.

Olivia smiled genuinely for the first time in days. "You'll never convince me that my mother didn't pay you to come to my first fashion show." Olivia had been so nervous she'd banned her mother from attending. But Randall had come. Nothing had dissuaded him.

"She didn't, I swear," Randall teased, then his eyes slid to Alex beside her in a considering manner. "And this is your next husband, I presume?"

Olivia was aware of the tightening of Alex's mouth. He obviously didn't like being thought of as a "next" husband.

But she nodded and pasted a happily married smile on her face. "Yes, this is Alex." She introduced the two men. "Alex, this is Randall. One of my stepfathers."

"Ex-stepfathers," Randall pointed out, shaking Alex's hand. "I was the rich, handsome one."

Alex appeared to relax. "Obviously."

Randall turned to look at Olivia. "Unfortunately, I'm not rich anymore." He sighed. "As much as I still love your mother," he said in an exaggerated fashion, "she absolutely took me to the cleaners."

Olivia suddenly felt uneasy. She didn't want Randall saying too much in front of Alex.

"Thank heavens she didn't ruin my looks," he said in a manner that seemed ludicrous because he wasn't joking. "And thank heavens she has you to pay off her debts now," he said, sending dismay through Olivia. "I've told her to get another husband but she won't."

Olivia felt Alex stiffen beside her. "Randall, how is Cybil?" she said to change the subject.

"Fine, darling. She's doing a show on Broadway. That's why we're here in New York. That and to see our first granddaughter."

Olivia knew that Randall had no idea of the pain his words caused her. She had lost her baby after he'd divorced her mother and Felicia hadn't shared that news with him. Her mother had never believed she wouldn't have a child so she probably didn't think of it as an issue.

She forced a smile. "Shari has a baby? How old is she?" It nearly killed her to ask.

"Just a couple of months and she's a little darling,"

Randall said, then went on to sing the praises of his first grandchild.

Olivia could see the glint of anger at the back of Alex's eyes. Oh, why had Randall said anything about her mother's debts? She didn't need this right now.

After that, they spoke of other things, then they kissed goodbye and promised to meet up another time. All the while Olivia could feel Alex's anger seeping through, despite his outwardly calm manner.

He said nothing until the function had finished and they were back in their hotel suite. Then, "Something else you didn't bother to tell me?" he said, an edge to his voice.

She played for time as she placed her purse down. "What do you mean?"

Irritation flared in his eyes. "The money I gave you to marry me paid for your mother's debts, didn't it?"

She inclined her head. "*Some* of the money did, yes. The rest helped pay off my own business debts." She frowned, pretending ignorance. "You have an issue with that?"

His gaze sliced over her. "I have an issue with you not telling me things."

Her chin lifted as her heart sank. "You mean about my infertility, right?"

For a moment his face closed up. "Yes," he

muttered. Then his mouth tightened. "And now this. I feel I don't know you at all."

"You *don't* know me, Alex. If you did, you'd know that there are some things I like to keep private, just as there are some things *you* like to keep private." She paused deliberately. "Such as the fact that your father expects you to father a child."

A momentary look of discomfort crossed his face, then he gave a jerky nod. "Point taken."

"Good."

"Just tell me one thing," he fired back at her. "Are there any other surprises I should know about?"

"No." She started to walk away. She'd had enough. They were tired and their nerves were stretched and this wasn't a good time to discuss anything further.

He blew out a breath. "It comes down to trust again, doesn't it?" he said, stopping her in her tracks. "You married me, but you didn't trust me about your mother's money problems. You thought I might let it leak to the media and make some publicity out of it."

It was all true.

Every word.

She sighed. "The point is that I married you, Alex. You must've had some sort of redeeming quality about you, though for the life of me right now I can't see what it is. I'm entitled to my privacy."

His eyes shuttered then he turned and poured himself a drink. "Go to bed, Olivia. I'll come in later."

Sometime during the night, Olivia was aware of Alex coming to bed. She'd been half-asleep, but now she held her breath, waiting for him to pull her close.

Only he didn't.

"I'm sorry," he said, his voice low and rough.

Silence fell in the darkness. This was the last thing she expected him to say. "Thank you."

And then he rolled onto his side, his back to her, and promptly went to sleep.

Olivia lay there for ages, listening to his breathing, a sense of hopelessness filling her. They were destined to be childless and that meant they were destined to be divorced. It was just a matter of time.

Alex had gone when she woke up and only the crumpled blankets on the other side of the bed told her he'd been there. Heavy-hearted, she drew on her silk bathrobe and walked out into the living room, fully expecting it to be empty.

But Alex was just placing the telephone back in its cradle. He glanced up when he heard her. "That was the specialist. He said he can see you later this morning."

She missed a step. "Wh-what? So soon?"

His jaw tensed. "We need to have it confirmed once and for all."

She quickly gathered her thoughts together. "*You* need to, Alex. I don't need to know at all."

His gaze softened as he came toward her. "Olivia, don't you want to know? Really?"

Panic stirred in her chest. "No."

He stopped in front of her and placed his hands on her shoulders. "You're scared. I understand, but isn't it best to know?"

Easy for him to say, she thought cynically. He'd drop her once he knew for sure and go make a new life for himself. While she…

She shrugged. "Maybe I'll just wait and see what happens in a few years. Who knows? I might marry again and find myself pregnant and that will be a bonus," she said, letting him know he wasn't the only one capable of getting on with his life.

He pressed his lips together and gave her a little shake. "The only person you're going to get pregnant to will be me, Olivia."

His words warmed her but she knew it wasn't fair to let him get his hopes up. "Alex, look—"

He sighed and dropped his hands away. "Olivia, I won't force you into this. The choice is yours."

She stared at him and all at once realized he really needed to know. She wanted to believe it was about them as a couple, but she knew it was about the baby.

Okay, so for *him* she would do it. Otherwise he would always wonder. And perhaps after this he would be able to move on.

From her.

"Okay, Alex," she said quietly. "I'll do it."

His brows drew together. "Are you sure?"

"Yes," she said with mild exasperation.

He fixed her with a candid gaze. "Right. Go get dressed. I need to make a few phone calls then I'll be ready to come with you. We have an hour."

Her mouth dropped open. "You're coming with me?"

He looked surprised by the question. "Of course. Just try and stop me."

Oh heavens. If she wasn't careful she was going to get all weepy.

She cleared her throat. "Thank you, Alex. It's just that Eric…" How did she say this politely? "He never…bothered."

"The bastard," Alex spat, his expression clouding in anger. After a second or two, his anger seemed to cool a little. "Well, I'm different. We're in this together, Olivia."

Her throat felt so tight with emotion, she could only nod.

"Now go get dressed," Alex said, turning away and reaching for the phone, but his voice sounded a little unsteady.

Olivia fled the room before she broke down altogether. It was easier being strong when she didn't think too hard about things, but have someone give her sympathy and she would probably turn into an emotional wreck.

Once they arrived at the hospital the specialist spoke to both her and Alex, then she was given a private room and a thorough round of tests began.

The doctor was totally noncommittal during their discussion and Olivia told herself not to get her hopes up. For the main part she didn't, but there was that rogue flicker of optimism that wouldn't be quiet no matter how much she tried to suppress it.

As for Alex, he was great. He stayed with her as much as he could, refusing to leave her side.

And then late that day they waited in the room for the news together.

And Alex sat next to the bed and held her hand tightly as the specialist delivered the bad news that she would never have a child. The damage from the ectopic pregnancy was just too extensive, he was sorry to say.

Not as sorry as she was, she thought, glad to be feeling hugely numb both inside and out.

She'd known.

Dear God, she'd known, but somehow she'd let herself hope.

Now there truly was no hope left.

Nine

"We should get another opinion," Alex said once he'd recovered his breath. It was almost impossible to grasp what the specialist was saying. Hell, he didn't *want* to grasp it.

From where he stood at the end of the bed, the doctor looked down at them with sympathetic eyes. "Mr. Valente, I understand, but it won't make any difference to the outcome. Our tests were very thorough." He paused. "I'm sorry."

But Alex wasn't convinced. He glanced at Olivia. "We should try elsewhere. We could—"

"No, Alex," she said firmly. "Enough is enough."

Up until this moment "no" just hadn't been in his mindset. Now, dear God, he just couldn't believe he was being told there was no other answer.

Then he looked at this beautiful woman who was sitting up in the hospital bed, dressed in a white hospital gown, and who had just been through a medical procedure, and her head was held high with courage and determination to get on with her life. He swallowed hard. If she could take the news and put it behind her then how fair was it for him to keep pushing her over this?

"You're right," he said, and lifted her hand held tight in his own to kiss her knuckles, letting her see the admiration in his eyes.

She held his gaze for a few seconds and soft pink colored her cheeks before she looked up at the specialist. "Thank you for all your help, doctor."

The doctor nodded. "I wish it could have been better news, Mrs. Valente."

"I know."

Alex stood up and shook the doctor's hand, then the other man left them alone.

Silence.

He looked at Olivia. "Are you okay?"

It took a moment, but a small, reassuring smile appeared. "Yes, Alex. I'm fine."

He wasn't. He still felt gutted. And how she managed to smile through all this was a—

He saw her bury her face in her hands and her shoulders began to shake. "Olivia?"

She gave a small sob.

He sat on the edge of the bed and gently pulled her up against his chest, his heart cramping with pain when he saw the hot tears slipping down her cheeks. "Oh, sweetheart, let it out," he muttered. "Let it all out."

That only made it worse. He held her like that for long moments while she cried.

Eventually she pulled back, sniffing and trying to unscrunch a tissue she'd been holding in her hand. "I'm sorry."

He let his hands slide to her shoulders, needing to keep on holding her. "No, I'm the one who's sorry. I shouldn't have put you through that."

She dabbed her eyes with the tissue. "It's better that I know for sure."

He swore. "Better for whom? You…or me?" His chest ached with an inner pain. "I was wrong in asking that of you, sweetheart."

She shuddered. "Alex, don't punish yourself. I did this for both of us."

A feeling in his heart began to morph into something he'd never felt before. It terrified him, so he quickly pushed it aside, not wanting to know. "Thank you," he said in a hoarse whisper.

She drew a shaky breath. "I think I'll go to sleep now. It's getting late. Do you mind?"

He cleared his throat. "Not at all."

The specialist had said he would keep her in the hospital overnight and Alex was more than glad of that now. She needed to rest.

And he suddenly needed to be alone.

"Get them to call me if you want anything and I'll come straight over."

She leaned forward and kissed him softly on the lips. "Thanks."

He hopped off the edge of the bed and helped her to make herself comfortable, then he kissed her and left the room, the door shushing closed behind her.

It wasn't until he walked into his hotel room that he dropped down onto the sofa, his legs no longer able to hold him up. He'd gotten this far but now the reality of it was sinking in.

Olivia would never have a baby.

His baby.

Dammit, he'd realized he wanted that more than anything in the world. And it wasn't just because his father wanted him to have a child.

Then something lodged in his throat and he realized he was wrong about this. Totally wrong. The only thing he wanted more than anything in the world was Olivia herself.

He loved her.

A sense of joy swept over him that went clear through to his soul. He had a heartbeat to savor it, contemplate it. Half a second later, pain slammed into him with the force of a wrecking ball.

He couldn't tell her, especially not right now. She had enough to cope with without him putting unnecessary pressure on her. And telling a woman he loved her and wanted her to stay married to him forever was definitely immense pressure. He couldn't do that to her right now.

If at all.

Olivia was glad to leave New York later that week and head back to LA, where they were to spend a couple of days with her mother. Felicia was full of talk about whether she could juggle both the television series and the movie next year, assuming she got the part. It was good to see her mother so enthusiastic and full of promise for the future.

If only she felt as hopeful for the future, too.

But she couldn't be.

She didn't want to burst her mother's bubble so she kept quiet about the conclusive tests for her infertility. Her mother would be devastated.

As she knew Alex was, too. It was the reason he'd been slightly aloof since she'd come out of hospital and hadn't tried to make love to her. Oh, he'd been wonderful—looking after her and giving her attention, but they were normal everyday things most husbands gave their wives.

Yet she understood where Alex was coming from. He had responsibilities to his father and to his brothers and nothing could change that. He had to step back from her.

Yes, she understood.

But it hurt.

She needed him to tell her everything would be all right.

She needed him to say he wasn't going to dump her before the twelve months was up.

And right now, as silly as it seemed, she needed him to *need* her.

"Randall told me he saw you in New York," Felicia said their first evening at dinner after they'd caught up on other things.

Olivia was glad Alex would be late this evening. It was best they didn't discuss anything like this in front of him. She didn't want to give him any reminders about what had happened.

"Yes, and he's a granddad now, I hear," she said,

pasting on a bright smile to show she could handle it all. She had to put one foot in front of the other and keep moving forward, not stop to think about what she had lost.

Felicia's mouth curved with affection. "Yes, he told me." Then her smile faded. "I hope it didn't upset you, darling?"

Olivia pretended to be surprised. "No, of course not. I love Randall and I'm happy for him." That was the truth.

"That's my girl," Felicia said, leaning over and briefly squeezing Olivia's hand. "I'm glad you're over it." Just as quickly her mother leaned back in the high-backed dining chair. "Darling, I've been wanting to tell you for some time that Eric has a child, too, but I wasn't sure—"

"Shut the hell up, Felicia," Alex growled from the doorway, taking them by surprise, and both women spun around in their seats.

Felicia started to gulp like a fish. "Well, I never!"

Alex glared at her. "Can't you see your daughter is upset? Or is that just a bit beyond your comprehension?"

"Alex, don't…" Olivia warned.

He waved a dismissive hand. "No, Olivia. I won't be quiet over this. Tell her the truth. Then she might look beyond herself and see your pain like I do."

Olivia blinked in shock. There was nothing aloof about him now. Her heart skipped a beat.

"What truth, Olivia?" Felicia demanded. "What is Alex talking about?"

Olivia slowly turned. This was going to be painful for her mother. She swallowed, her throat aching. "I can't have a child, Mum. It's been confirmed."

Felicia paled. "Never?"

"No, Mum."

Her mother's mouth worked without speaking for a moment. "Oh God, I'll never be a grandmother?"

"No, Mum," Olivia said as gently as she could. "I'm afraid this isn't like the movies. There won't be a happy ending."

Seconds ticked by as Felicia stared aghast at her daughter. Then amazingly, something seemed to change inside her mother. Olivia could feel it in the air.

When she looked across at Alex, he had left the room.

"Darling," Felicia's apologetic tone began. "Your husband is right. I've only been concerned about me, not you. I'm so sorry."

Shock ran through Olivia. "Mum, it's okay."

Her mother shook her head. "No, it's not. I know my faults. I'm self-centered and irresponsible at times but…" She took a shaky breath and her eyes filled with tears. "Darling, I love you more than life itself. You know that, don't you?"

The tears welled in Olivia's eyes, too. "Yes, Mum, I know that. I've always known that. And when it comes right down to it, that's all that matters."

"Thank you for that, darling," Felicia said, and grabbed her napkin, dabbing it at her eyes in a theatrical pose that Olivia knew wasn't a pose at all this time.

Her mother gave a watery smile. "You might need to go see how your husband is," she prodded. "And please tell him I'm sorry." She winced. "No, I'll tell him myself when I see him tomorrow. I need to take responsibility."

Olivia blinked away the last of her tears and looked again at her mother with new eyes. It had been a long time coming, but Felicia really had changed. Olivia got to her feet and hugged her mother.

Felicia hugged her back, then as Olivia moved away, she asked in concern, "Are you okay with what I said about Eric having a child?"

Olivia nodded. "Absolutely." And she was. Eric didn't affect her any longer. At last she was able to leave all that behind her.

Her mother looked pleased. She waved a hand toward the door. "Go see Alex."

Olivia found Alex in the bedroom, undoing his shirt. Just the sight of him made her heart beat fast.

"That wasn't a very nice thing to say to my mother," she said, matter-of-factly.

A pulse beat in his cheek. "She needed to hear it."

"I know. Thank you," she said sincerely, seeing him look startled. "It did the trick. I think she's finally growing up."

He stopped undressing and his eyes searched hers. "It's about time she did."

Olivia wrinkled her nose. "It's been hard for her to change."

"It's hard for anyone to change."

"Yes, but perhaps it was more difficult for her. She grew up being a spoiled little girl because of her looks, then she became a beautiful spoiled woman, and then a spoiled movie star. Everyone treats her like royalty."

He stared for a moment before shaking his head with slight amazement. "You don't realize it, do you?"

She blinked. "What?"

"Your mother may be royalty in the movie world but out here in the real world, *you're* the one who is true royalty. You not only have elegance and class, but you have a sense of compassion and understanding and generosity that shines through."

Her breath hitched, his opinion of her making her feel like jelly inside. No man had ever said such a nice thing to her. "You can't know that," she murmured.

He came toward her and put his hand under her chin, looking deeply into her eyes. "I *know* the person you are, Olivia Valente."

Then he lowered his head and kissed her, her pulse racing even more when his hands slid down to pull her up against him. He was fully aroused.

She kissed him back. He needed her and that was enough.

For now.

They returned to their apartment in Sydney overlooking the harbor and Olivia was immediately swept up in business dealings with her boutiques. It was a relief to keep busy.

Of their future together Alex didn't say a word, nor did he mention anything about telling his father and she was coward enough to accept that. Suddenly every moment spent with him was important.

Why, she didn't want to know.

And then she came home one evening and heard the muffled sound of voices coming from the study. She tapped lightly on the door and opened it and found Alex and his two brothers sitting on the couch, glasses of whiskey in their hands.

Their expressions were welcoming but she suspected they'd been discussing something important and didn't really appreciate the interruption.

"Oh, I'm sorry. I didn't know you were all here," she said, ready to step back and leave them to it.

But Alex was already coming toward her. "Sweetheart, you don't have to apologize," he said, the loving husband. "We're just discussing business." He swooped in for a kiss in a possessive manner she knew was only for show.

She kissed him back, welcoming the feel of his lips on hers after a day spent away from him.

"Um...I'd better go get some dinner," she said, once he eased back and let her go.

"There's a casserole in the oven."

Up close, Olivia could see his eyes already turning back toward business. "Great." She forced a smile. "Have you eaten?"

"Yes." She looked at the other two men to ask them if they'd like something, but Alex spoke before her. "They've eaten, too."

"Oh."

"Yes," Nick said with a polite smile. "We've eaten."

"But thanks anyway," Matt, the youngest, said.

She could see they were wanting to get back to their discussion. "I'll leave you to it."

She stepped back and closed the door, then went to take a shower before eating, but she grew more worried with each passing moment. Had Alex told them about his father's ultimatum after all? And not just about needing to marry but about having a child as well? He had nothing to hide from them any longer. He had already married her. And now there would be no baby.

Her heart ached. Then something occurred to her. Perhaps Alex had asked them here to discuss a new plan?

Or a new wife?

She gulped. No, she couldn't believe he would say anything about her infertility to his brothers. Not without her consent.

Still, later when he slid into bed in the dark she had to ask. "Is everything okay?"

"Yes."

"You all looked quite preoccupied."

"There's a small problem. We can deal with it."

She swallowed hard, hoping *she* wasn't the problem they would deal with. Then she pushed it out of her mind and tried to get some sleep.

But the next morning as she came out of the bathroom after finishing her shower, she heard Alex talking on the phone and she stopped dead.

"Dad, I need to see you about something," he was saying quietly, his back to her. "I'll be there in half an hour."

There was a pause.

"Cancel your appointment, Dad. This is important. It can't wait."

Another pause.

"Right. See you soon." He hung up, pushed himself to his feet and reached for his trousers. Then he saw her and he seemed to freeze. Or was that just her imagination?

He scowled. "You look pale. Are you okay?"

She forced herself to move. "Yes, I'm fine. The shower was a bit too hot, that's all." She half expected he would tease her about them making steam in the shower, only he didn't. He had that distant look back on his face.

"You take it easy, Olivia. You've been rushing around too much lately."

"Thank you for your concern," she said, unable to stop a hint of coolness to her voice.

He held her eyes for a beat, looking slightly puzzled, then turned away to glance at the bedside clock. "I have to go." He headed for the door, stopping briefly to kiss her on the mouth. "See you tonight."

He left the room.

But he left behind a very worrying silence.

Ten

Alex didn't come home until after ten that night. He had phoned earlier to say there was a problem and he had to work late, but Olivia had heard voices laughing in the background and wondered if that were true. She wanted to believe him and for the most part she did, but memories of her ex-husband's cheating kept flashing through her mind.

She knew Alex wasn't like that. Alex had integrity and was honest and—

Was this the same Alex she now suspected might not even wait the twelve months before getting rid of her? The same Alex who might be plotting even now with his father and his brothers to find a way to end his marriage?

The same man who—

No, she was jumping to conclusions. She seriously didn't want to believe any of that. Perhaps those voices had merely been his staff. There certainly hadn't been any music in the background to indicate a bar, nor any woman's voice specifically.

Still, when he stripped in the dark in the bedroom then went to take a shower, she found herself quietly sniffing the air for the scent of perfume. Thank God there was none. And when he joined her in bed ten minutes later, there was only the smell of Alex.

And it was wonderful.

And when he slid his arm around her and pulled her up against him, she waited for him to kiss her and make love to her. Only, he kissed the top of her head instead then promptly fell asleep.

Strangely, Olivia felt comforted and she must have fallen asleep, too, because the next thing she knew the telephone beside the bed was ringing. Her heart jumped in her throat and instinctively she reached for the phone in the pre-dawn light.

Her heart thudded with relief when she heard

her mother's voice. Felicia always got the time zones mixed up. "Mum, it's five in the morning over here."

"Darling, I had to call you," Felicia said urgently. "I'm afraid the newspapers know."

"Know?" Olivia's forehead crinkled as she sat up in bed. "What do they know?" She still wasn't functioning right.

"About you not being able to have a...a...baby."

Olivia's brain stumbled. "Wh-what?"

"It's in all the newspapers over here today. And my phone hasn't stopped ringing." Felicia took a shuddering breath. "I'm so sorry, darling."

"I don't believe this," Olivia whispered, vaguely aware of Alex switching the light on and coming around to her side of the bed.

"I don't know how they knew," her mother continued. "*I* certainly didn't tell them. I hope you believe that."

She was having trouble coming to grips with this. Why would anyone want to know about her and her infertility problems?

"Olivia?" Alex demanded, then when she didn't answer he took the phone out of her hand. "Felicia, what on earth did you say to Olivia?" He listened, then his eyes shot to Olivia and his jaw clenched.

"How the devil did that happen?" he growled. Felicia must have spoken as he paused, then said, "Yes, I'll look after her."

Olivia was only partly aware of him hanging up the phone.

"Olivia?"

She looked at him then. "How could they, Alex?" she choked.

His eyes darkened. "I know, sweetheart."

She bit back a sob. "I don't want the world to know about…about… It's private."

He pulled her into his arms. "Shh."

She went willingly, leaning on him for a moment, accepting his strength, before giving a shuddering sob. She wanted to cry but wouldn't give them—*any* of them—the satisfaction.

And then something hit her.

It was so obvious.

She pulled back, the words bursting from her, her nerves stretched to the limit. "I bet it was your father. He wants to get rid of me. He wants you to marry someone who can give you a child."

His eyes narrowed. "Do you hear yourself?"

It suddenly seemed more than plausible. "You told him, didn't you? You told him and now he knows and—"

"Don't be bloody ridiculous. I didn't tell him a thing."

"Then it was one of your brothers. That's why they were here the other night. You were telling them the whole thing, weren't you?"

He shook her lightly. "Stop it! No one knew but you, me and your mother."

She gasped, his shake hurtling her back to their surroundings. "Oh God, I'm sorry, Alex. I don't know what came over me." Heavens, she'd gone crazy for a minute there.

"It's understandable," he said, but there was a stiffness to his shoulders that hadn't been there before. He got to his feet and stood looking down at her, keeping a distance now that she very much regretted.

She hesitated, measuring how to explain it all. "I wonder how the media found out about it? Someone had to have told them. My mother's just as confused as we are."

His brow rose. "Maybe someone from the doctor's office in New York?"

"Yes, that's possible."

His eyes hardened. "Or your ex?"

She sucked in a sharp breath and considered the possibility out loud. "Yes…but why now? He knew it was unlikely I'd ever have a child. He could have told them about it years ago." She shook her blond head. "No, he'd come out of it smelling less than roses. Eric wouldn't want that," she added cynically.

"No, I don't suppose the bastard would."

She was surprised by the comment yet not. The thought of Eric always set her on edge, too.

She mentally pushed Eric aside. "I just don't understand why the papers need to print stuff like this. Why do they need to cause people pain? Isn't it enough that we have to live it?" she whispered, then gave a ragged sigh. "I guess I should be used to it."

He made a harsh sound. "Whoever leaked that bit of information had better watch out. I'll hunt them down. They won't do it again in a hurry."

He looked so angry she was reminded of how fiercely this man protected his own.

"Alex, I know I got it all wrong about your father and brothers, but what were you and Nick and Matt speaking about the other night? You went to see your father yesterday morning, too. I heard you on the telephone telling him there was a problem."

His angry expression faded and concern replaced it. "Dad's not well. We were discussing how to push him gently into retirement."

Her shoulders slumped. "Oh boy, I really got it wrong, didn't I?"

He held her gaze for a minute, seeming to delve into her thoughts, but then he broke eye contact and glanced at the clock. "Speaking of my father, I'm going down to the study to call him. He needs to know. If we don't tell him, the media will. No doubt they'll be hanging around the office today."

Dismay filled her. "That'll mean they'll be at the boutique, too."

"Yes. Perhaps you should stay home today and not leave the apartment."

She nodded woodenly. "Okay. And I'll phone Lianne and tell her not to go into work either."

"Don't turn on the television," he said, heading for the door. "Do some work or just try and relax. I know it's hard."

"Okay." Her throat closed up and her heart cramped. "I'm so sorry for causing all this trouble, Alex."

He stopped at the door and looked back. "Don't be crazy," he rasped, then left the room, taking her heart with him.

It was then she realized why he made her forget who she was. Why she found herself in him.

Oh God, she loved him.

Loved him more than life itself.

Oh my—she loved Alex. He had taken possession of her heart in a way she'd never thought possible.

He filled her completely, making her come truly alive for the first time ever. For a moment she took hold of that love, celebrating its beauty, honored that it had come to live in her heart.

Then reality struck with a bang.

She had no idea what Alex felt for her, but it didn't matter anyway. She couldn't let it matter. Despite knowing he was the right person for her, this just wasn't the right time or the right place. There could *never* be a right time for them. Not when she could only bring pain and heartache to him.

There was only one thing to do. She had to compose herself, somehow. She'd been given a beautiful gift that chose to rest in her heart, but showing him that gift of love would only cause more heartache.

Pain clawed at Alex's heart as he strode to the study to call his father. The pain was for the anguish Olivia was going through right now, and for the strength she'd need to get through the next few days. He'd be there for her of course, but damn the media's greed for a story—any story.

Damn them all.

He swallowed hard. Hell, she'd just apologized for causing *him* trouble. No apology was necessary for something like this.

In fact he wanted to apologize to *her* for putting her through all this. If he hadn't married her, if he hadn't tried to use her to help launch Valente's Woman, then she'd be going about her own business, designing clothes and getting on with her life.

But no, he had to come into her life and make sure the one thing she wanted kept to herself was splashed through the papers.

Bloody hell.

Entering the study, he sat in his chair and reached for the telephone. It was early and his father was going to get a rude awakening. Good. Cesare Valente shouldn't have started all this marriage business in the first place. If he'd just let things be…

Alex flinched. Then Olivia wouldn't have come into his life. He wouldn't have fallen in love with her. He wouldn't have known what true love was all about.

He sighed. As much as it was painful for him, at least his love for her was something to hang on to.

It took a few moments for his father to answer the telephone. "Dad, it's Alex."

"Alex?" Cesare's sleepy voice came down the line.

"Dad, I have to tell you something."

"Son, it's five-fifteen in the morning." There was a pause as Cesare replied to something Isabel said in the background.

"I wouldn't call if it wasn't important. You know that."

There was a grunt. "Let me just get comfortable, then you can tell me. I'm still trying to wake up." There was the sound of movement. "Right. Now what's the matter?"

Alex could feel his blood pressure begin to rise just at the thought of it all. "You're going to read it in the newspapers soon, or someone will call you and tell you anyway, but…"

"But what?"

Alex took a deep breath, his heart pounding in his chest. "Olivia and I can't give you a grandchild, Dad. She's infertile." He hated saying the word. Hated having to tell anyone what was essentially his and Olivia's private business. "And now, dammit, some-how the media have found out and it's in all the papers in the States."

There was nothing but the heaviest silence on the other end of the phone.

"So you're telling me Olivia can't have a child?" Cesare finally said, followed by Isabel's gasp.

"Yes."

It was hard to tell what his father was thinking and Alex could have kicked himself now for not going straight to his parents' estate, rather than saying this over the phone. At least then he'd be able to try to read his father's expression. He grimaced. And why the hell did he care what his father thought anyway?

"I'm sorry to hear that, son."

"Yeah, so am I." And that was the understatement of the century.

Time ticked by as though it was dragging its feet.

"You love her, don't you?" Cesare said with what Alex thought was deceptive calm. His father was always the ultimate businessman and rarely gave anything away of his thoughts. On another level Alex was surprised by the other man's perception.

"Yes, Dad, I do."

Cesare made some sort of sound, but Isabel said something in the background over the top of it, and it was hard to tell what reaction his father had given.

Then, "What are you going to do, Alex?"

Alex's hand tightened around the telephone. "The one thing I *won't* be doing is giving her up," he said in a warning voice.

"That sounds like an ultimatum to me."

"You should know. You're an expert at them."

There was a heavy pause. "What do you want me to say, Alex?"

"Nothing, Dad. There's nothing you can say that will change a damn thing." Alex gave a short pause.

"The only reason I'm telling you this is because we need to look at what the media will do next. They're bound to be calling you for comment or coming to the office."

"Maledizione," his father cursed. "I've got better things to do than let them waste my time."

"I agree, but we have to think about Olivia," he reminded his father. "I don't want anyone talking to them about her. She's going through enough as it is."

"Look, come and see me. We need to talk."

Alex's throat tightened with emotion. "I will, but don't think I'll be changing my mind."

"Don't jump the gun, *figlio mio.*"

Alex ignored his father's further lapse into Italian. He'd go but he already knew talking would be a waste of time. And right now he really didn't give a damn what Cesare Valente had to say.

Half an hour later Olivia had showered and dressed and, with a heavy heart, she went down to the study. Alex was sitting at the desk going through some paperwork. He looked up when she entered the room.

Her heart constricted. Dear God, she was breaking up inside, but she had to go through with this. She had to set him free so that he could make a life for himself with someone else, someone who didn't cause havoc in his life, no matter how inadvertently.

"Did you tell your father?" she asked, watching his face, trying to see how it had gone.

"Yes." His expression gave nothing away. "About half an hour ago."

"What did he say?"

"Not much. He was still trying to wake up."

She could imagine that Cesare Valente wouldn't be pleased. He'd seemed to like her but now that she was stopping him—no, stopping his son—from carrying on the Valente name, things would change. It wouldn't matter that Nick and Matt would undoubtedly have children of their own. Cesare was old-school and he would want his eldest son to have the first grandchild.

"I have an important meeting this morning, but my mother said she'll call you later. She doesn't want you to be alone. She wants to come over and spend some time with you."

"There's no need." She didn't plan on being here anyway.

"Yes, there is."

"Alex, I'm okay. I don't need Isabel to come over and stay with me." She swallowed past her dry throat, steeling herself to tell him why. "Alex, I—"

The telephone rang, cutting her off.

He sat there, his stare drilling into her, as if he suspected she was about to say something important.

It rang again and she nodded her head at it. "You'd better answer that."

His eyes narrowed. "It can wait."

She'd lost her momentum now. How could she say what she had to say with a ringing telephone in the background?

"Alex, we can talk later. You should answer the phone."

Frustration crossing his face, he grabbed the receiver and barked into it. Olivia dropped down on the couch, needing something to sit on while she gathered her strength again. As soon as he hung up she would have to speak up. There was no getting around it. Alex deserved better than—

All at once she noticed he'd turned pale with what looked like shock. Oh heavens, not more of this media crap? Didn't they ever—

"I'll be right there," he muttered, then put the phone back in its cradle.

She pushed herself to her feet. "What's the matter?"

He didn't answer, just sat staring at the phone.

"Alex?"

He blinked, seeming to come from a long way off. "Um…it's my father. They think he's had a heart attack. The housekeeper just called to say my mother's gone with Dad in the ambulance."

Olivia gasped. "Oh my God!"

He stood up and started toward the door, pale but focused now. "I have to go."

She put her hand on his forearm as he passed, stopping him. "Alex, I'll come with you."

His brows drew together. "No, you stay here. There'll be enough reporters at the hospital as it is." And then he kissed her cheek and continued out of the room.

Olivia let him go, shaken by his comment. He hadn't meant to be hurtful but it had cut her to the quick, showing her exactly how unsuitable and disruptive she was for him.

For his family.

She swallowed as a new anguish seared her. And now his father was having a heart attack and she was more than likely to blame for bringing it on. Oh Lord. She prayed Cesare would be okay. If he wasn't…

No, she wouldn't think about that.

She'd keep busy until she heard from Alex. He'd call as soon as he knew something, surely. For now, she'd go phone Lianne and explain it all. She was close to her business partner, but this wasn't something she looked forward to doing. She didn't want anyone's sympathy. The only thing she wanted was Alex.

The telephone rang again and she rushed to the desk to grab it. Could this be news of Cesare so soon? Alex would only just be getting in his car.

It wasn't.

It was a reporter and she hung up without answering his question. *How do you feel about your infertility?* She gave a choked sob. How the heck did he think she felt?

On top of the world!

Gloriously happy!

Ecstatic!

The phone rang again.

She froze. It could be Alex. Or Isabel. Or perhaps Felicia. With a shaky hand, she picked it up then dropped it back down just as quickly when she heard the same reporter's voice. And then she disconnected it.

Damn them.

She'd turn her cell phone on so that Alex could at least contact her. Only, when she took it out of her purse, as soon as she turned it on it began beeping with messages. None of the numbers looked familiar and she soon realized the messages were all about the same thing. Her heart thudded. No doubt for some it was easy getting her number.

At least with a cell phone she could leave it on

silent and still check the numbers in case Alex called. But first, she called him to let him know what was happening.

He swore. "Don't answer any of them unless you see my number, okay?"

She was warmed by his response. "Okay." She hesitated. "I'm so sorry about your dad, Alex."

"So am I," he muttered, then had to hang up because he'd just arrived at the hospital.

A sense of inadequacy swept over her as she walked back into the study and sat down at the desk. She couldn't be there for Alex when he needed her. She couldn't have his child. She couldn't even give her mother a grandchild. What the heck use was she?

She shuddered. Oh God. This was crazy talk. She was feeling sorry for herself, that's all. She had to stop it.

Right. She took a deep breath and gathered herself together. She'd phone Lianne shortly, but first she'd phone her mother just to let her know she was okay.

And she was, she told herself as she picked up the telephone from the desk and reconnected it, breathing a quick sigh of relief when she got a dial tone.

Surprisingly it was her mother who answered straight away, and not the housekeeper. Olivia briefly told Felicia about Cesare and promised to keep her up to date, then she told her about having to disconnect the phone temporarily and to call her on her cell phone if necessary. Her mother understood all too well.

Then, "Darling, I know who leaked the news. It was Brita."

"Your housekeeper?"

"Yes. Just now I caught her on the telephone to a reporter. Apparently she heard us talking about it when you stayed here." Her mother's displeasure came clear across the ocean. "She's packing her bags right now."

Olivia was shocked. "But she's been with you for years." And lasted the longest.

"Five, but apparently she feels hard done by." Felicia clicked her tongue. "It's hard to get good staff these days."

Olivia could have reminded her mother that even back "in the good old days" her mother had had trouble keeping her staff. It wasn't that Felicia wasn't nice to them, but more that she was too "precious," as one of them had commented when Olivia had contacted her to beg her to come back.

"Darling, I'm so sorry about this," Felicia said. "I don't know how I can make it up to you."

"Mum, you don't have to do anything. It's not your fault, okay?"

"Okay. Don't forget to call me when you know something about Cesare."

"I won't."

But as Olivia hung up the phone, she knew her mother was feeling guilty about it all, in spite of what she'd said.

And perhaps that wasn't such a bad thing where Felicia was concerned. It showed she was still growing and changing and becoming more aware of others. Olivia was relieved not to worry so much about her mother anymore. It was one less thing for her to think about.

Alex spent the morning with his brothers pacing up and down the hospital, racked with guilt. He shouldn't have woken his father up so early. He'd known his dad wasn't in the best of health and needed his sleep.

Not only had he woken him, he'd then gone on to hand Cesare a plateful of stress. Just the idea of all the hassle the media would cause was enough to stress a person out, let alone telling his father about Olivia being infertile, and worse, that he was sticking by Olivia's side no matter what.

Not that any of this would change his mind. He still intended to stay with Olivia and love her as much as he could. But perhaps dumping all this on a man who'd come close to having a heart attack wasn't the cleverest thing he'd ever done. He could have waited a few hours and gone over and broken it to his father more carefully than he did.

Just then Isabel came through the doors of the waiting room, and he held his breath, his heart thudding inside his chest. Then he saw she was smiling.

"He's going to be just fine," she told the three brothers quickly. "It was only a mild heart attack and they have every confidence he won't have another one. That is, if he changes his lifestyle. I intend to make that happen."

Alex felt sick with relief. His father was a pain in the butt at times, but this was his father and he loved him, dammit.

Nick and Matt started firing questions at Isabel. Alex listened while she replied as best she could, but he held back, taking it all in.

"He's sleeping now, so why don't you all go to work and come back later this afternoon? It's no use just sitting here doing nothing." She kissed Nick's then Matt's cheek. "Now I want to speak to Alex for a moment so you two go on ahead," she said, shooing them out of there. "It's nothing important."

Alex stiffened, aware of the curious looks from his

brothers before they left. Was there something more Isabel wasn't telling them? Isabel said it wasn't important but—

"Alex, I want you to know how sorry I am that Olivia can't have children," she said, giving his arm a squeeze.

Alex had been so involved in everything else over the last couple of minutes, he'd forgotten his own problems.

He nodded. "Thanks."

"Your father asked me to give you a message."

He tensed, feeling the blow already. "And that is?"

"He said he's sorry. He said he only wants you to be happy, and that if you love Olivia then that's enough for him."

Alex gulped. "He said that?"

"Yes. And he told me everything." Her mouth tightened. "If I'd known what he was doing I would have put a stop to it, believe me."

His stepmother was a formidable woman when she got riled.

"Thanks, but if he hadn't given me an ultimatum, I doubt I would have married her." Or maybe he would have—though it may have taken quite a while. She'd caught his eye right from the moment he'd seen her.

"Somehow I think you would have still ended up together." She kissed his cheek. "You'd better get home to your wife. She needs you right now."

Alex nodded, then left with the promise to be back later. Now it was time for Olivia. He hated the media for what they were doing to his wife. It gutted him to see their private business in the papers, but it must go to the heart of her even more.

Olivia got up from the sofa and rushed toward him when he opened the door. "How is he?" she said, full of concern for the man who had done nothing but manipulate her life for his own purposes.

Hell, not that *he* had done any different.

"He'll be fine. It was only a mild attack."

"Thank God!" She threw her arms around him and hugged him.

Delighted to have her in his arms, he hugged her back, inhaling the scent of her, loving the feel of her body against his. He wanted this for the rest of his life. He wanted—

She dropped her hands and took a few steps away. "I spoke to my mother again. Alex, it was her housekeeper who told the reporters. Brita heard us talking about it."

His brow furrowed. "Brita? I'm surprised. I would never have thought it."

"I know."

His brow cleared. "At least we know who it was."

She nodded. "Mum fired her on the spot."

"Good." Thank God it hadn't been someone close, he wanted to say but didn't.

She must have sensed his thoughts. "Alex, again, I'm so sorry I accused your father of it."

He had to be fair. "It's not such a far-fetched conclusion," he admitted. "Who knows what he would've done if I'd told him before the papers got hold of the story?"

Or before he'd told his father he loved her.

"Let's give him the benefit of the doubt," she suggested, making him love her all the more for her generous nature.

Right then, he caught something out of the corner of his eye. Turning to look, he saw two suitcases down by the bureau. The breath seemed to leave his body. "What the hell?"

Regret filled her eyes and she straightened her shoulders. "I thought it only fair I wait to speak to you."

His heart began to sink. "Wait?"

"I'm releasing you from our agreement, Alex."

He swore. "What are you saying?"

"I'm offering you a divorce."

His head reeled back. "Who said I *want* a divorce?"

Her blue eyes shimmered with sudden tears, but she blinked them away. "I don't want you feeling responsible for me anymore. I don't want you staying with me out of pity."

"Who the hell said I'm staying with you out of pity?" he grated, his gut clenching and unclenching.

She took a shaky breath. "Accept it, Alex. This is the way it has to be."

"No." His chest tightened with emotion. How could she even think about divorce? Didn't she know he loved her?

Oh Lord. No, she didn't know that. How could she? He'd never told her of his feelings.

He opened his mouth, then as quickly shut it again. She'd never told him of her feelings either. To tell her he loved her, he had to know that her love would meet him halfway. He didn't know that with Olivia.

In fact, he *knew* she didn't love him. That was the one thing he would have sensed. A woman in love wouldn't even think about divorce…about walking away from her husband. A woman in love would sacrifice herself for…

His heart jolted.

Wasn't she sacrificing herself right now by releasing him from their agreement? Could she actually *love* him? The thought of it captivated him, just as her beauty did. If that were the case he had to tell her, had to let her know. If she were afraid of love he'd help her through it.

"I love you, Olivia."

She went perfectly still. "Wh-what?"

"I love you, darling. You can't leave me."

Olivia fumbled for words as she looked at Alex. They were words she longed to hear. Words she dare not consider. "But I can't give you a child."

His gray eyes softened. "I didn't marry you for an heir. I married you for my father's sake and for the sake of my family's company." He paused. "And then I fell in love with you. You are everything I've ever wanted, ever needed. I don't want anything more than you."

Her chest tightened with emotion. "Oh, Alex," she whispered. If only she could believe it didn't matter. But she knew it did.

"Do you love me, too, Olivia?"

She hesitated. "Family is important to you," she said, ignoring his question. "To both of us. I—"

"Do you love me, Olivia?" his words cut across hers, a muscle ticking in the side of his cheek, making her realize he wouldn't give up until he knew.

"Yes, I do, but—"

"No buts."

Oh God. She couldn't let him fool himself. "No, Alex. I would always feel like I've cheated you by not giving you a child."

"No," he ground out. "Absolutely not."

"But your father...your brothers' inheritance..."

He stepped up to her and cupped her face with his palms. "Look me in the eyes, Olivia. Look deep and see my love. It's for you, for the person you are right now, the woman I fell in love with. Unlike our marriage pact, that love is unconditional. It has nothing to do with anyone else."

"Alex, I..." She hesitated, choking up, tears springing into her eyes.

"Darling, I'm asking you to trust me totally this time. *Trust* that I love you. Trust that you are enough for me and always will be."

It was that word—trust—that tipped the balance. All this time she'd been learning to trust him, but it was only bit by bit, no matter how much she fooled herself. Now she knew deep in her heart that she did trust him, fully, utterly, believably. She trusted what he said and the man he was.

"Yes," she said, swaying toward him. "I trust you, Alex. I love you with all my heart."

His gray eyes turned to dark silver and he pulled

her close for a kiss. Her head swam as love passed between them. Love and infinite joy.

Afterward he released her just a little. "I want to kiss you until we grow old together, darling."

She caught her breath. "Oh, yes."

He grew more serious. "I didn't want to say this before because I wanted you to make the decision, but we could always adopt."

Her heart rose in her chest. "I didn't dare let myself think about that option. Your father—"

"Is happy for us," he said, startling her. "I told him how much I love you. I told him I wasn't about to leave you and that the business could go to hell for all I care. My brothers would survive without it, just as I would."

Her eyes widened. "You said all that?"

"We Valentes don't mess around when we want something."

"That's true." She looked up at him, letting him see the love in her eyes, no longer afraid of hiding it. "And seeing that I'm a Valente now…" She began undoing his tie.

"You want me?" he said huskily.

"No, I *need* you." In that heartbeat, Olivia silently agreed that when it came to love there were no conditions.

Epilogue

Six months later, they held an adoption party for their new son. Eight-year-old Scott Portman, now Scott Portman Valente, had been orphaned by a car accident two years earlier, leaving him with no relatives. Despite initially hoping to adopt a baby, Olivia and Alex had fallen in love with Scott the moment he'd said, "All I want is a mum and dad to love me again."

Talk about a serious tug on the heartstrings! They'd asked about adopting him there and then and Scott had come to live with them soon after in the new house.

Today, Scott's adoption had been made official. He was well and truly *theirs*.

And now all the family were celebrating Christmas at Villa Valente. Cesare had retired just after his heart attack but was in good health. He and Isabel looked very happy.

Alex had taken over the business with the help of his brothers, taking the House of Valente toward outstanding success through more international settings.

Even Felicia had flown in from the States in between recordings of her television show, which had proven a winner. Someone else had won the part in the movie but Olivia's mother hadn't minded by that stage. Felicia had found a new medium to showcase herself. And she was doing it well.

As for herself, a month ago she'd held a showing of the Valente Collection designs and it had been a huge success. Her boutiques were doing well and Lianne had even suggested they expand more, but Olivia was rather enjoying being a mother right now. Besides, she and Alex had spoken about going back to the orphanage in the near future to find a brother or sister for Scott.

Life was good.

"Hmm, what's that perfume you're wearing?" Alex teased, coming up behind her in the sunroom where she was placing plates of food on the table.

She spun around in his arms. "You know it's Valente's Woman."

His mouth hovered over hers. "No, *you* are Valente's woman."

She smiled, loving the possessive sound in his voice, confident they were equal partners in this marriage. "Is that so?"

His brow rose. "Are you going to argue with the man who loves you more than life itself?"

She breathed in his words of love. "Yes."

"I thought so," he murmured, lowering his head for a kiss.

And as his lips met hers, Olivia changed her mind. Life wasn't just good. It was better than good.

It was fantastic.

* * * * *

THE THROW-AWAY BRIDE

BY
ANN MAJOR

Ann Major lives in Texas with her husband of many years and is the mother of three grown children. She has a master's degree from Texas A&M at Kingsville, Texas, and is a former English teacher. She is a founding board member of Romance Writers of America and a frequent speaker at writers' groups.

Ann loves to write; she considers her ability to do so a gift. Her hobbies include hiking in the mountains, sailing, ocean kayaking, travelling and playing the piano. But most of all she enjoys her family.

Dear Reader,

Many of you have written me asking if I intended to write about the missing twins from my Golden Spurs novels, and, yes, I always did.

The Throw-Away Bride is the first twin's story. When Leo Storm, the CEO of the Golden Spurs ranching empire, discovers that Abby Collins, the woman who lives on the ranch next to his, is one of the twins, instead of telling her, he beds her. Ashamed of their passionate night, she scorns him until she discovers she's pregnant. Leo has been down this dark road before, so when she confides in him, he's not about to risk losing his precious child. Thus, he forces her into a marriage of convenience.

When Abby finds out who she really is and the length Leo's gone to in order to keep her identity a secret, she wonders if he married her for the baby or because he's ruthlessly ambitious and wants to be wedded to a member of the legendary family he works for. Does their fragile relationship stand a chance?

Ann Major

I dedicate this book to my late, much-beloved mother,
Ann C Major, even though I know she was really
a true-blue horror fan.

One

Central Texas, near Austin
Abigail Colins's ranch outside Bastrop, Texas
Early morning, first of June

Predictable Leo Storm had seemed like a safe choice.

When you go to a bar on the rebound intending to dance with a wild cowboy or two, and you end up sleeping with the dullest, safest, most-buttoned-down guy there—your next-door neighbor of all people—you don't expect earth-shattering consequences…in his bed or afterward.

Abigail Collins's eyes burned, and not from mucking out her horse Coco's stall. She was suffering from a bad case of Poor-Me Syndrome.

Greedy, ambitious CEOs like Leo Storm were supposed to play it safe when it came to sex. They were supposed to carry wallets full of condoms and fall asleep after doing it once.

Apparently Leo hadn't read his CEO rule book on said subject. His skill and enthusiastic ardor as a lover had made Abigail's toes tingle and her bones melt. She'd opened herself to him in ways that had caused her to despise herself and blame him the next morning. They'd done it so many times, she'd been tender for days. Needless to say, she'd avoided the heck out of him ever since.

So, the discovery that she was pregnant—by Leo— sucked big-time.

You can have anything you want—as long as you're willing to pay the price, her mother used to say. Trouble was, the price was due, and Abby didn't want to pay.

Ever since she'd found out about her condition last week, she'd been wallowing in self-misery—not that she was proud of such childish behavior.

As soon as she'd gotten up this morning and had finished going to the bathroom, desperation had overwhelmed her again, and she'd flipped the toilet lid down and collapsed on it, sniveling like a baby. A little later she'd had another good cry while knocking her forehead against the wet tiles of her shower.

As if buckets full of tears or regrets—and don't forget whining—did any good. Some things just had to be faced.

Pregnant! By Leo Storm!

She was a control freak and single with no desire for a long-term alliance of any kind after being hurt so badly when her boyfriend, Shanghai Knight, had dumped her.

Since puberty she'd gone for short-term relationships with cowboys like Shanghai; not for boring, bossy, calculating, corporate, money guys without souls like Leo. She'd been the brains, and the cowboys been the brawn.

She licked her lips and wiped the sweat off her brow. Well, she wasn't going to cry again. No use indulging in any more pity parties. She was a big girl—whether she was acting like one or not. She could handle this. She *had* to handle this.

Which was why she was telling Leo today. Surely she'd feel better once that was behind her. She closed her eyes and tried not to think about Leo's white, drawn face and blazing black eyes the last time she'd seen him. He'd been furious at her. Not only furious—he'd said he was through with her.

Usually being in the barn with Coco, her gentle palomino, soothed her. Not today. Not when she dreaded driving into San Antonio and telling a certain stubborn, macho CEO, who was now refusing to take her calls, that *they* had a little problem.

Every time she bent over to scoop another pitchfork load of manure and dirty straw into the wheelbarrow, the zipper of her jeans slid a little lower, reminding her of *their* mutual problem and *that* night, that one night with him that she'd tried so hard to forget.

Not that he'd wanted to forget. He'd made it very clear he'd wanted her—again and again. He was nothing if not determined. He'd called her both at home and at her office. He'd dropped by, but finally when she'd rejected him for about the tenth time, he'd become so angry he'd issued his ultimatum—which she'd ignored.

Having rid himself of her, he wouldn't be happy to

learn that *that* night was now every bit as impossible for her to forget as it had been for him.

Heaving in a breath, she rested her pitchfork against the wheelbarrow and tugged her zipper back up. She was panting by the time she'd managed it, so she didn't even try to snap the waistband. The jeans had been tight when she'd bought them, but since she'd planned to take off a couple of pounds, she hadn't worried about it.

No chance of losing those pounds anytime soon.

As she stooped to pick up the pitchfork, the cell phone in her back pocket vibrated against her hip. She threw the pitchfork back down hard, and it stabbed a mound of hay so violently that Coco, who was just outside the stall, danced backward, her hooves clattering on the concrete floor.

Oh, God, what if her big darling slipped because of her thoughtlessness?

"Easy girl," she whispered, her tone gentle even as the stench of straw and urine and horse in such close quarters caused nausea to roil in her stomach.

She hoped against hope that Leo had relented and was returning her call like a reasonable individual. Maybe he'd even agree to stop by her ranch house tonight to talk. Much as she would dread seeing him, it would be so nice if she could avoid the drive to San Antonio and the humiliation of fighting her way into his office after he'd made it clear he never wanted to see her again.

Not that she could blame him for that. Her heart knocked as she remembered accusing him of not being able to take no for an answer and of stalking her. He'd hissed in a breath. But she'd seen the acute pain in his black eyes right before he'd whirled, pitched the roses he'd brought her into the trash and quietly walked back to his truck. Later he'd called her and had delivered his ultimatum, which, for some weird reason, she'd replayed at least a dozen times in her mind. Did she enjoy suffering or what?

Instead of Leo's name, the number of In the Pink!, Abigail's own company located on a side street just off Congress Avenue in downtown Austin lit up the blue LED of her mobile phone.

Kel, her executive secretary, best friend, unpaid therapist…and of late, her number-one shoulder to cry on, was calling.

Damn.

Abigail sagged against the wall of the barn. A tear rolled down her cheek as she caught her breath. Then she swallowed and squeaked out a hello that she'd meant to sound chirpy.

"Hey, Abby, do you have a cold or something?"

"Or something." Abigail felt frozen. "This thing has me all messed up."

"I know. Hormones."

Or the terror of Leo Storm, of what he would say and do to her this morning at her news, especially after the way she'd treated him.

"Other than feeling like I'm about to have a nervous breakdown, I'm fine. Never better." Somehow she managed a hollow laugh. "As fine as someone with morning sickness can be, mucking out a stall…before they face a firing squad."

"You need to hire somebody for that yucky-mucky stuff now."

A city girl through and through, Kel didn't get horses.

"I know. You're right. I will."

"So, anything I need to know before I start scheduling your day?"

"Yes. I-I'm going to tell him…today."

"Oh? When exactly?"

"This morning! First thing!"

"Wow. Well, finally!"

"Putting it off is driving me crazy. The only problem is it looks like I'm going to have to track him down. He won't return my calls."

"You should have listened to your smart secretary. Didn't I tell you, you should call him and apologize—"

"Smart-assed secretary!"

"Big-assed, too." Kel laughed. "And getting bigger. Jan brought in two dozen donuts this morning coated with yummy strawberry goo. I'm inhaling my second."

"Okay. Well, I didn't call him back or apologize. And ever since, he's avoided the ranch and me. Now he won't even take my calls or call me back."

"Why are we surprised?"

"I said it was urgent. I've left several messages with his secretary, too. Yesterday, she actually got snappy and said he had no intention of returning my calls. I can't tell you how humiliating that was. I'm not about to tell a witch like her to tell him I'm pregnant with his child, so I guess I have to drive over there."

"Right. You think you'll get back here this afternoon?"

"After lunch. I'll probably be a basket case after seeing him."

"Do you want me to cancel your afternoon?"

"No!"

"Is there anything I can do?" Kel's voice was soft with concern.

"Just be your smart-assed self and put out any and all home fires."

"Don't worry about us," Kel said. "Just take care of you."

They hung up.

Abigail's hands began to shake again as she slid her phone in her back pocket. Compulsively, she began marching back and forth in the barn, straightening tack that didn't need to be straightened, lining up bottles and brushes on shelves, trying to feel she controlled something. She got a broom and began to sweep the feed that Coco had shaken out of the feed sack when she'd grabbed it by her teeth earlier.

Coco walked up and lowered her head almost apologetically. It was her way of begging for her favorite treat, a mixture of oats and molasses.

"Not today, big girl. Not after this big mess you made!"

Setting the broom against the wall, Abby pushed the wheelbarrow full of dirty straw outside the barn and up a small hill where she dumped it before heading toward the house. Coco, who adored her, trailed behind her in the hope of being stroked or fed, but Abby was too distracted to notice her as she usually did.

Pregnant! By Leo....

Even though Abigail had taken the pregnancy tests a week ago—three of them—she still couldn't believe she was in this mess. She was a businesswoman, an entrepreneur with a staff of forty, the owner of her own ranch. Make that a ranchette. But still...she was *la capitana* of her ship! Even if she'd sailed headlong into the rocks.

She reached into her pocket and pulled out her phone. Quickly she scrolled down to Leo's cell number and punched it. Once again she listened to it ring until his voice mail picked up. So, he still refused to answer. She flipped her phone shut and began to pace.

So what else was new? She'd watched him screen his calls, so it was easy to imagine his black eyes grimly eyeing her name before his jaw tightened and he thrust his buzzing phone back in his pocket.

How eager he'd been for her to call him just two weeks ago…until she'd accused him of stalking her. He'd stormed home, but had called her back. She hadn't answered, but he'd left a message.

"Stalking? Is that what you think? I thought you were just embarrassed and wary because we sort of took our relationship too far and too fast that first night," he'd said. "I was hoping I could convince you that I think you're great, as a person I mean. That I was willing to slow things down. But if you really want me to leave you the hell alone, I will. Call me back today, or I'm through, and I mean through."

She didn't know him very well, but she imagined he was probably a man who meant what he said.

She clenched her fist. It was ridiculous how crushed she felt that he wouldn't return her calls now. She'd told herself all he'd wanted was more wild, uninhibited sex. Had she taken the intensity of his interest for granted? Had he meant more to her than she'd known?

In any case, when she hadn't done exactly what he'd wanted, he'd quickly thrown her away. Like her mother and her father had…after Becky, her twin, had vanished. Abigail killed that thought. She didn't like to think about

her long-missing twin or that she herself had never mattered very much to anybody.

She drew in a sharp breath. Yesterday after calling his
secretary, she'd tucked Leo's business card in her
dresser under her lingerie. Fisting her hands at her sides,
she marched toward her house. She had to find that card
again and call his office. Then she'd punch his exact
address into her GPS and drive there.

Letting her screen door bang behind her, she rushed
inside her kitchen and washed her hands before heading
toward her bedroom.

She took her time at the faucet. Why had she let him
pick her up that night in that bar? Why had she gone to
that bar when she'd felt so lonely and rejected and vulnerable after Shanghai had dumped her for Mia Kemble?

Why had she thrown herself at Shanghai, a wild-bull
rider who'd never been particularly fascinated with her
in the first place?

It was no use asking questions like that. She had to
go from here. She'd been hurting, so she'd had a night
of wild sex with Leo Storm. As a result, the next pair of
jeans she bought would have an elastic waistband.

Had he even used a condom? She wasn't sure. Except
for a few shamefully sizzling memories, the night was
a horrible blur.

Once inside her bedroom, she yanked the top drawer
of her dresser open and began ransacking her under-
wear. When his card wasn't there, she looked up and
caught a glimpse of a pale, thin woman with guilt-
shadowed eyes and clumps of butterscotch tangles falling about her shoulders. She stood up straighter and
sucked in her stomach.

Even though her jeans wouldn't snap, her tummy didn't look the least bit fat...*yet*. Still, thoughts of her future big belly panicked her.

Oh, God. Pretty soon she'd have to tell her staff. Shaking even harder, she squeezed her lashes shut and then yanked the second drawer open so hard it fell to the oak floor. She knelt and began clawing through her nightgowns and T-shirts.

Never again did she want a repeat of a week like the last one. After a visit to her doctor, Abigail had realized that she couldn't go through this alone...or end it as Kel had suggested. So, if Leo thought he could play Mr. CEO jerk and just give her that ultimatum and then walk away...the way everybody in her life had always walked away...well...at least, she'd tell him off first.

A final image of her mother packing her suitcase and telling her she was leaving her father—and leaving her—made her heart ache as she opened a third drawer.

Abby didn't know much about babies, but she knew enough to know her baby would want her to at least tell its father about the pregnancy.

She suspected that Leo had been staying in San Antonio and avoiding his ranch. Or rather the Little Spur, the ranch he owned with his brother, Connor, which was next door to hers and to Shanghai's Buckaroo Ranch. She hadn't seen him or his black truck—not once at the Little Spur—since his ultimatum, and lately she'd been watching. *Well, too bad, Mr. Rich Know-It-All, Macho CEO! You should have kept your pants zipped.*

The last thing she wanted to think about was that night in the bar after they'd danced dirty and she'd become as intensely aroused as he'd been. He'd kissed her, a second time, his tongue in her mouth, his hands sliding all over her, caressing, cupping, possessing. She'd melted, utterly melted like a slab of rich chocolate too near a flame.

Later in his loft in downtown San Antonio, she'd climbed onto his dining-room table and stripped. The next morning when she'd awakened next to his tanned, naked body, all she'd wanted was to run from him and forget.

She dreaded facing him again. He'd probably suggest the modern options just as Kel had.

"So, why even tell him?" Kel had said. "Just take care of it. In a week you'll forget it ever happened."

"You don't have my memories, Kel."

Some things, one never forgets.

Abigail hadn't ever told her about that fatal afternoon two identical eight-year-old little girls had run up a twisting trail after a wild turkey in the Franklin Mountains. The sun had been setting. The thin, impish face of her twin, Becky, had been rosily alight, her hair backlit with fire.

"Wait!" Becky had screamed. "Wait for me!"

Abigail had yelled back. "No! Come on!" Then she'd turned, expecting her twin to follow as she always did. But that had been the last time she'd ever seen her sister.

Abby opened the last drawer. She still dreamed about Becky, and now she dreamed about her baby, too. She'd never wanted to be part of a family again and open herself up for more hurt, so being pregnant was very risky for her. Still, she wasn't about to throw away her precious unborn baby. Not when she knew how sacred family was if you were lucky enough to have it and how easy it was to make irrevocable mistakes.

Don't think about Becky.

Abigail's hand closed around a card. Not Leo's card, but a Christmas card…from her father.

The money, fifty dollars in cash that he'd carelessly tossed in the envelope as a last-minute gift, was still inside it. Not that he'd spent Christmas with her. His only gift had been the card with that single bill, and it had arrived two weeks late, long after she'd given up hope he'd even thought of her at Christmas.

For a fleeting second she remembered that last Christmas before Becky had disappeared. She and her twin had conspired to make sure their parents didn't know they no longer believed in Santa Claus. They'd made cookies for Santa and set out small pink teacups filled with milk near the fireplace.

A dark feeling of loneliness washing over her, she hugged her tummy. When she'd been a little girl, she'd never felt alone. She'd had a twin, someone to share everything with. They'd both taken ballet and had had identical pink tutus and tights.

Don't think about Becky.

Abby was shaking as she tucked the Christmas card back under her sweaters. She smoothed the dark blond tangles out of her eyes. One thing she knew—no matter what Leo did, she intended to love her baby with all her heart. Bad as things seemed right now, maybe this was her second chance.

Finally, her hand closed numbly on Leo's expensive, engraved card. Lifting it, she stared at his name in bold black type. Dreading his condescending baritone, she swallowed hard, grabbed her cell and punched in his office number before her fear could escalate.

"Golden Spurs. Leo Storm's office. Miriam Jones. How can I help you?" The crisp, no-nonsense voice that had so annoyed her yesterday was as impersonal as ever.

"I need to see Mr. Storm. This morning. It's urgent."

"Mr. Storm makes his own appointments, and I assure you, he makes as few as possible. He's quite busy today. Perhaps you could send him an e-mail and outline the reasons why you need a meeting."

"N-no…no e-mail!"

"Your name please?"

She gave it—as she had yesterday. There was a long pause. Then his snoop of a secretary asked more questions before excusing herself to confer with Leo. The woman's voice, chillier than ever, came back on the phone almost immediately. The nosy witch was nothing if not efficient.

"He says he can't see you, and that you'll know the reason why."

"What? Did you say it was urgent?"

"Yes. Just like I did yesterday." Another long pause so this could sink in. "Is there anything else I can help you with, Miss Collins?" the impossible woman asked, her chilly tone holding polite finality.

"Did you really tell him it was urgent?"

The next thing Abigail knew, the woman had said a dismissive goodbye and Abby was listening to a dial tone.

Her heart pounding, Abby punched redial. "When is the best time this morning for me to see him?" she blurted before his secretary could say anything.

"I told you what Mr. Storm said—"

"You don't understand. He doesn't understand. I *have* to see him. Work me in."

"That could take hours. And even then, I can't promise—"

"Just do it!"

"He's been down in South Texas at the Golden Spurs for the last four days. I'm afraid he has a lot to catch up on. And...I'm afraid he was most emphatic about not wanting—"

Abigail snapped her phone shut. Scooping up a handful of clothes off the floor, grabbing a pair of heels, she stomped into her bathroom. Five minutes later, she looked more or less presentable with her hair in a tight coil at her nape and her body clad in a pair of black slacks and a blue knit top. Slinging her black jacket over one arm and her purse over the other, she barged out her front door and raced toward her white Lincoln.

Coco looked up and whinnied expectantly, but Abby marched past her.

She had to tell Leo her news—whether or not he wanted to hear it.

She hoped she ruined his day, his week, the rest of his life—just like he'd ruined hers.

Two

Immense paintings and photographs of the world-famous Golden Spurs Ranch, which was two hundred miles south of San Antonio, decorated two walls of Leo Storm's impressive outer offices. Sheets of glass along another wall looked out over the winding San Antonio River fringed darkly by cypress trees and buildings. Not that Abby was impressed by his showy office or the dramatic view as she scribbled a note to Leo and folded it again and again until it was a tiny wad.

If she'd been agitated when she'd walked in, she was totally charged after sitting here an hour, watching his secretary pointedly ignore her and escort others who'd come in after her, in to see him, the last of whom had been an elderly, unhappy-looking rancher.

She tried and failed to distract herself by studying his office. The massive photographs were of cowboys, oil wells, cattle drives and the legendary big house where the Kemble family he worked for had entertained presidents and kings, and lately, Arab sheiks. She'd been there—once. The museum-quality, nineteenth century oil paintings were mostly scenes of cowboys and Native Americans, although there was the inevitable clichéd landscape of Texas hill country, live oaks and bluebonnets.

The opulence and grandeur of the Golden Spurs headquarters were meant to impress, but Abigail merely felt incensed as she continued to languish in a huge red leather chair that dwarfed her.

Impatiently, Abigail looked at his secretary again. Naturally, the tight-lipped, string bean of a redhead with that awful knot screwed at the top of her head rustled papers and pretended to ignore her in that arrogant way waitresses in posh restaurants do when you need silverware and wave madly while trying to signal them.

Abigail glanced at her watch and then up at the photograph of the big house again. She'd been there once and did not have fond memories of it.

Damn his hide! Leo owed her. He'd ruined her life, hadn't he? She was through playing his games! She looked at her watch. If she didn't do something, Leo would never see her.

Getting up from the chair, she rushed up to his secretary's desk to plead her case for what had to be the fourth or fifth time.

Her forehead puckering, the redhead, who was clearly losing patience, pursed her mouth. "Yes, Miss Collins?"

"Would you give him this note—*please?*"

Arching her brows, the woman narrowed her eyes as she studied the tightly folded wad. Finally she took it, rolled her chair back and got up without a word. Abigail watched her walk briskly down a long, wide hall and open his door. A few minutes later she repeated that stiff-legged march, her heels clicking all the way back to her desk. Then she spun her chair and sat down.

"Well?" Abby said.

The woman shook her head. "Mr. Storm says he's very sorry, but he's busy—*all day*. I tried to tell you that you'd be wasting your time, that you'd be better off sending him an e-mail. He told me to remind you that you made the decision to break off your relationship with him."

What? He was blaming her and humiliating her at the same moment?

Rage and embarrassment sent fire blazing through Abby. How dare he deliberately humiliate her?

Relationship? Since when did they have a relationship?

Somehow she resisted the impulse to scream. "I have to see him," she repeated softly. "It's important."

"I'm sorry."

Clearly, she wasn't. She'd probably read some manual that told her never to meet anger with anger. Embarrassed for Abby, the woman stared down at her desk.

"I've told you repeatedly this is urgent."

"And I've told you he said he can't see you."

Abigail could feel herself hurtling toward some edge. She knew she had to get a grip. "Oh, really? Can't or won't?"

Behind her, she heard heavy footsteps. When she turned, two large, beefy men in dark suits were heading toward her. They looked like cops. Their purposeful gazes and tread both energized and terrified her.

His secretary followed her gaze. "I'm truly sorry, but he said he wants you out of the building. I'm afraid he called security. They'll escort—"

"Damn him!" Abigail barged past the impossible woman and raced down the hall toward Leo's office.

The men shouted her name and then thundered after her. His secretary cried, "Wait! You can't go in there!"

Just you watch me!

Abigail banged his door open, walked inside and slammed it so hard pins flew out of her hair and sprinkled onto Leo's polished oak floor.

"Maybe a lot of people admire you because you're the CEO of Golden Spurs, but I know you too well. You're a ruthless, cold-hearted bastard." Mike Ransom had to yell to make himself heard over the raised voices behind the door.

Leo's focus was on Abby's voice, too, and he grew angry that just knowing she was out there could rattle him. Security must have arrived to handle Abby, but it didn't sound like his men were succeeding. She'd made it crystal clear she dated cowboys—only cowboys and only short-term. That she disliked him, that she thought his type serious, dull and greedy. So what the hell did she want with him now?

"I work with dull city guys like you all day long, men who don't ever think about anything but making money," she'd told him at one point. "I don't want to play with them at night when I'm looking for a little excitement."

Why the hell had she broken her sacred rule then and slept with him?

More importantly, why the hell had he broken his

own sacred rule—which was never to combine business with sex? Dammit, the Golden Spurs board had hired him to find the late Caesar Kemble's missing twin daughter. He in turn had hired his brother, Connor, a security specialist, to look for her. Connor had stunned him when he'd informed him that their own neighbor, Abigail Collins, and her missing twin were probably the Golden Spurs heiresses.

Leo had tracked Abigail to that bar that night to obtain a DNA sample from her, not to bed her. The beer bottle he'd bagged proved she was a Kemble.

With immense effort he forced himself to concentrate on Mike Ransom. The old man looked frail and weathered. Despite his blustering, his thin shoulders were slumped in defeat, the fabric of his jacket hanging against his body like a broken bat's wings.

The snap and toughness damn sure hadn't gone out of the old man, and Leo suppressed twinges of admiration and sympathy. "If I'm a bastard, the world has you to thank."

"I wouldn't sell the Running R. Not for twice your offer. And never to you."

"You don't have a choice. Just like I didn't have a choice when you kicked me the hell off the Running R for getting Nancy pregnant when I was eighteen and didn't have a dime to my name. How does it feel to know you're helpless and at *my* mercy now?"

Strangely, Leo didn't feel nearly as happy as he'd thought he would now that he'd turned the tables on the old man.

The ruckus Abby was stirring up outside was growing louder. Not good.

Leo longed to storm past Mike and deal with Abigail himself but forced himself to remain at his desk.

"This is revenge, pure and simple," Ransom said, still glowering at him.

"You would know," Leo replied.

"You don't even want the ranch. You're just after it because you know I love it and want Cal and Nancy to inherit it someday…and because you've never gotten over…."

No, he hadn't gotten over his pregnant girlfriend, Nancy, refusing to marry him because he was broke and homeless. No, he hadn't gotten over Nancy marrying Ransom's son, Cal, instead. No, he hadn't gotten over losing his daughter. Not when he knew Ransom had caused all these things.

"Think what you like…."

Leo would have said more. He'd waited years for this day. He'd been psyched to finish Ransom off this morning in a cool, bloodless business battle of wills.

Suddenly he heard racing footsteps. His door opened and slammed. He shot to his feet just as Abigail locked herself inside his inner sanctum and whirled on him, her dark, gold hair tumbling over her shoulders like a silk curtain.

"Get out!" Leo yelled even as the memory of his hands in her hair as he held her close so he could kiss her came back to him. The memory made heat pulse through him.

Frozen, she stared at him with the wide, frightened eyes of a doe caught in his sights as she tried to smooth her wild hair. Her face was worrisomely thin and much too pale.

He remembered how her eyes had blazed after their

first kiss, her pupils dilating with passion that night. Now dark blue circles shadowed her lovely hazel eyes. Except for the bold blue of her knit top and all that butterscotch hair falling over her shoulders in such wild disarray, she was dressed as primly as a schoolteacher in a black jacket and slacks.

She stooped and retrieved several pins from the floor. Pulling her hair back, she secured it again, so that she looked much more severe. He remembered how sexily she'd been dressed in the bar that night. Still, despite Ransom's raised eyebrows and her attempt to look all prim and proper, her haunted, condemning gaze both burned him and drew him. He felt his body harden and heat even as Ransom's cold eyes drilled him.

Hell. He had to get rid of her. She'd made it abundantly clear that she considered sex with him a huge mistake and that she despised him and his type intensely and not just for seducing her, as she'd put it—which was a laugh if ever there was one.

Ever since she'd slipped from his arms and run away without a goodbye, she'd been telling him to go to hell in various ways. But she'd been as eager for it as he'd been. Then she'd had the gall to tell him she'd been pretending he was Shanghai that night. The final straw had been when she'd accused him of stalking her. Damn her, he was through.

He wasn't about to admit that that night had opened doors into his heart that had been closed since Nancy, Cal and Mike Ransom had ruined his life when he'd been little more than a kid.

"I'm busy," he said. "You're interrupting an important meeting."

"Believe me, I don't want to see you, either! But like I told your secretary, this is urgent! And, Leo, I swear— it won't take long," she whispered in a voice that cracked. "I've got to talk to you. After you hear me out, you don't have to see me again."

I don't want to see you, either. Both those words and her raw, hateful tone cut, but her shadowed eyes were scaring the hell out of him. What was wrong?

With an effort, he fought his concern and curiosity and kept his gaze and voice hard. "As you can see, I'm busy."

"Not anymore you're not. I'm just leaving," Ransom growled. "The bastard's all yours, sweetheart. Enjoy." His last word seething with sarcasm, Ransom shot him a murderous look before pivoting. Unlocking and opening the door, he slammed it behind him.

Seeing their chance, the two security officers rushed the door, but Abigail was faster. Swiftly, she shot the bolt. When the officers banged on the door, she leaned against it, her mouth trembling.

Her face was ashen, and the lack of brilliance in her wide eyes was beginning to frighten him. She was scared to death of him. She swallowed, or, at least, she tried to.

Gagging, she gave a little cry. Then, cupping one hand over her mouth, she lurched toward his desk. Was she seriously ill?

Fear gripped him even as her eyes grew even wider in panic. With her hand still covering her mouth and the other crossed over her stomach, she sank to her knees and retched violently. For another long minute she made horrible, dry-heaving sounds as she held on to his wastebasket.

"What the hell is wrong with you?"

Finally, when she lifted her desperate gaze to his, her hair wild again as it fell over her shoulders, he saw Nancy's white, terrified face from the past.

"Can't you guess?" Abby whispered.

And he knew.

Still, he had to ask her. "Morning sickness?" he muttered, hoping to hell and back he was wrong.

When she nodded, the stark pain in her mute eyes tore off a corner of his soul. Shuddering, he shut his eyes and took a deep breath, attempting to clear his head. Not that the trick worked. The air suddenly felt too thick to breathe. Or maybe his heart was thudding too violently.

"You'd better not be trying to nail me for somebody else's kid...for Shanghai's..."

She blushed, and when a single tear slid down her cheek, he bit his tongue so hard he tasted blood.

"I hate you," she whispered. "I think you're... you're horrible."

God, she was right. How could he have said that? He was the worst creep on the planet.

When she spoke again, her eyes flashed with real hatred and her voice had sharpened. "But it's yours. I wish it wasn't, believe me. I never wanted to see you again, either!"

Her barbs stung. "You would have preferred Shanghai! Even if he is married. You made that abundantly clear."

She ignored his comment. "There are tests that will prove it's yours...if you don't believe me. There's DNA."

He felt his neck heat guiltily. He knew way too much about DNA.

"That won't be necessary," Leo said through clenched teeth. "Look, I'm sorry...."

"Relax. You don't have to apologize. I hate you just as much as you dislike me."

"Right." No surprise that she didn't want his child any more than she'd wanted him.

He ran his hand through his hair, staring at her for a long moment while her eyes damned him to hell and back. When she knew the whole truth—why he'd been in the bar that night—she'd have even more justification for hating him. If the Golden Spurs board learned the truth, this could spell the end of his career.

Abruptly, Leo strode across his office and opened the door that led to his private washroom. He turned on the faucet and dampened a towel with cold water. He poured water into a glass. When he returned, he handed the towel and the glass of water to her.

"Sit down before you fall. Bathe your face, and we'll figure out what the hell you need to do next."

"I need to do? It's yours, too," she repeated dully.

"Right. I get that."

"But you didn't believe—"

"I said I get it—okay? It's mine. Unpleasant realities have a way of sinking in fast. Now this is what we're going to do—"

"You can't just boss me around. I don't work for you."

"You're carrying my child."

"You're supposed to be smart! Did you even use a condom?" she accused.

"Yes, dammit. Several."

She flushed as if it embarrassed her to remember once hadn't been enough for either of them.

"I wasn't some kid, in such a rush and so madly in love, that I didn't think…."

He'd done that once, years ago with Nancy when he'd been eighteen. Still, that aside, he'd been wild for her. He hadn't just happened to go to that bar. He'd known she'd be there. He'd had something very important to tell her.

Something very important to get from her.

Too bad for them both that she'd dressed so sexily and had looked so sad that he'd let himself get derailed before he'd obtained what he'd needed.

He remembered how many times they'd done it, and how every time it had just gotten better and better. How she'd moaned and sobbed and opened herself utterly, clinging to him with her legs and arms until he'd hardened again while still inside of her. He'd felt sexy and big and powerful.

He remembered her taking him between her lips, kissing him until he'd felt himself in a hot swirl of soft, wet satin and had climaxed in her mouth. She'd been sweet, hot and good. He'd been on a high for several weeks after that night. He'd been unable to believe that she would want to throw him and what they'd had that night—which had been that mind-altering, at least for him—away.

As if she read his mind, color flooded her face. "I—I don't remember much about that night."

"Right. Lucky you. I wish I could forget you and all that happened between us as easily."

"Well, I'll have the baby now as a constant reminder."

"So you want to keep it?" His rush of relief stunned him.

She sprang out of her chair, sputtering at him angrily. "D-don't you even dare suggest anything else the way Kel did, or I'll...or...."

"Hey…hey… Calm down." He rushed to her and placed his hands on her shoulders.

At his touch, something raw and true sparked in her eyes. Then hatred followed in its wake.

Heat flashed through every nerve ending in his body. As if burned, she jumped back, and as always he felt stung by her rejection.

Impossible relationships with women. Were they his specialty or what? But this was worse—because it involved his career. He was screwed on every level by this turn of events. Dammit, he liked being CEO of the Golden Spurs, and if he didn't think fast, his career was charred toast.

"Settle down," he muttered, but his voice was deliberately gentle now. "I-I'm glad you want my baby."

"Your baby?" she repeated, backing even farther away from his blunt, broad hands.

When he nodded, relief flooded her face. He fought the softening he felt as she sank slowly back into her chair. He had to remember she was dangerous, exceedingly dangerous on many levels.

He went to his own chair, and she sat in hers staring across his desk at him as if she were in a daze.

"What are we going to do?" she finally whispered. "This is such a shock."

It sure as hell was, and it was far more complex than she knew. He would have to act before she figured out that she held all the trump cards.

"You've had more time to get used to the idea than I have. I'm sure my secretary told you I've got a really jammed schedule today. Why don't I come over tonight? Say around seven? And we'll talk about options."

"I—I would really prefer to meet you in some public place."

"At night? Then you'd have to drive back to your ranch alone. Are you more afraid of me than of some stranger who might follow you home?"

"You don't have to worry about me. I'm used to living alone, to driving home alone."

"If you're having my baby, you and the baby are my responsibility now."

She bristled. As he stared at her narrowed brows, he could almost see a dozen arguments buzzing in that micromanaging brain of hers.

"Okay, forget I said that. I don't want to argue. But are you afraid of me?"

She shook her head furiously.

"Okay, why didn't you want to see me again?"

"I didn't want to see you again because you're pushy and arrogant, and because you're not the kind of man I like."

"Right. You prefer bull riders. Shanghai Knight in particular."

Why was he repeating himself? Because knowing that hurt, dammit. "You pretended I was him, and you wish this was his kid."

She wouldn't meet his gaze. "At least I didn't lie to you about him."

"Didn't you?"

Shanghai. Leo was sick to death of hearing about the guy. Goaded, hardly knowing what he was doing, he leapt out of his chair.

She jumped up, too, but he clamped his hands around her arms and pulled her to him before she could run. The heat of her body nestling against his torso and legs reminded him of her wet, enticing silkiness that night and why he'd been unable to stick to his original agenda in the bar. Hell, she'd filled him with a hunger it might take a lifetime to satisfy.

"Why are you so afraid of me? Did I hurt you? Have I ever hurt you? Forced you?"

He'd done worse than that by getting that DNA sample without telling her, by not informing her who she was. There was no telling what she'd do when she found out. But it was better to kill one snake at a time. He had to know what she thought of him.

"No, but—"

"Yet you called me a stalker…."

She was shaking as he tightened his grip.

She felt good. So damn good. She smelled of wind and trees, of wildflowers.

"I only said that so you'd leave me alone."

"All that Shanghai crap… Are you really in love with him? Or were you just throwing him at me because you couldn't face me after what we'd done?"

She didn't answer, but something in him relaxed a little.

He'd sensed her inner demons right from the beginning. He knew all about inner demons, and like a fool, he'd sympathized.

He should let her go now, but he couldn't. "If you didn't want me, then why did you make love to me again and again that night?"

"I don't know. I can't remember."

"Can't? Or don't want to remember? Do you really hate me the way you said?"

"Y-yes."

"Go on."

Fixing him with her huge, hazel eyes, she tried to form the words but couldn't.

Suddenly he noticed her heart beating in her throat as she swallowed convulsively. Did she want him... just a little? He remembered burying his face in her breasts. How soft she'd been. How sweet she'd tasted when he'd licked each nipple. How eagerly she'd kissed him back.

"Okay, so maybe you don't totally hate me. But we're still in a helluva mess, aren't we?" he said.

Cursing, he ripped off his glasses and crushed her mouth beneath his. Again, she tasted exquisite...like honey. He expected more fight, but like a terrified animal that had exhausted itself after being caught in a trap, she went absolutely still. Finally, when he didn't release her, when the heat of his body seeped into hers, she grasped his muscular shoulders and pressed her soft lips closer to his, opening them to him.

He loosened his grip. Not even then did she run. Slowly her tongue slid against his, mating with his, and she pushed herself tightly against his body. She didn't draw back, not even when she discovered that he was fully aroused. When he pushed himself against her, she caught her breath.

Moaning, arching her pelvis against his erection in bold invitation, she circled his neck and then caressed his cheeks with her hands, framing his face in her palms as she kissed his mouth again and again.

Instantly the sweetness and the passion and the primal perfection of that night she'd spent in his bed flooded him, and everything made sense again. No wonder he'd been unable to believe she didn't want him. No wonder he'd gone back again and again only to endure more painful rejections.

Her response to his kiss and his male arousal was instantaneous and instinctive and true—unlike the negative garbage she'd been dishing out ever since. He wanted this woman.

When he realized how acute and complex his need for her was, and what a terrible, complicated mess he was in, he jerked his mouth from hers and backed a safe distance away. As if there were a safe distance.

His breathing was hard and labored, but so was hers. Maybe she was pregnant, but he was equally trapped.

"Seven o'clock," he muttered, his tone low and fierce. "Your house. If you prefer to be in a public place, I'll drive you into town in my truck."

"You have no right to just take charge."

"Like I already said, you're having my baby. I think that gives me certain rights."

"This—and what just happened—is exactly why I didn't want to tell you. You'll take advantage…."

Hell. She'd liked it—every bit as much as he had.

"But you did tell me. So, I'll see you at seven. Unless you want me to finish what that kiss started…here on my couch."

Her eyes widened as she stared past him to his long, leather couch. Involuntarily, she touched her lower lip with a fingertip in a way that caused desire to pulse in his blood. "No…."

She must have seen the heat in his eyes that signaled how close he was to the edge because she turned and stumbled toward the doors. Twisting the knob, she seemed to panic when the door wouldn't open and began to beat against the wood with her fists.

He walked across the room. Without touching her, he turned the appropriate lock.

"Seven o'clock sharp," he murmured dryly against her ear before she jumped and ran through the open doors, past his secretary and the still-waiting security guards. Leo motioned for them to let her pass.

Watching her slim hips encased in black silk swing back and forth as she disappeared down the hall, he broke out in a sweat. He had to quit lusting after her and think. All hell would damn sure break loose when she and the board discovered who she really was—which meant it was time to consider damage control.

He shut the doors, went to his desk, punched a button and told Miriam to reschedule his late-afternoon appointments.

Sinking into the chair, Leo's mind flashed back to the afternoon his brother, Connor, had barged into his office and tossed his Stetson and several 8 x 10 pictures onto his desk of their cute neighbor from the ranch next to theirs, riding her palomino bareback.

"I'm pretty sure Abby's one of your missing twins, but we need a DNA sample to confirm it," Connor had said.

"Abby?"

"Like I said, we won't know for sure until you obtain the DNA sample."

"Me? You're the hotshot security specialist."

It hadn't taken Connor long to convince him that all he had to do was buy her a cup of coffee and bag her cup.

Leo called her office late one evening to make an appointment and had told her secretary he was Abby's neighbor. In passing, Kel had mentioned where Abby and she were going that night. He'd shown up at the bar and had taken it from there.

A week after Leo had slept with Abby, Connor had called and said they had a DNA match. Abigail was one of the missing Golden Spurs heiresses. Which made her long-vanished twin, Becky, the other one.

Abigail was the last woman he should have slept with. If he didn't figure out a way to turn this new disaster to his advantage, her pregnancy could cost him everything.

Three

Leo sat down in front of his computer, adjusted his webcam and moved his mouse. He was a firm believer in the theory that when the shit hits the fan, the best defense is almost always a good offense.

So, whose ass better to kick than his baby brother's?

Several mouse clicks later, Connor's square-jawed face and broad shoulders filled Leo's screen. They both nodded and said hello. Then Connor, who was obviously having a better day than he was, leaned back in his chair and flashed his trademark lady-killer smile.

"How can I help you, big brother?"

Connor swept a lock of blond hair out of his blue eyes. He'd put in quite a bit of hard time playing the baby brother from hell and wasn't always as easygoing as his present-day smile might indicate. Baby brother had definitely shown his dark side on more than one occasion.

Leo, who'd raised him after Mike Ransom had kicked them both off the Running R Ranch—not that Connor had been to blame for that—had bailed his baby brother out of plenty of messy jams before a nasty altercation with the police had finally convinced Connor to stay on the right side of the law. Connor had joined the Marines, served in Afghanistan, married and had been widowed.

Leo cut to the chase. "So why the hell don't you have any promising leads on Becky Collins? You been sitting on your thumbs or what?"

Connor loosened the knot of his tie and shifted in his leather chair. Not that his cocky, lady-killer smile wavered. "I have my top agent on the case, but so far…nothing. It's as if she vanished into thin air out there in that El Paso park. Hey, ever since I sent you the DNA report that confirms who our sexy neighbor really is, I've been waiting to hear from you. How'd she take it when you told her who she is?"

Counter-kick-in-the-ass. Baby brothers were good at that, especially baby brothers who'd grown up to be talented P.I.'s and in addition owned a large, multifaceted security business with branches in several major Texas cities. Hell, it could be argued that Connor was even more successful than he was. Not something Leo, who was as competitive as hell, liked to think about much.

"I haven't," Leo hedged testily. "Not yet."

"It's been weeks since I found her. A week since I sent the DNA results. What the hell are you waiting for?"

Maybe Connor was sitting in his office in Houston, but the gaze of his big blue eyes shaded by dense black lashes felt as hot as a laser beam.

"It's complicated." *And getting more complicated.*

"You were as excited as hell when I gave you the file on her."

"Yeah, I was."

"You said if the DNA proved I was right, you were going to tell her first thing."

"I intended to." Leo frowned, not liking the interrogation. "When I met her that night, she was still on the rebound because Shanghai, our neighbor, had dumped her to marry Mia Kemble."

"Right, Mia Kemble of the Golden Spurs Ranch; her famous half-sister, or is it cousin?"

"Cousin. Only Abby doesn't know who she really is."

"My point. So why don't you tell her?"

He'd been trying to when she'd accused him of stalking her.

"She was pretty vulnerable that night...and in a sort of self-destructive mood. She was acting crazy, and I got crazy. Things got personal pretty quick."

"Usually you put business before pleasure."

"Too bad I didn't that night."

"Tell me you didn't sleep with her."

"I didn't sleep with her," Leo repeated as if by rote. He probably could have fooled anybody but Connor. Connor had an uncanny knack for smelling out a lie.

Connor's smile changed into something more dangerous, and he leaned forward. "Don't just repeat what I said like a damn idiot. Say it like you mean it."

"I wish I could. Hell. Look, she didn't agree to that DNA sample I sent you. Worse, she's pregnant. I'm meeting her tonight to figure out where we go from here."

Connor whistled. "You knocked up the long-missing

secret Golden Spurs heiress you hired my agency to find? How will the Golden Spurs board react to that?"

"Favorably—if I figure out how to make this work for me…."

"Leo! Don't work it! Not this time! Just keep it simple."

Leo didn't say anything.

"Leo! You'd better listen to me. For once, keep your damned ambition in check and just tell her and the board the truth. This is your kid. You don't want to mess things up the way you did last time."

"The way I did? Have you forgotten how Mike Ransom and Cal threw both of us off the Running R when Nancy turned up pregnant, probably because they'd always wanted Nancy's family's ranch? How they convinced her to marry Cal instead of me because they could do so much more for the baby? For little Julie," he amended softly. He swallowed as he remembered Julie, his dark-eyed daughter, a defiant teenager now, a slim woman-child he barely knew, who hated him.

"No, I haven't forgotten, but you don't want that to happen this time, do you? Look, I know what you've been through. But I know these kinds of situations, too. People make incredible messes when they keep secrets or cover shit like this up. Things spin out of control."

"I'm not going to promise you anything. You know as well as I do that honesty got me into a helluva lot of trouble. So much trouble I lost everything. Nancy… Julie… And you—nearly. I used to think I'd never see myself clear."

"It wasn't your fault I went a little wild after Mother died, when it was just the two of us and you were working all the time."

"Maybe it was. I should have paid more attention to you. I shouldn't have let Cal adopt Julie. I should have fought harder be a part of my daughter's life."

"You've gotta forget…like I have."

"You're not me, little brother. If Ransom hadn't thrown me off the Running R…and cut off my college money, then maybe Nancy wouldn't have left me for Cal. I can't forget that."

"Right. Praise the Lord. You're swimming in success, and you still want that old man's head on a spike."

"You know something funny—Mike Ransom was in my office today. I had the bastard in the palm of my hand, but instead of squeezing, I let him walk out the door."

"Good for you! After all, he is Julie's only living grandpa."

"No! The only reason he got away was because Abigail showed up, looking haunted and ill. I started feeling sorry for her, and then she let me have it with both barrels."

"God speaks to us in strange ways. He has a plan. Why do you think she showed up at that exact moment—pregnant? Maybe to give you a chance to count your blessings and reconsider getting your revenge. Ransom made a mistake. A long time ago. Yeah, he was too rough on you, but haven't you ever made a mistake? He's an old man now. His wife's sick. The ranch has been in his family for generations. If you hurt him, you hurt Julie."

"I'm through with this conversation."

"Just think about it. Ransom's got plenty of problems without you going after him. Life has a way of making us pay for our sins. If you use Abigail to suit some ambition of yours, you'll regret it."

Connor said goodbye. Leo clicked his mouse, and the computer screen went blank. He sat staring at himself in the gray glare. Then he ran his hands through his hair. After a long time he got up, went to his bar and poured a shot and a half of scotch into a highball glass. Leaning his head back, he bolted it.

Normally, he never drank during the day, and never at his office. The stuff burned his mouth and throat as he sat back down in his leather chair for a long moment and waited for the liquor to ease his pain. When it didn't, he eyed the bottle across the room, yearning for another shot.

No. He'd been down that hellish road. It was always better to face pain, better to stay in control.

Instead, he opened up his top desk drawer and pulled out the file folder with Abigail's name on it that his brother had triumphantly pitched on his desk six weeks ago. Opening it, Leo thumbed through the various documents and photographs.

Several glossy 8 x 10 photos taken with a high-power lens of Abigail riding her golden horse, Coco, fell onto his desk. The DNA report was there, too. He'd told Connor that it was a helluva coincidence her ranch was next to theirs and Shanghai Knight's.

"More than a coincidence," his newly converted, ex-bad-boy brother had retorted with sickening, self-righteous assurance and an easy smile. "It's nothing short of a miracle. God definitely has a plan."

"I don't believe in miracles or plans."

"Someday you will. Maybe sooner than you think."

Leo went to his bookshelf and picked up Julie's picture. She had black hair and black eyes. He'd called her on her last birthday and she'd refused to talk to him. Nancy said that every day she looked more and more like him.

Julie was a teenager now…nearly as old as he'd been when he'd gotten Nancy pregnant. She had a bad attitude about school, said she didn't want to go to college, said she didn't want to do anything but hang out with her friends, who were creeps for the most part. She wanted a tattoo and some piercings. She wore tight clothes and too much makeup. Nancy said it was because she craved attention. Cal said it was because she felt abandoned by her biological father. But what could he do about that when Julie refused to take his calls or see him?

He'd never played a big part in her life, so for all intents and purposes Cal was her father. Now she was nearly grown, and Leo regretted having let his daughter slip away.

Bottom line: how far was he willing to go to prevent that from happening again?

All the damn way, he thought. All the damn way. He'd do whatever the hell it took.

Just one more minute….

The sun was low in the sky, and the shadows of the oaks and pines swept across the gravel road and the lush grasses where Coco grazed nearby.

It had to be close to seven. Abby knew she should get up from the stone bench and go back to the house to wait for Leo. But her heart was thudding because she felt so anxious at the thought of facing him again. She was exhausted, and the balmy warmth soothed her.

Why was it that she could go and go and go—until she stopped? Still, Leo Storm didn't strike her as a patient man, and it would only make things worse if she kept him waiting.

Not that she got up. The soft breeze caressing her cheek was too seductively delicious, and her body felt heavy as she continued to lie flat on her back on the cool stone bench. So instead of doing the intelligent thing, she stayed where she was, procrastinating, enjoying this fleeting moment of peace.

From her first dread-filled, wakeful moment, her day had been long and tense. This was the first second she'd had to herself, if she didn't count the hectic commutes from the ranch to San Antonio, from there to Austin, and then the commute home. The high-speed traffic had been dense and fierce, so there was no comparison to this alone-time lying underneath this wonderful tree.

Trees looked completely different when viewed from such an angle. Lying here took her back to her childhood, and she remembered how much she and Becky had loved climbing trees.

For a moment longer she forgot Leo and lay quietly, staring up at the spreading branches of the immense live oak tree and then beyond at the sparkling sunlight and brilliant blue sky that peeked between the dark leaves. The world was big and the universe even bigger. The problem of her pregnancy and dealing with Leo seemed tiny in comparison until she heard him thrashing clumsily through the trees, calling her name.

"Abby! Abby!"

She shot to her feet at the sound of his deep baritone and brushed a leaf out of her hair. "Over here!"

The intensity of his dark gaze had her trembling long before it slid knowingly to her belly and caused heat to scorch her cheeks. Could he tell that her waist was a little fuller?

She remembered standing on his table. He'd been beneath her as she'd undulated to "Wild Thing" and peeled her red jersey top over her head. When she'd wiggled out of her spandex denim skirt, his avid fascination with her body that night had made her feel feminine and reckless and strangely empowered. Like Pandora's box, once opened, needs had been let out that she was having a hard time containing again. But she had to.

Flecked with gold and rimmed with thick black lashes, his gorgeous eyes had followed her every move. When she was naked, he'd strode to the table, clasped her waist and had pulled her into his arms in such a way that she'd slid down the length of his body.

For a long time he'd simply held her. Then he'd kissed her hair, leaned her back down onto the table very slowly and tongued her body until she'd thought she'd surely turn to flame. She'd wanted wild sex and oblivion from the hurt of years of loneliness. He'd wanted more, and that had scared her.

Don't think about that night. Don't let him that close ever again.

He was tall, six-two at least, and rugged, as well. She knew he did hard, physical work on his ranch, and often when one of her fences had needed mending and she'd driven past while he'd been working on the Little Spur, she'd felt a twinge of envy. It would be nice to have a man around who could do things like that.

His skin was dark, the angular planes of his face thoroughly masculine even when he wore his glasses. He must have gotten home earlier than usual because he'd taken the time to discard his suit and glasses and put on a pair of freshly pressed jeans and a long-sleeved, blue chambray shirt. The soft collar was open at his tanned throat and his sleeves were rolled halfway up his muscular forearms.

Suddenly she wished she'd changed into something more flattering, but she'd been too tired to do anything other than shed her jacket.

She sucked in a breath because just looking at the V of dark hair, and his strong, tanned arms made her feel curiously weak. She had to remind herself that he was serious and dull, not her type at all, that she preferred cowboys and, of course, that he'd taken advantage of her.

Calm down. All you're going to do is talk to him.

"I saw your car, so I knocked," he said. "When you didn't answer, I went around back and found the door open. I yelled, and you didn't answer, so I'm afraid I went on in. When you weren't anywhere…" He stared at her again in that intent way that communicated his fear for her. "Well, never mind now. I've found you. I'm glad you're okay."

His evident concern and even his anger pleased her, which was ridiculous. She didn't want him to care. Most of all, she didn't want to need for him to care. There was nothing to like about him—not now—not after he'd gotten them into this horrible mess.

"Have you eaten?" he asked.

Men and their appetites; they either wanted sex or food.

She shook her head.

"We could drive into town."

"I've driven a lot today. I'm pretty tired. Maybe we could just talk…and then you could go."

"You want to get rid of me as soon as possible?"

"I thought I made it clear that I didn't think we had anything going for us."

"Except good sex…and now the baby."

She didn't deny it, so he pressed his point. "That's a lot to have in common, wouldn't you say?"

"Not nearly enough."

"Okay. Truce. Do you have a beer? It's been a long day."

"You're telling me."

His cell phone went off, and he flipped it open, frowning when he saw who it was. "Sorry. I can't talk now, Connor. Yeah, I'm at her place. No, we haven't gotten to that yet. Hell, no!"

Clearly irritated by whatever his brother had said, he hung up abruptly.

"You told your brother…about us?"

"Yeah. He likes you, so I did. Then he got religious on me. Thinks it's a miracle." He glanced toward her, his eyes both cool and yet disturbingly dark and sensual. "Haven't told anybody else, though. Not yet."

"You're close to your brother?"

"Close enough. We've been through a lot together."

"And you own the Little Spur together, too, right?"

"We both thought it was a good investment. Neither one of us can be here all the time. But we both know a thing or two about ranching, and the physical work after a long day or week at our offices releases a lot of tension."

"I love it out here, too."

"That makes three things we have in common."

Coco walked up and nuzzled him.

"Four. See, your horse likes me."

Abby got up and began to walk toward the house. He

and Coco fell into step beside her. His strides were long and easy, yet his pace matched hers. When she reached her front steps, Abby paused.

"I've got to put Coco in the barn."

"I'll do it," he said.

"But she won't let anybody but me—"

"I've been seducing her with little treats of oats and molasses when I see her along our fence line for quite a while."

"What?"

"Just go inside, and I'll join you in a minute." He headed to the barn with Coco following right behind him.

A few minutes later, when he opened her kitchen door, she nodded for him to come inside. He flashed her a smile and then made a beeline for her refrigerator.

"Give a guy an inch," she began, fighting a smile of her own. "Any problems with Coco?"

"She's a breeze compared to you. Too bad you don't crave oats and molasses…."

He grinned. She grinned back. Then, stooping, he opened the refrigerator and got out two bottles of beer. "Want one?"

"No. Not for the next nine months."

His long glance gently touched on her brow, her nose and last of all her mouth. Heat climbed her neck and scorched her cheeks.

He looked a little embarrassed himself before he turned away to rustle through a drawer. He found an opener and popped the top.

Pulling out a chair, he straddled it. Then, leaning back with a pretense of casualness, he took a long pull from the bottle.

"You certainly know how to make yourself at home," she said.

"Would you prefer to wait on me?"

Turning her back on him, she poured herself a tall glass of water.

"This is probably a bad idea, but I'm prepared to marry you," he said.

She whirled. "Don't do me any damn favors, Storm."

"I was thinking more about giving my child my name."

"Your child? My child, too."

"My point exactly. Our child. People with children do occasionally marry each other."

"For the child's sake?"

"Right. There could be other compensations."

Being a man, he was probably thinking about sex. "We're practically strangers!"

"I disagree. On several counts." His burning black eyes were locked on hers, causing her to blush as dozens of shared intimacies she'd fought to forget flooded her mind. She remembered lying on his bed, her legs parted as he lowered his head to kiss her. Cowboy or not, she hadn't been able to get enough of dull, corporate Leo Storm until long after she'd shuddered against his lips. And not even then. She'd clasped the back of his head and had held him against her for long moments, wanting more, several times. Never had she felt so open, so vulnerable, so completely trusting...or so connected.

Why him? She'd told herself that she couldn't ever let herself feel so vulnerable and trusting again.

She swallowed. "I won't marry you."

"You got a better game plan?"

"Not yet."

"Then that leaves me an open field. But, hey, I'm too hungry to come up with plan B." He set his beer on her kitchen table and went to her refrigerator again. "Why don't I cook us both something for supper?"

Before she could say no, he said, "Or I'm happy to take you out."

He was being entirely too agreeable. "But that would just make everything take longer."

"You mean if I cook, you'll get rid of me sooner?" He was chuckling as he knelt and removed a bag of carrots, two potatoes, mushrooms and two thick, frozen steaks.

Fuming because he didn't appear nearly as upset about all this as she was, she watched in silence as he poked holes in the steak's cellophane wrapper and stuck it in the microwave to defrost.

"You want to watch TV or listen to music while we cook?" he asked as he began clanging pots and pans as if their being together didn't bother him in the least.

"How can you act like everything is perfectly normal, when I'm pregnant and feeling so crazy?"

He put the frying pan down on the unlit stovetop. "I thought maybe we should take our mind off the crisis. And that maybe dinner would help us both to relax a little and get used to each other. That maybe then we could think better."

Relaxing with him was the last thing she wanted to do, but maybe he had a tiny point. "Okay. You're right."

She found her remote and turned on her TV because music sounded romantic and being romantic alone in her house with him scared her. Instantly, she regretted her choice when the news stories were all about crimes of passion. When there was one story after another about men killing their girlfriends, he cursed beneath his breath, picked up the remote and changed the channel to one about the hunting habits of large African cats.

Not that she could focus on pouncing cats tearing throats out of zebras. At least, not with Leo's huge, muscular presence filling her kitchen. His black hair was iridescent as he bent over the stove, and she found herself staring at it and remembering how soft and silky it had felt when she'd slid her fingertips through it. He was so broad-shouldered, she wondered if he'd played football in high school.

Gulping in a quick breath, she got up, grabbed a cutting board, a bag of carrots and a knife, and turned her back on him. Trying to ignore him, she began to cut and chop. But she was very aware of him when he edged closer to her as he washed the lettuce. Only when he went outside and lit her grill could she breathe normally again. But he was back in less than a minute, and so was her tension.

He knew his way around the kitchen; she'd give him that. Dinner preparations certainly went faster when there were two in the kitchen. Twenty minutes later the table was set and the side dishes were simmering. Saying the coals outside were perfect, he salted and peppered their raw steaks and then forked them onto a platter.

"Sun's going down. You want to sit outside and relax with me while I cook our steaks?"

Relax? "What is all this to you? A game?"

"No. But do we have to hate each other forever just because this has happened?"

"Yes. I've taken a vow."

"Have you now?" He headed out the door without

further discussion, letting the screen door bang noisily behind him.

Did he know he was totally stressing her out? Like a little kid with a hankering to bicker, she grabbed a bottle of water and stormed after him.

Not that she said anything when she plopped down in the chair across from his. The instant she sat down, she realized her mistake. The sun was going down in a blaze of scarlet. Stars were popping out in the purple afterglow. The fire and the night air and his closeness made her think romance even though all he was doing was sipping his beer while he watched their steaks. She unscrewed her bottle top and gulped, but an ever-thickening tension caused by the night and his nearness and the intimacies they'd shared was building inside her.

Finally, she blurted, "You know, I was doing just fine before you came along and ruined everything."

"Were you now?" he said easily. "That's why you were in that bar that night dressed in a pickup outfit."

She jumped up off her bench. "I'm single. I'll have you know I have every right to go out with a girlfriend."

"No argument here."

"Nobody tells me what to wear."

"Some outfits do strike a chord in the primitive male psyche, as you probably know."

"I don't have to take this."

For some reason instead of stalking back to the relative safety of her kitchen, she stayed put, her breasts heaving. His dark gaze skimmed the labored breathing of her chest much too appreciatively before he grabbed her wrist and pulled her back down.

"I liked what I saw. Too much. I still do." He paused, his eyes roaming lower than she liked.

"Look at my face, dammit."

He met her glare with an amused look. "Tight denim skirt. Short, too. Tight red jersey top."

"You've got a good memory."

"For things I like. You're a beautiful woman. You wouldn't have worn a getup like that if you hadn't wanted to go home with somebody."

"You took advantage."

"I took what was offered."

"Kel talked me into the bar that night. She said a wild cowboy was the only cure for a broken heart."

"But instead of a wild cowboy, you ended up with me...and a baby."

"Because you pushed."

"Sure I did. I wanted you. I go after what I want."

She'd gone with him because she'd felt lost and vulnerable, and he'd given her the illusory feeling of being protected.

He leaned closer. "And you wanna know something? Despite the way you've treated me lately, I still do. That's why I asked you to marry me. The way I see it, your horse likes me, we wouldn't be so good in bed together if you didn't like me a little, you're pregnant and we've both got places out here. That's a start. Maybe we're not madly in love, but if you tried to get along with me half as hard as you put yourself out to be cantankerous, who knows what might happen?"

"If I tried—"

"Yeah, you! If you did, who knows, maybe things could work out between us."

"You're a calculating guy. I can't believe you're serious about marrying me."

"Believe it."

"What you are suggesting is medieval."

"The Western idea of romantic love is far from universal. Lots of countries believe marriages should be based on more practical reasons. Take the Indians...."

"I am not Indian."

"Their divorce rate is probably lower than ours."

"Something is wrong here. I can feel it. Why are you being so nice when you wouldn't even talk to me this morning?"

"Did anyone ever tell you, you have a suspicious nature?" He shrugged. "Think what you like." He pretended to turn his attention to the fire.

When the steaks were nearly done, he tore off a piece. The gesture was savage, and she wondered if he was as calm and practical about all this as he pretended. "Want to test it?" he asked.

She'd barely nodded before his broad, tanned finger placed a bit of beef on the tip of her tongue.

"Delicious," she murmured, savoring the juicy tidbit.

He let his finger linger against her wet mouth until she turned her head away.

He caught her frightened glance. "What do you say we go inside and eat, woman?"

Four

Leo set his plate on the table, went to the counter and turned off her TV. "I've had my fill of lions. How about some music?"

"No! No music!"

"I seem to remember you got pretty excited over 'Wild Thing.'"

Which had led to a long night of lovemaking.

She remembered tossing him her red jersey top, remembered how he'd inhaled her scent while he'd watched her. The next memory that hit her was how she'd felt when she'd awakened the next morning with his long, lean body sprawled on top of her. She'd been naked, and her body had felt well-used. Her mouth had been bruised from too many kisses and sour with the taste of beer. She'd pushed him away, dressed and run. And she'd never wanted to look back.

But she had, first in her dreams, and then all the time this past week.

"Don't get started on that night!"

"My lips are sealed." He smiled as he sat down across from her at her tiny table. His thigh slid against hers. Funny, how mere denim against black silk could send a frisson of heat up her leg. She jumped back, bumping her knee into the table leg.

"Ouch!"

"Are you okay?" he asked.

Before she could stop him, he knelt to inspect her leg, running his hand beneath the silk and up her calf with unbearable tenderness.

"Good. You didn't even break the skin."

"I'm fine," she muttered through gritted teeth, tugging her pants leg back down.

Smiling broadly, he returned to his seat. "You're mighty jumpy."

Who wouldn't be with him so close? Even seated, he seemed huge. Dangerous. Was he bigger inside her kitchen? Or did the room just seem smaller and more intimate now that darkness pressed its velvet fingertips against the windowpanes and she knew they had the whole night ahead of them.

Slicing off a piece of steak, she tried to concentrate on chewing the tender meat. Impossible with his big muscular body so near…not to mention her memories.

He attempted polite conversation, but when she didn't encourage him, he soon stopped talking. After that, there was only the clatter of forks against china and the beating of her heart. Once or twice they reached for bread at the same time, and their fingers accidentally brushed. Both times she felt a jolt and jumped again while he smiled as if he enjoyed her uneasiness immensely.

The night grew ever darker, and she became ever more intensely aware she was all alone with him in the privacy of her house. A house with bedrooms…and beds. She was as bad as he was. She couldn't get near him without thinking about sex.

Oh, would this interminable meal never end? Would he never finish and get to what they had to discuss and leave?

Marry him? Eat with him every night like this? She would go mad!

He devoured his meal with more relish than she and was finished when she still had half her steak untouched. She wished he'd get up and go out on the porch or something so she could eat in peace, but no, he sat politely watching her toy with a bit of potato until finally she dropped her fork in frustration.

"All done," she whispered raggedly.

"You're sure? You're supposed to be eating for two now, remember?"

As if she needed reminding.

She seized her plate and stood up. "We talk now, and then you go. I've got an early morning just like you do."

"No. First we clear the table and wash and dry your dishes."

"You did say you realized that I'm anxious to get rid of you."

"I suggested dinner. I'm not sticking you with a sink full of dishes. Not when you have an early morning."

"As if you care about that."

"I do. I'm told pregnant ladies tire easily."

He turned from her and put his plate down and

splashed detergent into her sink. She heaved in a breath as he began scraping food into her garbage disposal. There seemed to be no stopping him once he was determined on a path.

"All right…we wash the damn dishes," she muttered, surrendering. "Then we talk and you go."

He was silent at first. Finally he said, "We can talk now. You said no to marriage. Does that mean you prefer money? A large check maybe? Or monthly installments?"

She frowned. "No large check. That sounds so…so cold."

"I agree. I want to assume responsibility for you and the baby. I'd like to know my child…be close to him or her…."

"Under the circumstances, the less you're around, the better."

"Does our baby get a vote?"

She thought better before answering that. Besides, she was too tired to argue.

"In any case," he said, "we'll have to make some legal arrangements—to protect ourselves and the child."

"I can't believe we're having this conversation."

"If we were a normal couple, we'd have fallen in love first."

"But we didn't." The thought made her strangely sad. She didn't believe love made you happy. What it did was make you ache for the impossible.

Studying her face, he lapsed into a thoughtful silence.

He couldn't know that he was making her feel guilty, making her long for things she did not want to long for. Damn the man.

When he dried the last glass, she yanked the dish towel

out of his big tanned hand and threw it on the counter. "Now, you can quit acting so concerned and nice and—"

"Careful." He took a step toward her. "Maybe you shouldn't have reminded me that you go for the bad boys. I might take it as permission to be bad. I've had more experience in that role than you might imagine, and we are very much alone."

"No…." She tried to back away from him, but her hips hit the counter edge.

He followed. Placing a hand on either side of her, he gripped the counter, imprisoning her. "You did go to that bar because you wanted a wild cowboy."

"Stop it."

"Who says only cowboys are wild?"

"Leo, this isn't funny. You were being so nice and so reasonable."

"Nice and reasonable doesn't seem to be working. Maybe you're not the only one here who's been made kinda crazy by what happened that night. I crossed lines, too, lines I've never—" He broke off. "Never mind! I haven't had a date or…woman since that night with you. You want to know why I've been sleeping in town? Well, I'll tell you. Out here I kept wondering about you, wondering if you were over here sleeping alone. Wondering if you'd been out with anyone. Some damn bull rider, maybe, who reminded you of Shanghai. Well, have you? Have you seen other men since me?"

Suddenly he was watching her so intently, she couldn't catch her breath.

"Y-yes… Yes! Many times! That's why I didn't want to see you again."

"I wonder." He was staring down at her mouth, which had suddenly gone dry.

She licked her lips. She wished he'd look away, but he didn't. His gaze burned her mouth. She hoped he couldn't tell she was trembling. She traced her upper lip with her tongue to cool it off. "I think you should go."

"Again we disagree," he said too smoothly, his eyes on her lips.

"You're the enemy."

"Depends on your viewpoint. I'm the father of your child. I want you. Even more now that I know you're pregnant and scared and vulnerable."

"I'm not any of those things!"

"You are, and I think that's a big part of the reason you're so mad at me."

She wasn't about to admit he had a point. She didn't want to feel dependent and needy.

"I hate being pregnant! Why do you get to be so strong and sure of yourself?"

"If you'd let me take care of you, maybe you wouldn't be so scared. Maybe you wouldn't hate being pregnant so much."

"What are you saying?"

"Marry me…at least until after the baby's born."

"But—"

"Look, when the sun came up this morning I didn't want to get married any more than you, but there's our baby to consider now. He'll be legitimate. I think that's important."

"He could be a she."

"Could be, but that's not really the point, is it? People don't think as much of babies who don't have fathers. Don't you want to give our baby the best possible start?"

She hated to agree with him about anything, but she was more old-fashioned than she'd realized. If she didn't marry him, she'd dread telling the baby why she'd never married its father. She'd told Kel, but she felt embarrassed about explaining this mess to the rest of her staff.

"We'll sort it all out as we go along," he said.

He was so close, so tall and dark and strong, and she felt so weary and sad and scared. Would marriage make things better or worse?

Despite her determination to dislike him and blame him, his nearness had an intoxicating effect on her. His clean male scent mingled with something tangy and lemony that she remembered from that night. Her skin had smelled of him afterward. Why couldn't she forget how their bodies had strained together in perfect harmony?

And her dreams... Fragments of half-remembered dreams about him had haunted her when she'd awakened hot and perspiring and clutching her sheets against her breasts in the middle of the night. Did she subconsciously hunger for him even though she fought thinking about him every waking hour?

"This conversation about marriage is ridiculous."

"For a minute there you had the look of a woman seriously considering my offer."

She actually had been. "You've got to go." Desperately, she began pushing at his thick chest.

"Not a good idea," he muttered thickly, crushing her closer.

She knew that if she fought him or screamed, dull,

gentlemanly Leo would let her go. For some reason she stood still in his arms and waited. Maybe to see what he would do next.

When she didn't fight him, something hot and exciting flashed in his dark eyes, but he didn't rush her. His arms stayed around her for another long moment. Then he leaned down, tipped her chin back with a fingertip and kissed her ever so lightly. The instant his mouth grazed hers, a ripple of hot, carnal need trilled from her lips all the way down to her toes.

Not that she was quite past the ability to think and admire his technique. Dull Leo was a superb kisser, her mind noted with cold approval.

His kisses at the bar that night had been the spark that had lit the conflagration that had landed them in this mess.

From that first kiss—a teaser, he'd called it—she'd been his. She remembered his second kiss after he'd told her he was going for broke. Talk about a meltdown.

Her breath came unevenly as she opened her lips. She hadn't realized until his tongue slid against hers how much she'd wanted his mouth and hands on her body again. Was that why she'd dreamed of him and feared him?

Quivering, she threaded her fingertips through the soft black hair that curled over his collar. Then with a little cry, she bunched fistfuls of his shirt, pulled him closer. Breathing hard, he was fully aroused. Holding on tight, she reveled in his passion.

"Where's your bedroom?" he demanded huskily after they'd kissed for a while.

"Right behind us," she answered.

"How convenient."

As his mouth left her lips to explore her neck and

trailed kisses upon her heaving breasts, the enormity of what she was doing washed over her. Weakly, she shoved at his chest. Then she began to push at him and struggle in earnest. But her efforts were puny and half-hearted at best because what she really wanted was Leo naked and wild on top of her. She wanted his knees to spread her legs. She wanted to open herself. She wanted him deep, deep inside her.

"Don't run out on me again," he begged between kisses. One of his big hands slipped down her waist to her knees, and he lifted her into his arms.

When she shook her head and murmured no, he kissed her again and again until she shivered. Then quickly, carrying her, he moved down the dark hall to her bedroom. He set her down on the bed and continued kissing and stroking her. His gaze lit her entire being as he tugged her blue top over her breasts and then over her head. She closed her eyes and lay still as he unhooked her bra and removed it. Very gently he lowered his head, causing her to gasp when he began to lick each rosy brown nipple.

Cupping her breasts, he murmured, "They seem larger." He ran his hand down and rested it on her belly, holding his palm there for a long moment with an attitude of such awe and possession that she began to feel on fire.

His reverence caused a tightness in her throat. Not since Becky had she felt this close to another human being.

Finally, she splayed her fingers against his warm chest. Beneath whorls of dark hair, she felt the violence of his pulsing heart.

He wanted her, but he was a man. He'd said he hadn't

had a woman since he'd been with her. What she couldn't account for was the fierceness of her own urgency.

"Leo…"

Wrapping her arms around him, she leaned her head against his chest with a sigh, reveling in his scent and heat and strength. "I'll regret this. I know it."

She sighed, unable to help herself. Being in his arms felt so right and safe.

What was wrong with spending one more night with him? She was already pregnant, wasn't she? The worst was done…horse out of the barn and all that. She felt strangely light-headed, almost happy knowing she had nothing more to lose and that she could gain such immense pleasure and comfort from letting him make love to her.

"I want you naked," she whispered, knowing she must be mad.

"What?"

"Your turn to strip for me. I stood on that table, remember."

His gaze burned her.

When he didn't move, she said, "Well, go on."

He gasped as her slim, white hands ripped at his shirt, encouraging him as she yanked it out of his waistband. When he still did nothing, she undid his belt and unbuttoned his jeans. Last of all, she tugged his zipper down. Never had any sound been more erotic than that rasp of metal as denim parted. When she touched him down there, he groaned loudly.

"Go on," she urged, "take your jeans off."

She removed her hand and stared at his dark body, her heart in her throat as he tore his jeans and shirt and briefs off and tossed them on the floor. There wasn't much moonlight, but there was enough for her to marvel at the heart-stopping perfection of his sculpted, male body. Maybe he was a CEO, but he did more than push pencils. Every inch of his lean body was hard and tough, as lean and tough as any cowboy's.

Dull Leo didn't seem so dull all of a sudden. He danced. He rode. He was great at kissing and great at sex. At least, he was with her. What other hidden talents did he have that could thrill a girl?

She closed her eyes, wanting to know more of him, and yet afraid. So afraid. He was what she'd been running from her whole life.

"Damn you! You'd better not be pretending I'm Shanghai! Not tonight!" he growled fiercely.

Her eyes snapped open, and she saw his cold fury mingle with hurt. "No," she whispered, feeling a strange sympathy. "Only you."

"Good. Tonight I don't want any ghosts in this bed. Just the two of us, understand?"

Swallowing, she nodded. Then she scooted across the bed into a pool of moonlight and kissed him, long and lingeringly on the mouth until they were both breathing so hard, she knew it was way past time for her to take off the rest of her clothes.

He helped her undress. When she was naked, he pulled her beneath the sheets and against his body, which was so blazing hot, she kicked off the covers.

"Why the hell have you been so damn set against me?" he growled.

She arched her body up to meet his. Just to tease him, she began to writhe. "Did anybody ever tell you that you talk too much, Leo Storm?"

And that was the last thing either of them said for a very long time, not until she was sobbing and he was crying her name hoarsely and crushing her so close she felt they were one.

Five

Abby awoke to burning heat. Why was she so hot?

When she began to squirm out from under the covers, she realized that she was buried beneath a tumble of sheets and quilts, and her legs and arms were tangled in Leo's. Her first thought was she'd better get out of bed and call Kel to warn her she'd be late getting into the office again. But Leo's warmth lulled her.

Who cared about the office anyway? Kel could handle anything, and from what Abby had seen of Miriam, she imagined Miriam could, too. Unlike the first morning after they'd made love, Abby did not disentangle herself and run. Instead she lay there, savoring the memories of his touches and intimacies of the night before.

Last night, dull Leo had definitely been anything but. Again and again she'd driven him over the edge until he'd clasped her, rasping for every breath, groaning her name as he'd shuddered in her arms.

He'd been so reasonable and nice all evening, cooking supper, washing dishes, putting up with her mood. Had he been intent on this happening all along?

He'd made love to her with such passionate, primal determination—as if he'd been staking his claim and making her his. It had all been very primitive and wild, and just thinking about it made her shiver and feel reluctant to leave the bed.

She stretched, reliving each and every one of the torrid memories. No man had ever wanted her with such intense urgency, and she had certainly responded in kind.

A black lock fell over his dark brow. She marveled that the sharp angles of his virile features could seem so much softer this morning. He'd been so driven and relentless last night.

Despite his dark, unshaven chin, he looked as innocent as a small child. At the same time he looked like a man who'd gotten exactly what he'd wanted.

She was still marveling at his look of contentment when his black eyes lazily opened and met hers, claiming her.

His arm came around her possessively, and he grinned, showing off his perfect white teeth. "Good. You're still here."

"It's my bed. My house," she said. "Where would I go?"

"So—are you going to marry me?"

"There are a million logical reasons why that's a very bad idea."

"You're pregnant. If we're unhappy, we'll get a divorce. Big deal."

"Divorce *is* a big deal."

Her parents had divorced. She still wasn't over it. She'd always dreamed of a romantic start at marriage, of making it work. "I can't just marry—casually."

When she started to ease away from him, he bolted upright, and the tension became palpable between them. He looked fiercely masculine.

"Stay here a minute," he whispered.

She sucked in a breath and swallowed.

"Please. I need to tell you some things."

"Okay."

"I got a girl pregnant when I was a kid. I won't go into the whole story now, but I couldn't marry her. For one thing, she wouldn't marry me. Hell, maybe it was for the best. That's what I try to tell myself. But, I hardly know my daughter, Julie, and I regret that more every day. So, your pregnancy isn't just about me and you, you know."

The pain in his voice touched her deeply.

"I'm older, settled in a career. I have plenty of money. I can afford a wife and child. I would try very hard to make our relationship work."

But he didn't love her, and she didn't love him. Maybe that was a good thing. Maybe when they divorced, she wouldn't suffer so much. If they married, at least their child would never have to be ashamed of the circumstances surrounding its birth.

She mulled over his proposal for a long time. Finally, she met his gaze again. "I know this is crazy. I know it won't work. I'll regret it. But for the baby…yes."

"Hey," he said gently. "How can you still be so damn negative after last night?"

Before she could tell him that sex, even great sex,

wasn't really all that important in marriage, he rolled onto his back and pulled her down on top of him.

"So, we're getting married," he said as if that was going to take some getting used to. "How about that?" His gaze was tender as he kissed her lightly on the brow.

When she didn't budge—fool that she was, was she actually hoping for more?—he said, "I'd better brush my teeth and shower so we can get to our offices."

He went into her bathroom, and her shower ran for quite a while. Later, when he appeared in her kitchen, his wet black hair gleamed, and his breath smelled like peppermint.

Dull Leo Storm was nothing if not fastidious.

"How about a cup of coffee, *dear?*" she quipped.

"*Dear?* I like the sound of that. Coffee sounds good, too, but I can get that anywhere. I'd rather have a kiss…from my bride to be."

"Hmm." Slowly she went into his arms and nestled close as if she belonged there.

He grinned. "I've just got time for one kiss, so I'd better go for broke. Don't want you changing your mind as soon as I drive off."

"Going for broke… That's what you said the night you got me pregnant."

He smiled as she lifted her lips to his. One taste, and they were both starving again. She really did think maybe she ought to promote Kel and give her more executive responsibilities.

"I've got an early meeting," he muttered several kisses later when things had really begun to heat up. "Buy a white dress and veil and decide who you want to be at our wedding. I'll handle the rest of the arrangements and call you back about the date. Let's get married as fast as possible—say in a week or ten days."

"A week? Weddings take a lot of time."

"Trust me. A week!" His quick male smile was both superior and all-knowing.

Men. Women could spend a year orchestrating a wedding. Being a CEO, he'd probably dictate his guest list, turn the arrangements over to the hard-hearted Miriam and think nothing more about it.

Ten minutes later when he loped out to his truck, Abby followed him, still feeling bemused. He kissed her again on the bottom step. Then she stayed there, licking her mouth, tasting him as she watched until his truck disappeared in clouds of red dust.

Her bruised lips were still warm from his kisses. She was wondering if he'd come back tonight and make love to her again. How could she want that? How she could feel almost happy about this, when so much could go wrong?

Was it because he was so good in bed? Yes, that had to be it. After last night, she was still in a brain fog. When she came to her senses, would she even like him?

Doomed. Abby felt trapped and alone as she stood beside Leo one week later before the carved altar of Mission San José in front of a hundred wedding guests, pledging herself in marriage.

If only her father had showed up, just this once. She thought about Becky and her long-dead mother and the perfect marriage and family she'd dreamed about having someday.

She missed the family she'd lost so much, missed

her father. Here she was, alone, marrying a man she barely knew.

"You may kiss the bride," the preacher said, his deep, sonorous voice ringing inside the thick stone walls of the ancient mission chapel.

As Leo's warm lips touched hers, Abby began to shake with the realization she was now married to this darkly handsome stranger. Was it only a week ago that he'd proposed and she'd marveled that he'd thought he could arrange everything so quickly?

Except for the night he'd dropped by to slide a three-carat engagement ring onto her finger, she'd hardly seen him. Miriam, however, had called her constantly to confirm various details. If Miriam was surprised by this sudden turn of events, she'd given no indication. She'd been deferential, respectful and, above all, exceedingly capable and efficient.

All Abby had had to do was buy a dress, invite her father, her friends and her staff…and show up. Not that her father had made the effort to do even that. He'd promised he'd be here to give her away, but an hour before the wedding, he'd called her on her cell with an excuse, wishing her the best wedding day ever but saying that his flight out of Colombia—where he was interviewing terrorists in the jungle—had been cancelled. As always, the adrenaline high he got from hanging out with a dangerous terrorist was a bigger lure than anything having to do with her, so Leo's brother, Connor, had given her away.

Even as Leo's warm lips lingered over hers, her father's absence tugged at her heart.

"It's okay," Leo whispered, releasing her. "He'll make it next time."

How had he known what she was thinking? That seemed sweet until a thought occurred to her and new fears filled her eyes. Was he already thinking of their imminent divorce and her future marriage to another man?

"Next time?" she asked in a tremulous tone.

Sensing her doubt, he squeezed her hand. "When the baby's born."

Still gripping her hand, Leo turned to face the congregation with his new bride. For an instant she was aware of Leo staring at his brother. In a sea of happy faces, Connor was the only man who looked grim. Leo smiled, so she forced a smile, too. When everyone stood, Connor was the last to rise, and he didn't join in the joyous applause for the couple. Was Connor, who knew the situation, as dubious about their union's ultimate success as she?

Leo's guest list had turned out en masse. Not counting his glum-looking brother, most of the guests worked for the Golden Spurs. She'd met many of them when she'd gone down to the Golden Spurs to wait for Shanghai to bring Mia back from Mexico after he'd rescued her.

Joanne Kemble, the late Caesar Kemble's widow and the mother of Mia and Lizzy Kemble, was the first to rush up to them and congratulate Leo.

"My, you're certainly a dark horse," she said a little too brightly. "You didn't even bring a date to the ranch for our Memorial Day family reunion. And a week later you call me and tell me you're getting married? Who is this woman who could make you change course with the speed of light?"

Leo's face darkened. "It happened suddenly."

"You're an ambitious man. You never make a move without thinking about it from every angle. You hardly seem the type to rush into marriage."

"It's called falling in love," Leo said, shooting Abby a tender glance. "Cupid's arrow is but one of the many reasons why it is impossible to predict the behavior of any human being."

"Well, someday I hope to learn the whole story." Joanne's all-knowing, speculative gaze zeroed in on Abby and stayed there, making her feel the woman saw too much. "Your bridegroom called every guest and invited each of us personally. He bragged and bragged about you. He said you were beautiful and smart. He sounded so in love. It was really…quite sweet. I had to change some vacation plans, but I wouldn't have missed this. Not for the world! Leo married. Who would have thought?" She paused. "I can't tell you what an asset he is to the Golden Spurs. And you will be, too, I'm sure."

Only she didn't sound sure.

"Still, this will certainly take some getting used to. I'm afraid we keep him hopping with all our crises. But he's so cool and collected. So logical. So ambitious—globally—for the ranch. He has a way of solving problems with the least emotional energy and the greatest efficiency, which is great, since we Kembles seem to have a flair for drama." She paused, her eyes growing even more intense. "How's your father?"

At the sudden unfortunate change of topic, Abby started guiltily. "He couldn't come."

"And I was so looking forward to seeing him." Joanne looked away.

"You know him?"

Joanne blushed. "Y-yes. Not all that well—I mean, personally—but he is a famous man...at least in some circles."

Abby felt she was missing something. She had never considered her father famous even though he was a multipublished, award-winning, nonfiction writer. "He's in Colombia, working. His plane was cancelled at the last minute. He really wanted to be here."

"I'm sure. Your father is so dedicated." Joanne's forceful, veined hands were cool and yet perspiring as they clung to Abby's. "I admire his work so much."

"Many people do."

"I wish...." The older woman blushed again and then frowned. "Never mind. Just tell him that I—I...that Joanne Kemble said hello."

"I will."

Joanne's gaze held hers a moment longer. There was depth and hope and an inexplicable tension in her gaze, but before Abby had time to dwell on this, a woman named Mona called to her, and Joanne turned and ran eagerly, as if welcoming the chance to escape a conversation that had felt increasingly awkward to them both.

What had that been about?

For a long moment, Abby felt confused and a little lost even though she was surrounded by people and Leo stood at her side with his hand on her elbow.

Joanne seemed to know her father very well indeed, and she'd taken much too great an interest in Abby for comfort. She would have to ask her father about Joanne Kemble someday.

Mia and Shanghai Knight and their dark-haired little girl, Vanilla, were the next to come up. Shanghai held her hand too tightly and kissed her a little more passionately than was proper for a former boyfriend. Was he relieved to have her safely married?

"You're a lucky man, Storm," he said gruffly, shaking his hand after releasing Abby. "You'd better take good care of her. You know you can't work as hard with a new bride."

Leo nodded, rather fiercely she thought.

"Hey, maybe you two could buy me out of the Buckaroo Ranch since your ranches both touch mine on different corners. I don't get up there much since I married Mia."

Leo nodded again. He didn't look like he was enjoying Shanghai kissing Abby or talking to them much. Then Vanilla raced away. Shanghai laughed and, catching Leo's eye, said, "Well, that's my cue. I'd better go," and chased after her. Mia laughed and followed after them at a more leisurely pace.

Funny, Abby didn't feel the least bit jealous of Mia anymore.

"Maybe we *should* buy him out of the Buckaroo," Leo said.

Shanghai's brother, Cole Knight, strode up with his wife, Lizzy, Mia's sister.

Kel, who was next in line, hugged Abby and quietly told her that if she was going to keep the baby, marriage to a guy as cool as Leo was definitely the best way to go.

"He's not the least bit dull. And he holds his own pretty well with all these hunky Golden Spurs cowboys. He's handsome and suave. And he's got to be smart. Still, I can't believe a straight guy could pull this off," Kel said.

"This?"

"You. This wedding. I mean, an historical mission—

the queen of missions, no less—what a great venue for a wedding! So memorable and romantic. And he did it in a week! Cool! Everything's simply gorgeous. Even the weather cooperated." She began to rave about the band and caterer.

Kel knew a thing or two about event planning since everybody who worked at In the Pink! had to constantly arrange photo shoots and coordinate media events, too often with very little notice.

"It's a little too perfect, and it was a little too easy for him, if you ask me," Abby said moodily.

"You'd prefer to be marrying a doltish, wild cowboy with no social aptitude?"

"Let's not go there. Just don't give him too much credit. His secretary probably did everything."

Kel, who thought secretaries ran the world, nodded. "Well, who hired her? Who keeps her happily working? You'd better watch out. Now that he's got a smart wife to go along with his super-brilliant secretary, he'll be invincible."

When the next person in line nudged Kel, she said, "I think I'll go introduce myself to his hunky brother. What was his name?"

"Connor. Over there…."

She nodded toward Connor, who was standing beneath a live oak tree with a glass of champagne in his hand. Why did he keep studying his brother so deliberately?

Connor was an investigator, she told herself. He was probably suspicious by nature. Maybe he thought she'd trapped Leo and felt protective of his older brother.

There were champagne toasts and dancing. Not that Abby drank anything other than sparkling water. Leo held her close when they danced, too close, and she was reminded that dancing close was what had led to that first going-for-broke kiss in the bar that had made her decide to go home with him.

She and Leo cut the cake and fed each other, licking cake and icing off each other's lips. When she passed on the white wedding cake and ate only the groom's chocolate cake, he made her confess that she was something of a chocoholic.

On the surface the reception was gay and happy, but Abby couldn't ignore Connor's unsmiling face every time his glance fell upon his brother or her. Nor could she forget her own doubts or Joanne's awkward comments. This was a marriage of convenience—not a real marriage. And, therefore, not a happy occasion.

Still, why dwell on those things? Maybe she would have stopped worrying if she hadn't overheard a snippet of the brothers' hushed conversation when they thought she was distracted by Miriam.

"So, have you told her?" Connor demanded.

"Butt out!" Leo replied.

"If you don't, and someone else… If she learns what you did that night from someone else, there will be hell to pay."

"You heard me," Leo said.

Abby must have made some sound, because they turned, and, when Connor met her gaze, he broke off in mid-sentence. Flushing darkly, both men rushed up to her.

You married a stranger.

She'd been a fool to go through with this, she thought miserably even as Leo took her hand reassuringly and tucked her possessively against his tall body.

"Told me what?" she asked.

"Sorry?" Leo said, frowning as if in confusion.

"I couldn't help overhearing…."

"We were talking about business. Dull stuff. I hire Connor from time to time."

"What do you need a private investigator for?"

Joanne, who'd been standing nearby chatting to Mona, was suddenly beside them again. "Oh, that's Lizzy's fault," she said, staring at Abby in that way that made her so uncomfortable. "I don't know how much you know about our family, but my late husband had two daughters by another woman, who was rather famous. Electra Scott. Have you heard of her?" A shrill edge had crept into her voice.

Leo's mouth thinned. The color drained from his face. Everyone around them fell silent and looked uneasy, too. Not that Joanne backed off. She seemed hell-bent on making some point.

"Oh, yes," Abby finally said. "I believe I have. Electra Scott. Didn't she die recently? In some jungle?"

"Yes." Joanne's eyes were as coldly blue as ice shards.

"And she took wonderful pictures of children and animals and wildlife?"

"Among other things," Joanne said.

"I think maybe my father may have collaborated on a book with her," Abby said.

"Did he? Well, that wouldn't surprise me. They were both well-known."

Leo was frowning and shifting his weight from one foot to the other, but again Joanne ignored him.

"Electra was my best friend in college. She was incredibly adventurous and very…independent. Lots of fun back then. She wasn't made for marriage. She always said, she'd never settle down. That life had too many possibilities. 'Why should I only live one little life, in one country, with one man?' she used to say.

"I brought her to the ranch, and Caesar fell madly in love with her the second he set eyes on her. I was in love with his older brother, Jack, who died, back then."

"I'm sorry."

"Thank you." An ugly shadow passed across Joanne's face. "But it was a very long time ago. I'd grown up knowing the Kembles, so after Jack died and Electra went away, Caesar and I eventually married. Not long after his death, I came into possession of Electra's journal and discovered that Electra had secret twin daughters by Caesar. Eventually Lizzy insisted we ask Leo to find them, and he hired Connor." She looked from Abby to Connor, her eyes seeming to ask much more than her question. "So, how's that coming?"

Leo's hand tightened ever so slightly on Abby's. When she glanced at him, he smiled and deliberately relaxed his fingers.

"I've made some real progress, but lately I've hit a few snags," Connor said, his eyes glued to his brother like an actor waiting for a cue. "Hopefully we'll have some good news for you before long."

Leo heaved in a breath and managed a thin smile. Not that his eyes warmed.

"How old would his daughters be now?" Abby asked, curious about these secret sisters.

"Twenty-six...nearly twenty-seven."

"Like me." Abby looked at Connor. "And these missing twins...they have no idea that they're Kembles?"

Joanne froze. "No. I am quite sure they don't. And it may come as quite a shock when they find out." Then, without another word, she turned and walked away.

Lifting his glass of champagne, Connor gulped it dry. "It's late. I'd better go." He turned to leave without so much as a glance toward his brother.

His abrupt departure, as well as Joanne's, struck Abby as odd.

"Is your brother happy about our marriage?" Abby asked when she was alone with Leo.

"Of course. What makes you ask?"

"I don't know him, but he seems…worried. And Joanne… I don't think she likes me."

"You're wrong about Joanne. As for Connor, he's always been moody. I should know. I raised him. I'm sure it has to do with work. He takes his work very seriously."

Leo's mouth was tight, and he seemed edgily defensive. Abby sensed he probably knew more than he was willing to admit. "Like you say, you know him. I don't. Whatever his misgivings, at least Connor showed up. Unlike my—"

"Your father would have been here if he could have been."

"It's easy for you to believe that. But then you don't know him like I do, do you?"

"Right." As if stung, he shut up.

She was remembering all the school performances her father had missed. He hadn't come to even one, not even those in which she'd starred. She thought about the Christmas card in her drawer that had arrived two weeks late.

This wasn't a real marriage. What did it matter if Joanne acted strange or Connor disapproved or her father wasn't here? Leo, who looked as tight and strained as she felt, took her hand and brought it to his lips. "I'm sorry," he said, squeezing her fingers.

She looked away just as an older man, who introduced himself to her as B. B. Kemble, came up and began to rant about the high winds and drought in South Texas. Leo fell into this discussion with relish, probably because he was anxious to forget her and about their tense conversation. Soon he was smiling again, and she was sure he'd forgotten her entirely. So, feeling lost and forgotten, she let go of his hand and wandered away.

All too soon the reception was over and Leo and she were holding hands again. Bending low, they ran through their guests, who blew environmentally correct bubbles over their heads as they made a dash for Leo's waiting stretch limousine, which whisked them toward the center of the city.

Leo hadn't attempted conversation since they'd discussed Connor and her father. When the driver didn't take the downtown exit that would have taken them to Leo's loft apartment, Abby tugged at Leo's sleeve.

"Airport. Weekend honeymoon," Leo said brusquely. "Sorry I can't get away for longer. Didn't Miriam tell you to pack a bag?"

"She said, 'Be prepared for warm weather. Two nights. And be sure to bring a bathing suit.' I thought she meant you had a pool in your building."

"I do. But Miriam was wrong about the bathing suit. Where we're going, it's so private, we can swim naked. I hope you'll want to."

The sudden heat in his eyes made her breath catch. "Where are we going?"

"It's a surprise."

She couldn't stop looking at her lean-muscled husband. With his black hair and tanned skin, he was devastatingly, moody-broody handsome. Fierce looking, too.

Her heart sped up. Boy or girl, their baby would be beautiful if it looked anything like him.

Leo held out his hand. When she took it, he pulled her closer. Her head fell against his shoulder, and the rasp of his warm breath in her hair made her scalp tingle.

That first night they'd made love, he'd held her curled against him like this for hours. She'd fallen asleep as if drugged from his lovemaking, never wanting to leave his arms—only to wake the next morning to profound guilt at her wanton behavior.

They'd both been forced into this marriage. They barely knew each other. What chance did their marriage have?

Six

When Abby and Leo got off the Golden Spurs jet, warm, humid, salt-laden air blew her hair back from her face. The inky sky swam with stars, and she could hear the surf pounding noisily.

The airport was a strip of asphalt laid on top of sand. Palm fronds clattered noisily beside a lone hangar at the end of the strip.

"Where are we?" she cried as he hurried her through blowing grit toward a strange-looking beach buggy.

"A private barrier island off the Texas coast. It's owned by a Texas rancher and oilman who owes me a favor or two. He offered to let me use his beach house for our honeymoon. His house is about a mile down the beach."

Even if the beach house hadn't been vast, yet cozy, she would have been glad to get inside and out of the wind. Nestled behind towering sand dunes and surrounded by dense vegetation, which included lots more noisy palms, the mansion had the ambience of a Caribbean plantation house. Big open rooms made for stunning interiors with soaring beamed ceilings and furnishing in beiges and browns with the occasional bright plump cushion and potted plant.

Leo ended his tour of the immaculate house in the master bedroom. Beside a massive, textile-draped, four-poster bed, a magnum of champagne and a bottle of sparkling water stood side by side chilling in a silver ice bucket.

As Leo deftly opened the champagne and poured himself a glass, she wondered who kept the mansion in such pristine shape and where Leo's pilot would sleep tonight. Not that she asked.

Leo opened the water and poured a glass for her. When he handed her hers, he tipped his glass toward hers, and she did the same. Crystal clinked.

He didn't make a toast out loud, however, she eyed the bed and made one silently. *To luck. To miracles. To happiness…together…forever.* She knew she was naive to even entertain such hopes.

"You look scared," he said. "At times like this, try to remember that Coco likes me."

"That's definitely a big point in your favor." Another point was the fact that he'd hired an excellent groom to take care of Coco while she was pregnant.

"I'll take all the points I can get," Leo said.

He smiled at her as she lifted her glass. When she gulped deeply, his smile broadened. He was about to lift his to his lips, when his cell rang.

He frowned when he saw who it was and excused

himself. "I've got to take this. Why don't you get ready for bed?"

The word *bed* was still hanging heavily in the air as he let himself out onto the balcony so he could speak privately.

Why was he being so secretive? Was this a business call or personal? She remembered Connor's grim attitude. What was going on?

Have you told her?

What if Connor had been referring to her? Leo had definitely seemed more strained since she'd asked him about their conversation.

Well, the empty bedroom wouldn't give her any answers. It was late. She decided to take Leo's advice and get ready for bed.

A wedding dress wasn't the only purchase she'd made when she'd gone shopping. She'd bought several sheer nightgowns, as well.

Hesitating for a moment, she went to her suitcase and removed her toiletries and the filmiest of all her new nightgowns, which was a transparent beige.

In the marble bathroom, she undressed and showered. She opened her legs and lathered herself. For long moments she let the warm water run down her neck and her breasts to her belly and thighs. Even after all the bubbles were gone, she stood under the water thinking about the two nights she'd spent with Leo.

He was so sexy. He could do anything, everything to a woman. She'd thought a corporate type like him would be unimaginative in bed, but he had no inhibitions. And he'd made her forget hers. Now that they were married, she wondered if he'd be willing to fulfill her wildest fantasies.

The tensions of the wedding and the reception drained away, and an all-consuming fiery hunger ate at her. He hadn't slept with her since she'd agreed to marry him. She wanted him—again. Just thinking about it made her heart beat faster and faster.

She turned off the water, stepped out of the shower and ripped a towel off a bar. Drying herself and her hair, she pulled the nightgown over her head. Last of all, she brushed her teeth so that she'd taste of peppermint, since peppermint seemed to be Leo's favorite flavor.

Racing into the bedroom, she turned out the lights, got into bed and waited for him to return. When thirty minutes passed and he still hadn't come, she got up and opened the doors to the balcony.

There was nothing out there but the screaming palms, the roar of the surf and the blowing sand. She slammed the doors and leaned against them. Where was Leo? Why hadn't he come to bed? Didn't he want her?

Had he had his fill of her already? Did he feel trapped and therefore uninterested? Some part of her wasn't quite ready to believe that. And yet…how well did she really know him?

Without bothering to search for her robe, Abby left the bedroom in search of Leo. When she heard his deep baritone issuing commands as decisively as a general, she ran down the hall. Pushing open the last door, she found him seated at a huge desk in the study, holding two phones, one against each ear.

She paused in the middle of the door so that the hall light came from behind her.

His gaze met hers and then ran the length of her backlit body before returning to her face. Something dark and powerful made his eyes flame. She read male appreciation and maybe more. Whatever his emotion, he turned it off with an abruptness that chilled her. Closing his eyes and then opening them, he regarded her levelly.

"Just a second," he said in a hard voice to whoever was on the phones.

Frowning, he shook his head at her. "Sorry. There's a grass fire at the Golden Spurs. It's huge, and it's my fault because I authorized a controlled burn yesterday. The fire jumped a road and got away from our men. The grass is dry and the wind is horrible. I should have gone down there myself to see to it. But I didn't."

Because he'd married her.

Not that he seemed to blame her.

"I have to deal with it now. Go to bed. I'll sleep in here near the phones. No need for us both to be up all night."

"I don't mind the phone ringing, if only you'll come to bed."

"We'll see," he said. "Maybe later."

"It's our honeymoon."

"I know." A muscle in his cheek jumped, but he lowered his head, his complete attention on his callers again.

Feeling rejected and desolate, Abby lay awake most of the night. She tossed this way and that, her emotions tearing at her. When she did sleep, she had weird dreams. Connor kept appearing in them like a dark spirit with his constant refrain.

Have you told her?

Every time she woke up, she felt like a fool for wanting Leo so much and even more of a fool for feeling so hurt because he preferred the study to being with her. Three weeks ago she hadn't ever wanted to see him again, and now she was pining after him like a lovesick idiot—just because she was a romantic when it came to marriage.

Around five o'clock, she got up and tiptoed down the hall to check on him. She found Leo, still dressed in his tux, asleep in the big leather chair in the brilliantly lit study. He looked so tired, she didn't want to wake him and urge him to come to bed. All she did was turn off the lights and cover him with a soft throw. Then she returned to the master bedroom and lay down alone. Finally, she fell into a dreamless sleep.

An hour or so later he walked into the bedroom and checked on her. She heard him, but false pride made her pretend to be asleep.

He neither spoke nor touched her. He simply stood there watching her "sleep" as she'd watched him. He walked back to his study, and her heart ached as she listened to his retreating footsteps falling ever softer as he moved back down the length of the hall.

Once more she drifted to sleep, awakening a few hours later to the smell of coffee. She combed her hair, put on her makeup and dressed in white shorts, a T-shirt and sandals. Hoping the fires were out and his mood improved, she scampered down the hall and found him in the kitchen talking on his cell again. Only this time, when he saw her, he ended the conversation abruptly.

"Sleep well?" he asked, his face grave.

She nodded, not wanting to admit how much she'd longed for him.

"And you?" She tried to sound casual.

"Not the best night, but I've had worse." His weary

smile failed to reach his eyes. "I'll make you some breakfast."

"What about the fire?"

"Not good. I'm afraid I have to go down there as soon as possible. I'll fly you to San Antonio. Then I have to go to the Golden Spurs. Ten thousand acres have burned. We've lost several structures. The fire seems to be getting worse. We need to cut or hose down the grass on either side of more ranch roads to make firebreaks and move cattle."

"Wouldn't you get there faster…if I went with you?"

"Yes, but I don't expect…" His black eyes narrowed. "I mean the Golden Spurs is my concern. Not yours."

His expression changed, and she wondered what he was thinking

"What?" she said.

"Nothing," he muttered grouchily.

"I'm going with you then. It's my concern now, too. I'm your wife."

"Suit yourself." His face remained guarded and impossible to read, but he nodded.

After a long moment, he said, "Look, I'm sorry I'm such bad company. I just got word that Black Hawk and Chinook helicopters capable of pouring hundreds of gallons of water in one sweep can't join our firefighters until the winds decrease. By the way, my pilot's standing by."

"I can be ready in five minutes."

"No, first we eat. I'm pretty tired after last night, but it wasn't anything compared to what's in store for us."

Like before at her house, he was at ease in a kitchen. Within minutes they were seated at the table in front of freshly squeezed orange juice, eggs, toast and bacon. Even though a maid would probably be flown in to tidy the place, he cleaned the kitchen perfectly. Then they packed, and he carried her bags to the dune buggy.

"Sorry that we didn't have much of a honeymoon," he said once they were airborne and she was glancing wistfully down at the house on the island and the strip of long white beach in front of it.

Not that he seemed sorry. His face was tense and drawn. He was completely preoccupied by his worries about the fire. Still, every few minutes she caught him watching her, almost in the same way that Connor had watched him during their reception, as if he really were worried about something concerning her, too.

Connor's question kept repeating itself in her mind. *Have you told her?*

Was she being self-centered to think he'd been talking about her?

Fifty miles out from the ranch headquarters of the Golden Spurs giant plumes of smoke billowed higher than a mountain against a hellish, purple-orange sky. When they got closer she could see cowboys on horseback were moving cattle. Leo went to the cockpit and ordered the pilot to fly low all over the ranch. He took pictures and made notes while talking constantly to Kinky Moore, the ranch's foreman, on his cell phone.

When they finally landed behind the tall, red-roofed Big House and its outbuildings, the air was heavy with the acrid smell of smoke. A white sun burned a hole through the slate-gray sky. Winds whipped the mesquite and palm trees on every side of her. Kinky ran up to them and told Leo that because of the wind direction, the house wasn't threatened.

"We've got a hunting lodge to hose down and cattle to move just south of Black Oaks. Mia, Cole and Shanghai are down there now trying to save the old Knight homestead at Black Oaks."

Leo studied the black sky and then turned to her. "I shouldn't have brought you down here. The fire's bigger and closer to the house than I realized."

"There was no time to do anything else. I'll be fine."

"Stay inside until I come back. Keep your cell phone charged and handy." He turned to go.

"I want to go with you."

"No!"

She would have argued, but Leo's expression was harsh and unyielding. And the situation was too chaotic. Fire trucks and bulldozers were everywhere. Adrenaline charged the air. Exhausted-looking firemen streaked across the lawn in dirty orange overalls, shouting orders over cell phones and bickering with sweat-streaked, soot-faced cowboys about how best to fight the fire.

When the cowboys saw Leo, they shouted and waved to him, and before she knew it, he'd left her to join the quarrel between the cowboys and the firemen.

The firemen wanted to start some controlled burns, but the cowboys yelled that if the wind changed, they'd lose valuable livestock and maybe the Big House. Leo battled long and hard, speaking in a firm, rational voice, but the firemen refused to listen and soon sped away in their fire trucks to start more burns.

A second later Leo was on his phone again. "Shanghai! The firemen are going to set pasture seven on fire! We've got hunting lodges down there, and if the wind changes—"

Then Leo was running, shouting to Kinky. As the two men got in Kinky's big black SUV, Abby ran up to them and grabbed Leo's door handle.

"Leo... Take care."

His hair was unkempt, his countenance hard and carved with exhaustion and worry. She wanted him to get out of the SUV and pull her into his arms and crush her close, to press his mouth to hers, to say something, anything, before he left, but his dark face remained frozen even as his black eyes seared her.

Kinky twisted the key in the ignition, and the big vehicle roared to life.

"Leo... Don't leave me."

He clenched his jaw and nodded to Kinky to go.

Her last glimpse of him etched itself into her mind. Broad shoulders, steel-like jaw, anxiety emanating from him, virile sexiness.

What if he never came back?

Her heart felt hollow. A fist squeezed her throat closed.

Except for two nights of sex, she barely knew this man. How could she feel this intensely about him when, obviously, he didn't return her feelings?

Her shoulders sagged hopelessly as she backed away from the SUV. She didn't matter. She never mattered. He was leaving her, just like Becky had...just like her parents had. Everybody always left her.

Speechless, motionless, she watched Kinky back the big vehicle out of its space and then edge out onto the road. A minute later the SUV vanished in the thickening smoke.

She notched her chin up. Nothing had changed. She'd been alone for years and years. She had to get a grip. She couldn't let illusions about marriage and what it should mean and her growing attraction for this man make her hope for something impossible.

When she went into the house and descended the stairs to the basement, she found Sy'rai Moore, whom she'd met at her reception, downstairs in the kitchen, cooking and washing dishes along with Lizzy and Joanne. Off in one corner, Vanilla was on the floor building a high wall out of a set of blocks. From time to time, Joanne would fold her dish towel, kneel and add a block to the towering structure, which Vanilla would knock down and then rebuild.

Cowboys and firemen were down at the house between shifts. The men were smiling and laughing, fighting valiantly to pretend they were cheerful and brave as they sat at tables in small dining rooms off the kitchen, eating beans, charred venison, roasted nilgai antelope, gravy and mashed potatoes.

Sy'rai told her they'd hurried home as soon as they found out about the fire and repeated that Mia, Shanghai and Cole were struggling to save the Knight's ancient homestead.

Not wanting to dwell on her fears for Leo, Abby grabbed an apron. "What can I do?"

"Same thing we're doing," Joanne said. "We've got a lot of tired, hungry men."

By six o'clock the smoke was so thick in the basement that Abby's throat burned and her eyes and nose ran constantly. News reached them that things were bad near Black Oaks. Panicking, she tried to call Leo to find out what was going on over there, but he never answered.

The television anchormen gloomily reported that more than thirty thousand acres were on fire and that a wind shift was expected. "There have been two fatalities on the Golden Spurs Ranch over near Black Oaks, but the names of the individuals are being withheld until their families can be notified."

Panic cut through Abby. With her heart pounding in her throat, Abby dialed Leo again. Still no answer. What if…?

She clutched the phone against her chest as aerial shots showed one hunting lodge exploding in flames. Just as the camera panned to the homestead at Black Oaks, reduced to a pile of burning, red-hot rubble, Kinky stalked into the kitchen.

Sy'rai ran to him and threw her arms around him. His face and clothes were black with soot; his voice hoarse. His dark eyes held no emotion.

"Leo…is Leo with you?" Abby whispered.

He shook his head. Then his weary eyes passed over her. "We're evacuating the headquarters. Everybody get your stuff and be ready to get the hell out of here! We've got thirty minutes max!"

"But have you seen Leo?"

"What about Cole…and Mia and Shanghai?" Lizzy asked.

Without looking at Lizzy, Kinky shook his head. "Last I saw of them, they were in the thick of it over there at Black Oaks. You saw the pictures on TV. You know as much as I do."

"But you drove him over there," Abby cried.

"Drove him into hell. That's what I did."

Kinky stomped back up the stairs and began yelling orders. Soon cowboys were lifting priceless antiques and paintings and carrying them out of the house to load into the beds of their pickups.

Frantic, Abby punched in Leo's number again. When he still didn't answer, she ran outside where Lizzy and Sy'rai had begun hosing down the house and grounds and nearby trees with garden hoses.

Sy'rai was hooking more hoses together to make them long enough for her to haul one up the stairs, so she could climb out on the roof and hose it down, too. The roof was made of red tile, and although Abby wondered if hosing it was really necessary, she offered to help her. Then Sy'rai began hauling hoses into the house and up the stairs while Abby hooked more together.

When the trucks loaded with antiques and paintings were ready to leave, Kinky told her it was time for her to go. Joanne was sitting in the front of one of the pickups holding Vanilla in her arms.

"Leo told me to wait for him here."

"Nobody's heard from Leo in more than an hour. His last order was for me to see about you. Why don't you get in with Joanne."

"I'm staying until he comes."

"Hell, girl. Only really stubborn fools like me and Sy'rai are staying to fight to save the house or die trying. Caesar's ghost would haunt me forever if this old place burned just 'cause I ran off and left it."

"I'm staying, too."

"You've got nothing invested here. We're family."

The way he said the word *family* made her feel jealous.

"Leo's out there! Would he leave if I were out there, and he were here?"

"He wants you safe."

"He told me to stay."

"Funny, you don't seem like the obedient type." Kinky glared at her, trying to stare her down, but she squared her shoulders and folded her arms across her breasts. A full minute passed before he finally shrugged and glanced away.

"There's nothing worse than a stubborn woman," he finally said. A grim smile touched his black-rimmed lips as he glanced toward Sy'rai, who was yanking on a hose. "I should know. Hell, I've been married to one damn near my whole life. Grab a hose then before Sy'rai has a heart attack. Help her spray the Spur Tree and the grass around it."

"The Spur Tree?"

"Over there! On the other side of that far road. It's the puny-assed mesquite with all the spurs dangling off it."

Kinky turned to a couple of cowboys. "Guys, we need a firebreak around the house. Fast!"

Dark, black clouds billowed from the south where Leo was. The smoke was thickening, burning her nostrils and lungs.

"Leo," Abby whispered as she ran toward the tree that was covered with sparkling spurs, dragging a hose behind her.

Seven

Half a mile ahead Leo saw a wall of flame and clouds of black smoke. Behind that was the Big House. The loss of the old Black Oaks homestead was still fresh on his mind. The Big House appeared to be square in the middle of the fire…or gone. He couldn't tell yet.

They'd almost saved Black Oaks.

But almost didn't count. Maybe he didn't really want to know about the Big House.

Houses, even a legendary, historical house like the Big House, were just houses. Kinky would have evacuated everybody hours ago, so at least he didn't have to worry about Abby and the baby.

If he lost them… He refused to let this mind go there. He had to believe they were safe.

Leo's hair and wet clothes were singed. His muscles ached. Every sort of thorn was stuck in his skin. His eyeballs and eyelids felt dry and scratchy from too much smoke. His lungs burned.

He wanted to lie down in the road. He wanted a drink, but he kept walking, one slow, trudging step after another. Behind him, he heard Mia's leaden footsteps and her occasional whimper. She was leaning heavily on Shanghai and Cole. Leo couldn't believe Shanghai had let her fight the fire with him, but then knowing Mia, he could. She'd survived being kidnapped by a drug lord.

They say bad people go to hell when they die. Leo wasn't a damn bit sure about that. Today had taught him you didn't have to die to go to hell.

He remembered screaming "Run!" to Shanghai and Cole and Mia as the flames had swept into the oak mott surrounding the Black Oaks homestead. Blackened tree limbs had crashed around them, splintering into pieces and sending showers of sparks in all directions. One had caught Leo's shirt on fire. He could still hear the crackling wall of flames as he'd dived into the creek; he'd felt the burning limbs crashing into the water on all sides of him as the three of them had huddled under the overhang of a huge rock.

They were damn lucky to be alive. If the creek behind the homestead had been ten feet farther away or the fire faster, they never would have made it. But the flames had raced through the trees without burning all the oxygen, only half burning the branches before sweeping north toward the Big House.

Leo pictured Abby as he'd last seen her. Her eyes had been wide and so fear filled when she'd told him good-bye. He'd wanted to jump down and haul her into his arms and never let her go, but he'd known that if he'd so much as spoken to her, or touched her, he never would have been able to leave her.

Why this woman? Why her? He'd never particularly wanted to be a father again, but ever since she'd told him about the baby, he'd felt strangely protective of her. Was it solely because she was who she was, and he was an ambitious bastard? Or had she always meant more?

Abby clung to Lizzy in the humid dark of the basement that was lit by a single flashlight. A cold, deadly fear gripping her heart, Abby couldn't stop shaking.

The thick walls seemed to close in upon her. All she could think of was Leo somewhere outside in that raging inferno. If Lizzy hadn't been holding her, surely she would have gone mad.

"He has to be all right," Abby whispered. "He just has to be."

"He's a quick thinker," Lizzy said, stroking her arm. "If anybody can take care of himself out there, it's Leo."

"Do you really think so?"

"Yes."

The flashlight flickered and went out, and darkness lapped at Abby in terrifying waves. Even though her arms tightened around Lizzy, she nearly screamed. Then another beam flared, and she swallowed a shallow breath when she saw Lizzy's tremendous smile.

It seemed hours that they sat huddled together, waiting.

Then Kinky threw the lower basement door open. "You can come out! The fire's past us! We lost the garage, but the Big House is safe."

As they climbed the stairs, Lizzy said, "This room

was built to protect the family and cowboys from Native and Mexican bandit raids in the 'olden days.' Who knew we'd ever need it for a grass fire?"

Holding hands, Lizzy and Abby climbed the last of the shadowy stairs. The house was still standing. It smelled of smoke and would have to be thoroughly cleaned, of course. When they got outside and saw the scorched oaks, palms and smoldering lawn and garage, they clung to each other. As far as they could see, blackened grass stretched endlessly to the east and south.

Letting go of Lizzy, Abby's eyes had wandered from the huge mansion to the glittering spurs of the Spur Tree. A deathly quiet wrapped around her when she gazed toward the south again in the direction of Black Oaks.

Where was Leo?

Abby saw the desolation in Lizzy's eyes and sensed her concern for her husband and sister, as well. Not that either of them said anything. They were too afraid of losing control.

Abby folded Lizzy into her arms. "For now it has to be enough that the Big House and everyone who stayed here is safe."

Lizzy bit her lips. "We can still hope and pray, can't we?"

Then Kinky began shouting orders, directing them to grab shovels and throw dirt on top of hot spots. "See if we've got any water pressure. We've got some spare hoses in the basement. Get them and spray the trees again. They could still ignite."

Abby busied herself spraying the trees. A couple of hours later she was sitting on a lawn chair, wiping her brow, when she heard Kinky shouting. She looked up and saw several dirty-looking men in the distance walking up the road, waving wearily. One of the bedraggled figures was a broad-shouldered, blackened scarecrow of a man, his shirt hanging in strips against his tall, lean body. He looked tired and footsore as he shuffled across the burned grasses toward her.

"Abby!" The man's deep voice was hoarse and strange, but it made the hair on the back of her neck stand up. She felt a new alertness, a lessening of her exhaustion. There was something about his walk, something about the set of his wide shoulders.

Her heart began to throb fiercely. Her hand went to her throat. When she tried to stand, her knees buckled, and she had to push herself off the ground with her free hand.

Then Lizzy screamed Cole's name and ran past her and flung her arms around two of the scarecrow's companions.

"Leo?" Abby whispered in a breathless croak that didn't sound a bit like her voice. She felt tears on her cheeks. *"Leo!"*

Abby's pulse leaped, then stopped and then sped up again. She felt sick to her stomach, and she was afraid she'd faint. Leo started running. She sprang to her feet and flew across the yard, hurling herself into his arms.

He winced when she grabbed his back, and she said, "I'm sorry. So sorry." But his grip was still strong as he snuggled her against the long length of his body and bent his dirty face to hers. His kiss was urgent and hot, demanding and devouring. His chin was rough against the softness of hers. He tasted of soot and grime and the brush country.

She didn't care. She framed his filthy face in her palms. He was alive. His mouth was vital, and his kisses filled her with a warm, surging tide of sheer desire and wild joy.

He released her so abruptly, she would have stumbled backward if he hadn't seized her by the arms. "What the hell are you still doing here?" he growled. Then he cursed vividly.

"Shh. The baby might hear. You did tell me to wait for you."

His dark eyes glittered with anger. For long minutes his fingers ground bruisingly into the flesh of her upper arms. "Right, blame me. You little fool, don't you know you could have died?"

"But I didn't, so there's no reason to get so mad."

"No reason? The baby could have—"

"What about you? You scared me, too. Do you think I could leave, knowing you were still out there?"

Something in her expression must have gotten through to him because his harsh face softened ever so slightly.

"Abby… Abby…" He lowered his voice to a soothing purr and cupped her chin with his fingers. "Oh, Abby…"

He crooked his head and kissed her again, gently, tenderly, until her fingers were curled against his chest. He held her as she had dreamed of being held, as if he never wanted to let her go. In that moment she was so happy it was hard to remember that the thought of loving and being loved scared her more than anything.

The early-morning sky was a cerulean blue as Abby, Lizzy and Leo stood in front of the Spur Tree.

"I'm going to miss you," Lizzy said. "Except for that one other visit, I've only known you—what—a day or two, but already you seem almost like a sister."

Abby thought of Becky running away from her down that desert trail in El Paso so long ago. "Maybe because we've been through a lot together."

"Leo, did I tell you she helped me save the Spur Tree?" Lizzy asked.

"Only about ten times."

"I couldn't have done it without her."

As Leo watched them together, his stern face tightened.

"We were lucky," Abby said, taking his hand and trying to draw him closer.

"No, it was a miracle," Lizzy said. "We have many, many miracles to be thankful for this morning."

Abby threaded her fingers through Leo's. He was alive, and so were Mia, Shanghai and Cole. The Big House was still standing, and this morning six brand-new flags hung limply from its wide roof. *The six flags of Texas.* The ranch had survived one hundred forty years of Native raids, war, drought, debt and now fire.

Maybe Lizzy was right. Maybe it was a miracle. The wind had shifted and then had died. The flames were now under control, and a storm in the Gulf that was moving toward shore promised rain.

"There's something we have to do before you and Leo can leave," Lizzy said. "Close your eyes, Abby, and then open your right hand."

With quiet excitement tingling inside her, Abby smiled. "I feel like I'm eight, playing a game with Becky."

Leo's face tightened.

"Becky?" Lizzy asked.

"My twin." Abby explained.

"Now hold your hand out," Lizzy ordered as imperiously as Becky might have.

Something heavy and spiky jingled in Abby's hand.

"You can open your eyes," Lizzy said softly.

Abby gasped. "Why, they're spurs. Thank you. I'll treasure them."

"Oh, you're not going to keep them. You see, since you're leaving us, they're for the tree. We have a tradition here that's nearly one hundred and forty years old."

Lizzy touched a pair of spurs dangling from the tree and made them tinkle. "These are my daddy's spurs." Her hand touched a second pair. "And these are Uncle Jack's. Every time a cowboy who's worked the ranch dies or quits, we hang his spurs here. When people like you, who've been important to the ranch, leave, we hang his—or in your case, her—spurs on the tree, as well. Even Leo keeps a pair on the tree when he's in San Antonio."

Abby's hand closed over the spurs in her hand. "Why…why, thank you, Lizzy."

"My real mother's are hanging on the tree, too."

"But isn't Joanne…"

Lizzy shook her head. "Joanne was pregnant with Mia by Uncle Jack when she married my father. The woman Daddy loved was pregnant with me. A horse threw Uncle Jack, and he died. Electra, my real mother, wouldn't marry Daddy. So Joanne and Daddy pretended that Joanne was pregnant with twins. That way they could raise Mia and me as twins. In fact, we didn't know until a little while ago that we're really cousins, not sisters. I didn't know that my biological mother was really a woman named Electra Scott."

"The famous photojournalist? Joanne told me about her."

"Did she? Well, good, maybe she's at peace with Electra at last. They were best friends once."

"She said Leo is looking for your dad's missing daughters."

"My sisters. Joanne was pretty torn up about them when she first read Electra's journal and found out that Daddy had resumed his affair with Electra after she and Daddy were married."

Leo shifted his weight restlessly from one foot to the other. His mouth was thin, his cheeks darkly flushed. He seemed extremely edgy all of a sudden.

"So how's that investigation coming, Leo?"

A muscle flexed in his hard jawline. "What?"

"So—are there any new clues about the missing twins?"

"Maybe a few." He dropped Abby's hand and took a step backward. "Are you two ever going to hang the spurs on the damn tree or not?"

"Hey, are you okay, Leo?" Abby whispered.

"You said five minutes. The jet is waiting."

"Go on then," Abby said. "I'll just be a minute."

He hesitated, obviously skeptical. Then he pivoted on his heel and strode toward the landing strip.

"Men," Lizzy said. "Cole can be so impatient sometimes. But I've never seen Leo like this. He's usually so calm and controlled."

"He's tired. He could have been killed yesterday. We were at the emergency room half the night. I guess it's understandable."

"He's okay?"

"Except for a few cuts and bruises. Smoke inhalation, too. And he seems unusually irritable all of a sudden.

But like you said, we have a lot of miracles to be thankful for."

"You'd better hurry then. If ever a man needed a good night's sleep and a lot of TLC from his bride… You didn't have much of a honeymoon, did you?"

"No. At least, not yet…." Abby felt her cheeks heat.

Last night they'd slept together, but they'd both been so exhausted that they'd fallen asleep the minute they'd lain down in their third-floor guest room despite the fact that it had reeked of smoke. When she'd awakened, Leo's side of the bed had been empty. He'd left without a word or a kiss or any show of affection. She'd found him downstairs in the kitchen talking to Kinky and the cowboys.

Not wanting to dwell on the lack of romance last night or to keep Leo waiting, Abby held her spurs up and approached the tree, where dozens more twinkled.

Finally, after studying every branch and reading the engravings on several spurs, she hung hers on the thick branch right beside Caesar's.

Leo was striding purposefully across blackened ground and had made it halfway to the runway when his cell phone vibrated in his shirt pocket. Impatiently, he jammed it against his ear.

"How's it going down there?" Connor asked. He'd called several times, and they'd talked. He'd been watching the news, so he was up on things for the most part.

"Great. When we evacuated the ranch, Abby stayed. She helped save the Big House and the Spur Tree. Hell, she's the heroine of the hour. The family loves her."

"*Her* family. I'd say that's real, real good."

"Lizzy just gave her an honorary pair of spurs. As I

speak, she's about to hang her spurs on the same tree as her father's."

"You'd better tell who the hell she is then. And fast."

"I'd like to make sure she's on my side first."

"Always looking out for yourself, aren't you, big brother?"

"I'm real short on patience this morning. Real short."

"I can understand that after what you've been through. I don't want to get all sappy on you, but you had me going there for a while yesterday when nobody knew where you were and I saw those body bags on TV. I have to admit I said a prayer or two."

"Illegals crossing the ranch."

"Poor bastards. You know, it might help if you asked Abby about Becky. Maybe you could get her talking about the kid's hobbies and dreams. You never know…it might help me find her."

Leo grimaced. The thought of grilling Abby about her sister made him feel even guiltier than he'd felt the night he'd stolen the DNA sample from her before sleeping with her.

"All right," Leo agreed.

"Good. I gotta go, but before I do, I'll say it one more time. First chance you get, tell her."

"Hey, maybe you're my only brother, but sometimes when you stick your nose in my business, you can be a real pain in the ass."

"What's a brother for?"

Leo flipped his phone shut.

Tell her? The thought scared the hell out of him. What if he lost her?

Eight

Abby's nose was pressed against the jet's window. The sky was bright and cloudless, and the fields beneath her were abnormally brown as the jet approached the outskirts of San Antonio.

Leo, his head bent over a ledger Kinky had given him, had scarcely spoken a word on the flight. Every time Abby had even glanced his way, she'd imagined that his square jaw tensed and that his gaze narrowed.

Why was he deliberately ignoring her?

Was something bothering him? Was it something she'd done? Did he feel trapped by their marriage? He'd been so cool and controlled last night in their bedroom. Did he regret…

Stop with the negative questions. You'll drive yourself crazy. It's not like you wanted to marry him.

They'd been married all of two days. He'd barely

touched her, but somehow she felt bound to him, tuned into him on deep, unconscious levels.

What was wrong? Considering all he'd been through, he'd seemed friendly and normal enough this morning. Until Lizzy had taken them out to the Spur Tree and had handed her those damn spurs. But why would he care if Lizzy had honored her in such a way? He couldn't be jealous because the Kembles seemed to like her. But if it wasn't that, then what?

Thinking of Lizzy and the spurs made her think of Caesar's missing twin daughters. She knew Leo was conscientious to a fault. She knew he felt responsible for the fire. Lizzy had asked him about the twins. Did he feel as guilty about not having found them as she felt because Becky had never been found? Apparently he'd been looking for them for quite a while.

"I hope you don't feel bad because you haven't found Lizzy's sisters," she whispered. She thought about Becky, who'd vanished without a trace. She, of all people, knew the frustration of trying to find a missing person.

He hissed in a deep breath but didn't look up. That telltale muscle tensed in his jaw. She had the distinct impression that he definitely didn't want to talk about Lizzy's missing sisters.

"You'll find them," she said reassuringly.

He swallowed. "I'm tired, okay?"

"Of course. I understand." But she didn't look away.

"Connor's responsible for finding them. I imagine it's on his conscience more than on mine." As if to put an end to their discussion, Leo flipped a page of the ledger loudly and lowered his head over the large book.

"What happened to them? Why is it so difficult to find them?"

He slammed the ledger, and she knew he wished she'd leave him alone. Well, it had been his idea to marry. Maybe it was time he learned that if they were stuck together, she couldn't stand the silent treatment.

"Leo, I asked you why it was so difficult—"

"I heard you, okay?" He drew a long breath. "Look, Electra was famous, and so was Caesar. She didn't want to damage Caesar's marriage, so she was very secretive when she put them up for adoption. She used an agency that agreed to a closed adoption. As a result, getting those records has been extremely difficult and time-consuming."

"But you got them?"

His mouth thinned. He nodded. "But often when two people adopt in a situation like that, they're secretive, too," he said. "Maybe they don't ever intend to tell their children they're adopted. And since the girls would be…er…in their twenties now…"

"You said they were nearly twenty-seven. My age."

He swallowed again.

"Right," he said. "People in their twenties move around a lot. They could be anywhere."

"So, Connor's really, really good at finding missing people?"

"That's what he does."

"You know, I have a missing sister, too. Do you think maybe I could talk to him about her sometime? We lost her when she was eight. Ever since then, it's like a part of my soul is still missing."

He grabbed a decanter of scotch from a low table and

poured himself a glass, which he gulped in a single long swallow. "That's awful," he replied.

"We're twins, too. That's sort of a strange coincidence, don't you think?"

"What? You are? Right! Yes, it is! Damn right it is!"

"Becky, that's my sister who disappeared when she was eight," Abby persisted. "I loved her, and I still miss her. I still wonder if she's alive…if she's happy…if she remembers me."

"I'm sorry," he said. He took her hand is his. "Look, I'm really sorry about her." The jet hit an air pocket just as the blood rushed from his face. He was as pale as a ghost, and his eyes blazed queerly. When she squeezed his hand to reassure him, he jumped. Then the jet hit real turbulence, and his stare became so wild and intense that she sucked in a panicky breath. "What? Is…is something wrong with the jet?"

"No. Just a bit of bumpy air. Sorry if I scared you. See…the jet's leveling out. Nothing's wrong."

"It's such a coincidence, me being the same age as the missing twins…and me having a missing twin."

"Yes, I suppose it is." He took a deep breath as if he were choosing carefully what he intended to say. Then he stopped, shook his head and closed his eyes for a long moment. He took two long breaths, and when he opened his eyes again, she was relieved that he seemed almost his old, assured self. Then he ran his hand through his heavy, black hair, she saw that he had a slight tremor.

She felt profound sympathy for him. It must be the turbulence. She hadn't realized he was such a nervous flyer. Maybe he wasn't usually, but he'd been through a lot. Obviously, he wanted to appear tough and unruffled.

He met her gaze. "You say your twin is missing? How did it happen? When?"

Abby didn't want to upset him. Not when he was this worried about flying. Still, he seemed so concerned and interested, that suddenly she couldn't stop herself.

"We were eight," she began in a breathless rush. "We'd been making too much noise in the tent where we were camping in the Franklin Mountains in El Paso, so our parents had made us go outside. We were playing this silly game, chasing each other and hiding from one another. Then we ran after a wild turkey. When the sun began going down, I suddenly realized how far we were from the tent, so I turned to run back down the hill. Becky yelled for me to wait... But I didn't, even though she sounded terrified."

"And?"

"I thought she would follow me like she always did. She was more afraid of the dark than I was, you see. Oh, why am I telling you all this, when you already have way too much on your mind?"

"Because I asked." His voice was low and soothing.

"I never saw her again," she whispered. "Nobody did."

Leo took her hand in his, and his tense, dark eyes shone with compassion. That's when the worst of the pain that she'd carried inside her for years and years burst forth.

"My father thought it was his fault. He'd been down in Mexico just before that, writing about stuff powerful people didn't want exposed. He thinks she was taken across the border. But I knew it was my fault. If I hadn't run away and left her, maybe she wouldn't have gotten lost. And maybe my parents wouldn't have gotten divorced. Maybe Mother wouldn't have died. And maybe I wouldn't have dated all those cowboys who could never have loved me. I didn't want them to love me, you see. Not even Shanghai. Because then they'd leave me. And maybe if I hadn't run away from her that day, my father would do things with me. Like, for instance, maybe he would have come to our wedding." She felt like a fool when she sobbed out that last.

"Shh. You're being way too hard on yourself." He yanked a tissue out of a little box from the nearby table and handed it to her. "Here. Blow your nose."

"T-this is…is why I never talk about her," she sobbed. "Why I try to never think about her." More hot tears fell. "B-because i-it upsets me too much. She was scared, and I left her out there in the dark all alone. And…and I can't stop wondering what happened to her. All this talk about the missing twins has stirred me up I think."

Abby felt weak and exhausted and absolutely raw after her tearful outburst. Fighting the fire was nothing compared to talking about Becky. She sat back, drained.

"I see." Leo's thoughtful gaze studied her. "A while ago you asked about talking to my brother." He seemed to consider his words. "Maybe you should phone Connor and tell him everything you know about Becky. *Everything*."

"It's been such a long time. I hardly dare to hope that even he can find—"

"Hopefully, he'll surprise us," Leo muttered gloomily. His grip on her hand tightened, and she wondered why he suddenly sounded so morose and hopeless again.

As if sensing she was worried, his arm came

around her, and his touch was so soothing she loosened her seat belt so she could curl up against him. She wished he would keep talking to her, because she'd liked sharing with him about Becky, but he said no more.

Instead, a heavy silence fell between them. His body felt tense and hard. Soon she realized an even thicker wall had gone up, a wall that she had no idea how to tear down. Why was he so quiet and uncommunicative all of a sudden when he'd been so attentive after that first night she'd slept with him? Before they'd married, he'd wanted to see her again constantly. Only minutes ago he'd listened to what she'd shared about Becky, but now he was shutting her out again.

"Leo? Are you okay? Did I say something or do something…"

"I'm fine. Just tired."

His tension seemed to increase. After they landed, he drove them in silence to her ranch house, stopping briefly to buy groceries. Without a word he pulled up to her back porch and unloaded their bags and the food. Then he told her he had a lot to catch up on. He called his office and stayed on the phone with various people for hours. She spoke to Kel briefly. Five minutes was all it took for her to catch up on things at In the Pink! When Leo remained in her second bedroom with his phone, she prepared and ate a cold supper of cottage cheese, carrot sticks and sardines—alone. As she'd done on their wedding night, she bathed and brushed her hair until it gleamed. She put on her sheerest nightgown and left her robe seductively unfastened, but when he finally came to bed, dressed only in his pajama bottoms, he gave her a light peck on the cheek. Then he rolled over to his side of the bed, turned his broad, powerful back to her and was silent.

Blinking back tears, she glared at him.

Why didn't he try to seduce her as he had the night he'd proposed?

"Leo?"

He stirred. "Hmm?"

"Is something wrong?"

"I'm just tired," he whispered. "Go to sleep."

She was a new bride. They'd both come close to death. She'd sat in that basement, terrified he was dead. She wanted him to wrap her in his arms, to make wild, violent love to her. But she would not beg.

Go to sleep?

As if she could.

The bloodred neon of the alarm clock was blinking 2:00 a.m. when Abby's breathing finally slurred to a soft and regular rhythm. At last, Leo thought. Maybe soon, he'd be able to fall asleep, too. God knew, he'd better.

He'd known by her choice of nightgown—the damn thing left nothing to his imagination—that she'd wanted him. Just as he'd known by her crushed tone that he'd hurt her when he'd kissed her coolly and turned his back on her. He'd lain there, his heart pounding with desire while his mind was tormented by guilt.

It had taken her hours to fall asleep. Leo knew because he'd been driven crazy by the blinking clock and by her fidgeting.

Asleep now, she snuggled closer to him, her delicious warmth invading his side of the bed. God. He bit his lower lip and turned to stare at her slim body molded by the quilts beside his.

In the moonlight, her loose, butter-gold hair gleamed like silk on the pillow. His heartbeat sped up.

He wanted to touch her hair, to thread his fingers through it, to kiss it, just as he wanted to brush her pale throat with his mouth. He craved her smell, her satiny softness, her taste. He'd wanted all those things last night, too, but he knew just as he'd known last night, that if he so much as held her hand, he wouldn't be able to stop. His deception and sex had gotten them off to the wrong start, and only honesty would set things right. But was she ready for the brutal truth? He'd known who she was, and he'd set her up.

Leo swallowed. Surely lying beside Abby without touching her, knowing she was awake and as needily restless as he, had been the cruelest of tortures. He'd lain there, remembering the fear blazing in her hazel eyes when she'd walked up to Kinky's SUV before they'd headed out to Black Oaks. Nor could he forget the wild joy in her eyes when she'd realized he'd survived. He'd never forget how she'd flown into his arms after the fire had passed the house.

Nobody could fake such emotions. Her heart and soul had been in that kiss. So had his.

If anything, his feelings were even stronger than hers, maybe because he'd lived most of his life in such a cold place. Ever since that moment in front of the Big House, he'd known he cared for her more than he'd ever imagined possible.

When he'd been in the thick of those flames at Black Oaks, fighting the fire and then fighting for his own life, she and the baby had held an inexplicable, almost mythical power over him. He'd wanted to live, solely to get back to them. He'd wanted a chance to be Abby's lover, her husband and the father of their child.

He'd prayed for a miracle as he'd dived into the creek as the trees on all sides of him had exploded in flames. Then he'd seen Abby again, and she'd kissed him so fiercely in that blackened pasture, he'd almost thought he could have his miracle. But his wild hope had made him more afraid.

How could he trust her not to break his heart when she learned the truth? Somehow he had to figure out a way to win her—permanently. Because if he lost her now, he knew from past experience how unbearable such pain would be. When he'd lost Ransom's respect and support, and Nancy and Julie and his mother, he'd lived in a bleak, lonely place fueled only by the cold brilliance of his ambition.

It had been a long, ruthless climb up from his hellish losses. So he didn't have the guts to face losing Abby. He had to calm down and woo her slowly, deliberately.

Ignoring difficult conversations wasn't going to work very long. He had to talk to her, confide in her, listen to her. But not tonight.

In a few months, after he'd won her trust, maybe then he'd find the courage to tell her everything. He could only hope that by then he would have proved he cared and she'd have enough invested in their relationship to forgive him.

In her dream, Leo was cupping her breasts and kissing her endlessly. Then something screamed outside the window, the owls maybe, rudely awakening her. The next thing she grew aware of was Leo's steady breathing.

Slowly she realized that Leo was on his side of the bed—as far away from her as possible. He lay on his back with his arms crossed. His eyes were open, and he was staring up at the ceiling.

He was awake.

"Leo?" Abby whispered, reaching for him before she thought.

His reaction to her lush voice and caressing fingertips was instantaneous and undeniable. As he grabbed her hand and stilled it against his abdomen, his breath caught in his throat. She could tell by the sheet bunched at his groin that he was hard, erect. His skin was burning hot, and his heart was pounding as fiercely as hers.

He wanted her, every bit as much as she wanted him. Yet he was pretending not to.

"Go back to sleep," he growled, pushing her hand away. Then he rolled to the very edge of his side of the bed and lay facing the far wall.

Why was he rejecting her? She should respect his wishes, shouldn't she? And she would, if only he would tell her why.

"Leo…did I do something…?"

"No, I said—"

"But I'm not sleepy."

"Well, I am," Leo said.

"Are you? I wonder."

Her dream made her bold. Giggling, she scooted beneath the sheets until her soft breasts grazed the warmth of his broad back. Her nipples grew hard the instant she felt his smooth, hot flesh. He hissed in a breath, tensing when she stayed there with her breasts mashed against his back. For a second she thought he might jump from the bed. Just to tempt him, she slid her hand down his side to rest upon his buttocks. Gently, slowly, her fingers kneaded.

"I want you," she whispered finally, splaying her fingertips. "I want you so much."

Her hand traced back up the length of his side with exquisite tenderness. He turned, caught her hand and kissed it. Then he went still, slowly he pushed her away, sprang out of the bed and went to the window, where he stood, fists clenched at his sides.

"Leo?"

He sucked in a harsh breath and stayed where he was.

She punched her pillow in frustration. "All right," she finally said. Getting up, she threw on her robe and walked down the hall into her kitchen. Closing the door, she pulled out a chair. Sitting down at the table, she buried her head in her hands.

Did he hate her? Hate himself for desiring her? He'd been so sweet and understanding on the plane when she'd told him about Becky. If he didn't hate her, what was wrong now?

She thought of their child. Did he feel trapped as she had? She wished her dream hadn't made her so brazen. Her stomach tightened.

Why had she touched him, pushed him? Like her, he was used to being in charge. How could she have been so conceited as to think she could seduce him when he was set against her? Why hadn't she given him the time he needed? He'd been through a lot...the news of her pregnancy, their rushed marriage, the fire, blaming himself for all of it, probably. Then she'd pushed him about the missing twins on the plane.

She began to berate herself as being the most selfish, pushy person ever. She didn't know him that well. He was used to his own space. She needed to slow down, to be careful for a while.

He'd been injured in the fire. Last night he'd been in the emergency room. He was probably still exhausted. Maybe he was in pain.

Scalding tears slipped from her eyelids. He'd probably despise her forever now.

Her sobs blocked the sound of his soft tread, so she didn't realize he was anywhere near until he said her name.

When she looked up, he towered over her. He was still bare-chested, wearing only his pajama bottoms.

He knelt and pulled her into his arms. "I'm sorry."

"I'm sorry, too," she whispered as she threw her arms around his shoulders. "Oh, Leo…I-I'm so sorry."

He pressed her close, stroked her back, her hair. She clung to him and was amazed that she was so starved for any show of kindness or affection from him. Never had she wanted any man's caresses and interest as she wanted his. What were these new feelings?

He stared into her eyes for a long moment with a burning intensity that left her breathless even before he traced the back of his hand against the softness of her cheek and then down her throat.

"My precious wife. My darling…"

Her nipples tightened. She swallowed, hoping for more. Then his hand stopped moving.

"Do you hate me?" she whispered.

"God, no. How could you even think…?"

He crushed her to his chest and held her tightly. She felt the thunder of his heart, the warmth of his powerful body.

Her sobs subsided, and she clung more tightly, laying her head, cheek to cheek, against his. He was alive and so solid and strong, so dear. She liked simply being held in his arms. Her dream had not been nearly so good as this. Closing her eyes, she prayed that he would kiss her. Afraid to encourage him, she remained still and breathless in his arms, waiting.

His hand began to move up and down her back. Then he caressed her neck, her shoulders, her arms, and whispered, "Sweet. You tempt me to…"

But he did not kiss her lips or touch her breasts.

Instead, he said, "Come back to bed, my darling."

My darling. The gentle endearment chimed in her soul. *He'd called her his darling. He didn't hate her.*

Threading her fingers inside his, he led her back down the hall.

As he slid the covers back, she saw that his pajama bottoms were tented at his crotch. So, he did desire her.

When they were both in bed, he said good-night. His voice was husky, and he was shaking slightly. He wanted her as badly as she wanted him. Why was he doing this? Why wasn't he going to take her? Why?

She closed her eyes and took a deep breath, willing him to kiss her. But he didn't.

"Good night, Leo," she finally rasped.

Tears beaded her lashes as she lay in the dark, hungering for more.

"Good night," he muttered in a low, choked tone.

She lay in the dark beside him, too aware of his big, long body just inches from hers. Still, as frustrating as his nearness was, his being there made her feel safe. It wasn't long before she fell asleep, and in her dreams he clasped her to him and made love to her as ardently as she desired.

In the morning when she awoke, he was staring so with such intensity that she blushed.

She realized the sheets had come off, and in her sheer nightgown, she was practically naked.

"What?" she whispered, smiling at him because she felt exposed and liked the way his hot eyes burned through the thin fabric to her skin.

"Sleep well?" His voice was gruff and tight.

She sighed. Then she stretched, just to tempt him. "Never better."

He didn't yield; his eyes remained glued to her face. Was he afraid to look at her body in the revealing night-gown? She could see his pulse knocking in the hollow of his tanned throat. She hoped so.

"Did you know you cried out my name...several times?" he said.

"I must have been having a nightmare."

"Didn't sound like it to me."

"Oh, really?" She got up and threw her pillow at him. Without bothering to throw on her robe or cover herself, she scampered off to her bathroom and locked the door. Not that it was necessary. She'd locked it solely to taunt him.

The heat of his gaze had seared through her night-gown. Maybe he hadn't wanted to stare at her, but he hadn't been able to look away. Once she was safe inside, she leaned against the door for a long time, trembling.

Where did she go from here?

Nine

Later that morning, to Abby's surprise, Leo had supervised the high-school kid he'd hired to see to Coco and had scrambled eggs and cooked bacon by the time she'd showered and dressed. He'd hauled out the garbage, as well.

Now he was dressed in dark slacks, a white shirt and tie. His dark jacket hung over a kitchen chair, and his bulging black briefcase stood by the door.

"You're fast and capable and handy to have around," she said as she sat down at the table on her back porch that he'd set. "I'll give you that."

"Hey, who knows, maybe you'll decide I'm a keeper. Beautiful morning," he murmured as he unfolded his napkin.

Sunlight slanted through the oaks and pines. Birds twittered in their branches.

"Yes."

Why were his knuckles white as he held his fork? Why was his face so hard and set? She'd barely slept. Maybe he was as tired as she was.

They ate in silence. When they were done, he stacked their plates and headed into the kitchen. Obviously in a rush, he began rinsing and putting the dishes into the dishwasher.

"I'll be home at seven," he said when he'd finished. "What's your schedule?"

"It'll probably be pretty hectic, but I'll try to be here by seven, too."

His smiled. "Good. We can cook or go out, whatever you'd prefer."

"You're being so agreeable."

"Why is that such a surprise?"

Remembering his rejection last night, she looked up, but his dark, smiling eyes were unreadable.

He went to the door and picked up his briefcase. Hoping he would kiss her goodbye, she chased after him. Instead, he turned and nodded. Then he said shortly, "See you—"

See you. She was a new bride. They'd missed their honeymoon, and he was treating her like a sister.

He pushed the screen door open. Feeling forlorn, she ran after him and watched from the porch when he drove away.

All through the day, she found herself hurrying to get finished with her phone calls and even her pet projects so that she'd make it home to him at the stroke of seven. And when she did make it, by recklessly speeding, and five whole minutes early, her heart fell when his truck wasn't there.

Thirty minutes later he called and said he'd be home at eight.

"I'll have dinner ready."

"Not sardines and carrots, I hope."

She laughed. "No. Steak and potatoes and green beans and chocolate cookies with ice cream. Store-bought, I'm afraid."

"Maybe you're a keeper, too."

"You think?"

"I think. Let me get back to this so I can get home." The eagerness in his low voice warmed her heart.

That night he brought her a box of chocolates and a single red rose. Not that he kissed her at the door or anything, even though she'd come running as soon as she'd heard his truck.

Sexual tension thrummed in her blood as she found a vase and stuck the rose in it. With shaking fingers, she set the vase on the table. All through dinner she found herself turning from his dark face to the rose and wondering why he'd bought it when he wouldn't even kiss her.

After supper they took a walk with Coco following them as the sky turned violet and stars popped out. Leo told her about his day, which had been every bit as crazy as hers, and she told him amusing stories about her meetings and unreasonable clients. He smiled and laughed a lot, and she was aware of him watching her when he thought she wasn't looking.

How could she have ever thought him dull when just being with him around the house was fun? Not since she'd had Becky around had she had someone to share the little things that made up her life. She'd thought he couldn't possibly be interested in hearing about one client's fit over naming and marketing ideas for a new product, but he was either fascinated and held her talent in awe, or he deserved an Oscar.

When it was dark and the moon had come up, they returned to the house and watched part of an old black-and-white Western on television. He confessed he was a sucker for all John Wayne movies.

"I guess in my heart I always dreamed of being a cowboy," he admitted.

"I'm a sucker for anything with a horse in it, too," she said. "A book, a movie…"

He was attentive from the moment he got home until they went to bed. They did nothing out of the ordinary, but the evening was special in so many ways, at least for her, as only simple pleasures can be special when shared with a friend or lover. Was that what he was doing—trying to become her friend?

But again, when they went to bed, he kept to his own side of the bed. Only tonight he didn't even kiss her on the cheek.

Why didn't he push for sex? She quit asking. She decided to try to be patient. Thus, a week passed in this pleasant if frustrating fashion, and with each new day the sexual tension inside her built. Every night he was a perfect friend, a perfect gentleman, but never her lover except in her dreams.

When Connor flew to Austin Friday afternoon to meet a client, Leo set up a late-afternoon appointment for Abby to meet him in her office to discuss Becky. As always, she promised Leo she'd be home at seven. When Connor didn't make it to her office until six, she didn't think to call Leo and warn him. She was so anxious about the interview, she simply shook hands with Connor, closed her office door and turned her cell phone to silent, so they wouldn't be interrupted.

"Sorry I'm late," he said grinning. "Airport. Airplane. Client."

"Say no more. Would you like something to drink?"

"Just water. Lots of ice."

By the time she returned to her desk with two bottles and two glasses of ice, he had his laptop up and running.

He asked all the same questions about Becky she'd answered too many times before, and as always, as he entered her replies into his laptop, she tensed and hunched over, her head pounding.

"What did Becky want to be when she grew up?"

Abby closed her eyes. If she grew up. "A teacher. But she was only eight. How many of us know at that age?" Funny, how she always thought of Becky as eight…as if her life had stopped…Abby's throat tightened.

"Did she like horses, too?"

"No, she was scared of them. Our horse, Blacky, stepped on her big toe and broke it, and she wouldn't go near the barn after that."

"What else was she scared of?"

"Mostly the dark. Snakes. Bugs, especially scorpions. All the usual suspects little girls are afraid of. Goblins under the bed. Disney villains like the witch in *Snow White*. Oh, and the tooth fairy. We always left our teeth under my pillow."

Connor smiled. "Was there anything unusual about her, anything at all that set her apart?"

"She was very sensitive, unusually compassionate.

She would always notice if anybody's feelings were hurt and try to comfort them."

As they talked, Abby lost track of the time. It was almost seven-thirty when Connor said he thought he had enough to go on.

"But do you really think there's a chance that you might find her?"

"Maybe. But you've got to understand that this case is very cold."

Feeling weary from all the emotions his questions had stirred, she nodded. Without another word, she got up and walked him to the door.

He insisted on following her down to her Lincoln. "Are you staying at the Little Spur or in town?" she asked as she flung her purse and briefcase onto her passenger seat and then sank behind the wheel.

"Neither. I'm flying back to Houston tonight."

"Thanks for looking into this."

"No. Thank you." He shook her hand.

Her mind whirled with memories about Becky as she drove home. Connor seemed cocky, but she was afraid to hope.

She was still thinking about Becky as she drove into the garage. No sooner had she gotten out of the Lincoln than Leo ran out of the house. He looked tall and strong and handsome in snug-fitting, faded jeans and a long-sleeved white shirt as he waited for her in the drive. His black hair fell loosely over his tanned brow. She wanted him to take her in his arms, to hold her. Would he never, ever kiss her again?

She drew in a long, shaky breath. Maybe part of her exhaustion had to do with her pregnancy, but she was utterly drained from her long day, the meeting about Becky and then the drive home.

"I'm sorry I'm late," she said as she wearily picked up her briefcase.

He stood in the dark, silently watching her.

"Is something wrong?" she whispered when his silence began to grow heavy.

"Where have you been? I tried and tried to call...."

"You called? Me?"

"You. I sent a text message, too."

She fumbled in her purse for her cell phone and saw that he had. "Oh, I—I guess I turned it to silent ring when I was in that meeting with Connor. Yes, I did."

"You scared the hell out of me."

"Oh, Leo, I-I'm sorry."

She could tell he was upset. His lips were pale and thinner than usual. When he pushed that lock of hair back, she saw that a vein pulsed in his forehead. Yet, the next time he spoke, his voice sounded remarkably controlled, even calm. "It's okay now that you're here, safe."

He grabbed her briefcase. "So, how'd the meeting with my brother go?" he asked as they began to walk to the house.

"He asked me so many questions. Talking about Becky made me so tense I have a headache and a backache."

"I was afraid. I imagined all sorts of wild scenarios. A flat...your Lincoln spinning out of control...a wreck...you hurt..."

He certainly didn't sound like an indifferent husband.

"Oh, dear. Leo, the last thing I wanted to do was upset you."

"I wasn't upset," he said, but his teeth were tightly clenched.

"Why were you so worried?"

"Break in routine, I guess. Let's forget it."

His strides became so long and quick, she had to run to keep up with him. He wasn't dull or cold. His emotions were fierce and all-consuming. Tonight she needed passion.

She needed to be kissed and held. After talking to Connor, she was afraid she'd never see Becky again. After the interview had ended, all she'd wanted was to get home to Leo. She'd imagined his arms around her, longed for them. Tonight she wanted Leo the lover, not Leo the friend.

When she stepped into the kitchen, he had a pasta dish ready to serve. She knew she was being thoughtless and selfish, but she wasn't in the mood for one of their friendly evenings.

"You know what I really need tonight, Leo?"

He turned and glanced past her. Sparks lit her blood. Not that he met her gaze.

She felt awful chasing him, but she couldn't stop herself. "I—I feel as if tension has settled in every nerve and muscle and ligament. If I weren't pregnant, I'd have a beer or a glass of wine. I'll never be able to relax unless I take a warm bath and maybe…maybe, if you wouldn't mind, you could massage me a little."

He closed his eyes and clenched his fists. "Not a good idea."

She shouldn't—she wouldn't—beg him.

Swallowing her pride, she did. "Please…"

The silent kitchen surrounded them. When he

frowned, she felt a horrible certainty that he was about to refuse her.

"Leo. I got so upset thinking about Becky…"

"All right," he said. "You win."

"I'm ready," Abby called to him huskily.

Leo's heart was rushing way too fast as he pushed open the door. He went still, staring at her.

He couldn't do this. But he had to.

Vanilla candles flickered, their soft glow bathing the exposed curve of her slim back in warm, golden light. Sheets were bunched at her rounded hips. Her hair gleamed like dark gold. Hungrily his eyes devoured her. All week he'd held himself in check even though he'd lusted for her constantly. Every night her nightgowns had seemed to grow thinner. Now, tonight, she was naked.

Soft, serene music played. A bottle of her favorite, lavender-scented lotion stood on the bedside table.

Leo was convinced they needed more time, several weeks maybe, to get to know each other. He had taken a long walk, telling himself that he could massage her without letting it go any further…that he had to.

He knew what talking about Becky did to her. Abby was pregnant, shattered and exhausted tonight. He kept reminding himself that they'd gone to bed before they'd trusted each other, and how ashamed she'd been of the dark, wild things she'd done with a near-stranger. He wanted to become her friend, someone she trusted before he touched her again. Tonight was too soon.

He must have made some sound because her fingers tensed, clawing the sheets. Desire raced through his veins and made every muscle in his being tense even as he fought it.

He went to the bed and fumbled to loosen the bottle's cap. Squirting a big blob of cold lotion into his hands much too violently, he waited awhile for it to warm.

"Leo?"

"Just heating the lotion up a bit."

"Or stalling?"

She had him there. "Sorry." He hastily knelt beside the bed and placed trembling hands on her bare shoulders.

For a long moment his hands remained still as her heat seeped into his fingers, causing his muscles to wind tighter. He sank his teeth into his bottom lip until it bled.

He couldn't do this.

"Your hands feel so good. Big and warm. I feel safe tonight with you," she murmured.

Damn. His heart was pounding like a drumbeat gone wild. He was as hard as a brick. He felt like a beast. She was naked under that sheet. Was she trying to drive him crazy or what?

Desperately, he swallowed. Then he forced his hands to move in ever-widening circular motions.

"That feels so good," she whispered huskily.

He shut his eyes, but he still saw her golden hair, the slope of her shoulders, the curve of her hips, and imagined the rest.

His breathing grew ragged. His pulse raced out of control. He wanted her so much he couldn't trust himself a second longer.

His hands stopped. For a long moment he stayed beside her, frozen.

Then she turned, the sheets falling away so that he

saw the triangular wedge of gold curls that concealed the secret of her womanhood. Her pale breasts with their shadowy nipples were uncovered to his gaze.

"Leo, I want to touch you, too. Please…please let me."

He stood up and stared down at her lush golden body, at her soft, wet, red lips. Then he ran.

"Leo?" she whispered in a tiny, bleak voice.

Every organ in Leo's body pulsed with blood and felt on fire as he stood in the guest bathroom splashing cold water onto his face and hair.

"Don't you want me at all?" she murmured from the doorway.

She was probably naked. And so close.

Hell. He stiffened. Why couldn't she just leave him alone?

When he glanced up into the mirror, he saw that her golden hair tumbled about her shoulders in wild disarray and that she wasn't naked anymore. She was wearing a thick red robe that was tied loosely at her waist…and probably nothing else. Her mouth was trembling. Her big sad eyes were asking questions he wasn't sure how to answer. The last thing he wanted to do was to hurt her.

"I think you know I want you," he said.

"Then why have you…or maybe I should ask why haven't you…"

A dark flush crawled up her neck and stained her cheeks.

"Dammit. Because I selfishly seduced you the first night and made you hate me. Then you told me you were pregnant and miserable because of me, and I seduced

you to get you to agree to marry me. I've been a bastard.
Because of our sexual history, I thought that maybe we
should try to become friends before we did it again."

Her face softened. "Really? You were trying to be
considerate?"

He nodded.

"That's so sweet."

"Believe me, I'm the last thing from sweet."

"What if I don't choose to believe you?"

"I assure you, my motives are extremely selfish."

A huge smile lit her face. "I'm so glad." Then she
laughed and came into his arms, gasping when she felt
his male hardness pressing against her pelvis.

"So you do want me?" she whispered huskily. "You
do!"

"I do," he murmured, ruffling her hair.

"I'm glad. Very pleased. But I want more than friendship. We're married now…you know."

He knew. His heart was pounding violently.

The bathroom shade was up. Outside, the night was
velvet black with only the faintest shimmer of silver
moonlight. In that strange, gray light, her normally fiery
hair gleamed like platinum.

His arms tightened around her. He'd never felt so
close to any woman. Not even Nancy, the girl he'd loved
as a boy. And he'd thought he'd never get over Nancy.

His lips found Abby's in a long, hard kiss, his tongue
plunging into her mouth. Fumbling with the tie of her
robe, she yanked it loose. When she wiggled, it slid off
her body. At the sight of her naked, he gripped her arms
so hard she cried out.

"Sorry," he whispered. Then he began to tear off his

belt and jeans. Stepping out of the denim, he tossed his jeans aside.

He pushed her against the wall. She was wet with lotion and as slick as satin, open. He stepped back, panting hard. Beneath her long lashes, her eyes were brilliant. Her lips looked swollen and bruised. He remembered that first night when she'd been so hungry for him. Not that they'd been any hungrier for each other than they were now.

"Wrap your legs around me," he commanded roughly. Grabbing her buttocks and pulling her tight, he drove himself into her.

When he filled her the first time, he went still, and she sighed.

"Yes," she murmured. "I thought you'd never…do this…again…."

She said more, but he didn't hear the rest. Still inside her, holding her bottom tightly against his pelvis, he carried her down the hall to her bedroom. With her legs laced around his waist, he lowered her to the bed and then followed her down.

Her pleadings, or whatever the hell they were, fell against his ears in broken whispers, but his desire drove him. He was past hearing her, past everything but the insane, pulsing need that drove him to make her completely his.

Again and again he plunged, each time more forcefully, each time finding a pleasure and a satisfaction unlike any he had ever known until finally he rushed over that final edge, shuddering as he exploded. She wept, clinging, stroking, trembling.

"Did I hurt you?" he whispered.

She kissed his mouth and shook her head back and forth on her pillow. Then she touched the tip of her nose to his.

Vaguely he hoped it wasn't too soon, but he'd wanted her too much and she'd been too sweet…and too hot to resist. He was still burning up.

He'd intended to go a while longer without sex, to court her slowly, to make her like him. So much for good intentions. There were those who'd said he'd been on the road to hell since birth.

He fell asleep while still inside her, with her arms wrapped tightly around him.

Ten

When Leo awoke the next morning, streamers of pink light drifted across the bed. The window must have been cracked an inch or so because he heard wild turkeys gobbling and morning doves cooing.

Glancing at his watch, he saw it was too early to get up. When Abby whispered his name, he pulled her warm, luscious body close. Then he ran his hand down her arm, which was velvety soft and deliciously warm. He kissed the curve of her elbow where a faint pulse throbbed.

She sighed and then reached over and framed his face with her hands. He stared at her before kissing her on the lips. She opened her mouth, and his tongue dipped inside.

"Wait! I've got to get up and brush my…"

"I can't wait."

He circled her with his arms and slid on top of her,

holding her down and parting her legs. His sex found hers. She was slick wet, and so hot. Satin wildfire.

When he went still instead of entering her, he swallowed convulsively. He kissed her again and again, on her throat, on the tip of her nose, on her lips, until her skin felt feverish all over.

"Now it's me who can't wait," she teased, nipping playfully at his bottom lip.

"All right then." He lunged, and her eyes flashed open as she cried out in pleasure.

"Don't move. I want this to last," he said.

"So do I. Oh, so do I."

He tried to slow down and keep his strokes featherlight, but her body gloved him tightly, causing too many exquisite sensations to course down every male nerve ending. It was as if they were wired for each other.

He'd hungered for her too long, and the taste he'd had last night wasn't nearly enough. She moved, causing hot bursts of thrilling sensations to course through him. It wasn't long before he lost all control and began thrusting faster and faster himself. Then they were both crying out at once and holding each other, swept away in a volcanic riptide that left them shaken and yet happy, too.

When he finally got up that morning, he tiptoed from the room. Several minutes later, when he was dressed for work and sitting down to a couple of fried eggs with his newspaper, dammit if the little minx didn't crawl under the kitchen table, unzip his slacks and make him forget all about breakfast and his office. She was insatiable.

Afterward, he pulled her into his lap and told her that was the most memorable breakfast he'd ever had.

"But your eggs are cold," she teased, nuzzling her lips against his throat.

As if he gave a damn. "I'm calling Miriam to tell her I'll be very late."

"Why?" she asked, but she winked at him.

He ripped off his tie and unbuttoned his dress shirt. "Because I've got a favor or two to return. I like to stay even. Why don't you call your office and tell them you won't be in until ten? I promise you won't regret it."

After he returned the sexual favor that she had bestowed on him, she told him again how sweet she thought he was for trying to make her know he respected her.

"But really, surely you could have done that some other way. Not kissing you, not being kissed, not being held, and all the other things we didn't do, was pure torture…at least for me," she said.

"For me, too. Believe me, I sympathize. But you do remember how mad you got at me after that first night. You called me a stalker."

She blushed. "I'm sorry. I thought I had to say something awful to make you go away."

"Why were you so determined you wanted nothing to do with me?"

"I—I was afraid of you, I think. Of how you made me feel…and lose control."

"Are you still afraid?"

"More than ever."

"Because you lost Becky?"

"And my parents, too. Still, avoiding sex wasn't a very practical idea, since we seem to think about it a lot when we're together."

"You can say that again."

"How long did you intend to stay celibate?"

"I don't know," he said. "A few more weeks. I thought maybe we should get to know each other a little better before—"

"But we're married," she murmured. "Hey, do you think we could stay home today?"

"And do what?"

"Are you going to make me keep chasing you?"

In the end, they stayed home all day. Leo told Miriam since he'd skipped his honeymoon, he deserved to spend one day with his bride. And Miriam, bless her practical, capable heart, didn't put up a single argument. The woman she'd once disliked was becoming one of her favorite people.

Bliss-filled days and nights became the norm for Leo and Abby.

They spent the Fourth of July at the headquarters of the Golden Spurs. It had rained, and except for the scarred trees, much of the damage to the pastures from the fire was brightened by leafy new foliage. Fences had been repaired and buildings were being reconstructed.

The Kembles made a fuss over her and her growing belly. It was funny how she felt so close to Mia and Lizzy. She liked to hang out in the barn with Mia and her horses or just sit and chat with Lizzy. It was strange how easily she got along with the Kemble sisters.

Although the summer was long and hot, and the drought, especially in South Texas was a fierce one, Abby felt happier than she'd ever been.

Not that life was perfect. Despite her frequent conversations with Connor and his determination to find her sister, Becky's disappearance remained a mystery. Nor had her father called or answered her e-mails once since their wedding. It was as if after he'd called to say he wasn't coming to her wedding, he'd disappeared off the face of the earth.

"He doesn't care about me," Abby said to Leo one evening in early September as he lay on the couch, perusing some papers from his briefcase that had to do with a pending oil and gas lease on the Golden Spurs.

"He cares," Leo said. "He just doesn't know how to show it. Sometimes when you're running from the crap in your life you can't face, you bury yourself alive in your work so you don't hate yourself. I should know. I did that for years after Mike Ransom threw me off his ranch. Do you remember that day you came to my office to tell me you were pregnant?"

"As if I could ever forget it."

He smiled. "Do you remember that old man who left when you came in?"

She nodded. "The skinny old gentleman who called you a bastard?"

"My mother worked on the Running R, his ranch, as his housekeeper when I was a kid. My father was dead, so Ransom became like a father to Connor and me. He invited us everywhere he took his own son, Cal. Took us to football games and theater road shows in Dallas. Taught us to ride, shoot and rope. Hell, he was even our Scout leader. I grew up loving him like a father."

"What happened?"

"Cal and I both fell in love with Nancy, a neighboring rancher's daughter. She chose me over Cal even though he was rich, and I was poor."

Leo broke off, remembering.

"Go on," she whispered.

"Money didn't make any difference to Nancy when we were kids. But when I got her pregnant my freshman year in college and I had no way of supporting her, I guess Nancy got scared and thought she had to be practical."

Abby nodded. She could sympathize with an unplanned pregnancy coming as a shock and blasting a frightened girl out of her romantic dreams.

"Well, Mike, the 'gentleman' you met, was an upright, teetotaling, religious sort who never took a false step in his whole damn life. He'd been sending me to college. He'd even promised me he'd let me run his cattle operation after I graduated. When Nancy got pregnant, he kicked me off the ranch and withdrew his financial support, called me trash and worse. I told Nancy I'd marry her, but Mike convinced her I was a worthless so-and-so who'd never amount to anything without his help, so she got scared and married Cal. Now her daddy's ranch is part of theirs." His dark face tightened at the memories.

"Go on," she urged softly.

"Mike had had his eyes on Nancy's folks' ranch for a lot of years, so I guess he could look past the moral issues where she was concerned. Eventually they talked me into giving up my rights to my daughter, Julie, too. Everybody, including me, thought I'd be a bad influence on a girl." He swallowed as if he were ashamed and looked up at her.

"I think you turned out all right."

Still, he'd lost Julie. She couldn't imagine giving up her baby forever, and yet if she believed it was really the best thing for the baby... Even so, it would put her in hell for the rest of her life.

"Back then...I convinced myself it would be better for her not to be divided between two fathers, especially since I was so damned bitter."

"Maybe someday you should pursue a relationship with Julie."

His troubled gaze met hers briefly. "I have. I've always been rebuffed. She thinks I abandoned her, which is understandable, I guess."

"Maybe someday...."

"Yeah. Maybe someday. She's kind of running wild right now. Nancy and Cal got so desperate they even lowered themselves to ask me to help, but she refuses to talk to me. She says she's gotten along without me all these years, so she reckons she doesn't need me now. Hell, maybe she's right."

Abby winced. Imagining how that must hurt, she went over to the couch and sat down beside him. Her thigh touched his. Gently, she took his hand.

He threaded her fingers through his and held on tight. "We have a lot to be thankful for. Maybe we should concentrate on that," he said.

He buried his face against her neck. His breath felt warm against her skin. She took his hand and placed it on her stomach.

Holding hands while resting on her tummy, they sat together like that for a long time. He was right. She knew they should concentrate on the baby and the joy they found in each other, on their successful careers and everything else that they had to be thankful for. She must be a very spoiled person to go on moping about Becky being missing and her father being inattentive.

"You know," Leo said. "I did something crazy earlier this week, something I was ashamed of at first."

"What?"

"For years I wanted revenge on Mike Ransom. A few months ago the chance to buy his ranch cheap for the Golden Spurs fell into my lap. This week I had the papers finalized, and I forced him to come into my office to sign them. I knew taking the Running R away from him was worse than pointing a gun at his head and pulling the trigger. I thought I wanted that until he hobbled in with a cane, still blustering and trying to act tough. But he was as pale as a sheet after he picked up his pen, I got scared he was about to have a heart attack."

"What did you do?"

"I grabbed the papers and tore them in two. I told him to get the hell out of my office. He growled at me and then headed toward the door, yelling he didn't want my charity. I started remembering how patient he'd been when he'd taught me to ride as a kid, so I asked him how Julie was.

"'Wilder than Connor ever was,'" he said.

"Ransom looked so lost and desperate as he stared at me that I couldn't just let him leave, so I said, 'Why don't you sit down while I call my banker? Maybe he could help you.'

"'Don't you think I've been to bankers?' he asked.

"'Not to mine.'

"'Like I said, I don't want your charity,' he told me.'

"'You're stubborn, old man. But so am I. It would just be a loan that you'd pay back…with interest.'

"'But you'd be pulling strings to get it.'

"'Look, whether we like it or not, we're family. You're the only grandfather Julie has. I know what you've done for her. And what I haven't done. Let's just say I'm repaying an old debt.'"

Abby took his hand. "I think that's wonderful."

"I think I was a damn fool."

They say time passes quickly when you're having fun. Autumn rushed by even faster than summer had. The long, hot days with summertime cicadas gave way to cooler, crisper mornings and breezy evenings. Being pregnant, Abby was glad the heat had abated.

She couldn't get into her regular clothes any longer, and when Leo constantly touched and stroked her belly, acting like he found her expanding figure more appealing than ever, she felt beautiful and sexy and loved.

How could a man she hadn't wanted to marry make her so happy? But was he happy?

As the months passed, and her due date neared, she wondered about his feelings. Deep down, did he still feel she'd trapped him? Would those feelings surface again?

She asked him constantly if he loved her. They'd be doing chores and having a conversation about work. Or he'd be getting into his truck to drive to San Antonio and suddenly she would touch his forearm and ask, "Leo, do you love me? Do you?"

One such evening they were walking toward the porch when she interrupted him with that question. He whirled and took her in his arms. Without taking his eyes from her face, he said. "I love you. How many times do I have to say it before you'll believe me?"

"I don't know. Again and again, I guess. Forever."

"Why can't you believe me?"

"Because no one ever has loved me. A least not so that I could count on them…."

"Hell, maybe I should be the one worrying about you loving me," he said.

"Do you…worry?"

"Yeah, I do," he admitted.

"But you know I love you!"

"Do I?"

"Yes!"

"Maybe you think you do now. What if you found out something…" He stopped, his expression tensing.

"Like what?"

"Nothing." But his face was dark and haunted, and his gaze was so piercing.

"Sometimes you watch me, just like you're looking at me now," she said, feeling uneasy. "Is there something you're not telling me?"

That telltale muscle jumped in his jawline, but he said, "I like looking at you because I love you. That's all."

But his voice was too smooth.

Something really was bothering him, eating at him. She was sure of it. Too often, she was aware of him watching her, his face silent and tense. If she asked him what was wrong, he would smile or snap at her that nothing was. He would touch her stomach and kiss her and say she was beautiful and that he'd never been happier. Then it would happen again. She would catch him watching her in that way that was beginning to worry her so much.

She wanted to believe that he loved her and that they

would have a happily-ever-after life, but she'd lost everyone who'd ever loved her, so maybe she'd been damaged in some way that made her be the kind of person people left.

He went out of his way on a daily basis to be thoughtful and kind. Maybe his kindnesses and passionate responses to her at night should have reassured her. Part of her thought that she shouldn't doubt him, that by doing that maybe she would make something bad happen. And yet something lay hidden beneath the outwardly peaceful surface of their marriage. She knew he wasn't being entirely truthful.

Everyone in her life had thrown her away. She prayed with all her heart he wouldn't do it, too.

When she wasn't worrying about her marriage, she wished her father would call or come. She wanted Connor to hurry up and find Becky.

Every time she mentioned her hopes about Becky to Leo, he would tense and then watch her in that worrisome way she hated, like he was afraid. But of what? Why did talking about Becky bother him?

Often Abby wanted to be with Leo so much she carried her computer to San Antonio and worked in his office. They could take breaks together and lunch together beside the lazy, brown river under giant cypress trees. Sometimes when she had meetings she couldn't get out of in Austin, he brought his computer to her office, and Kel would set up a desk for him beside Abby's. All too often Kel would breeze inside without knocking and catch them kissing, which she loved.

In fact, Kel became disgustingly, smugly conceited about Abby's newfound connubial bliss. When she dropped Abby at the San Antonio airport to meet Leo for their flight down to the Golden Spurs for Thanksgiving, Kel couldn't resist saying something.

"Look at you," Kel said, patting Abby's tummy. "All smiles and prettily pregnant. You all are so cute, the way you kiss all the time. Didn't I tell you he was great? Can't wait to see him, can you? How long has it been—all of eight hours?"

"Seven and a half. Hey, but don't you dare act like I owe all my newfound happiness to you. Besides, who knows how long it will last?"

"Don't borrow trouble, okay?"

"It's just that… Kel, I'm so afraid that it'll all go away."

"Honey, don't be." Kel's voice was soft with compassion. Then her eyes sparkled. "Hey, who's that tall, dark guy in the Stetson over there, devouring you with his black eyes?"

"Leo!" Abby squealed, the sight of him filling her with joy and fear. Then he swooped her into his arms, and she forgot to be afraid as his hard mouth claimed hers. She loved him so very much. Putting her arms around his neck, she clung, kissing him again and again while Kel made faces at her from behind his back.

"Abby!"

Abby leapt eagerly away from the foal she and Mia had been petting. The barn doors rolled open, and the next thing she heard were Leo's boots clicking on the concrete as he kept shouting her name. Even though she enjoyed Mia's company, she'd been missing Leo all morning while he was in the ranch office, discussing business with Cole and Shanghai.

Shanghai loped into the barn after Leo just as she pushed the stall door open.

"Mia!" Shanghai shouted.

"No, it's me," Abby said. "She's in the stall brushing Angelita, who's incredibly darling."

"Most young things are," Shanghai said, "which is why the world is overpopulated."

"Kinky broke into our business meeting and said he's ready to cut the turkey," Leo said, taking Abby's hand and bringing it to his lips. "I missed you."

"You've got him besotted," Shanghai said. "His gaze kept drifting toward the barn all morning. He didn't seem the least bit interested in discussing our renovations since the fire."

Abby smiled and squeezed Leo's hand. "It's Thanksgiving. You all shouldn't be talking business."

"Ranchers don't take holidays," Shanghai said.

"Have you made any progress locating the twins?" Mia asked as she closed the stall door.

"Some," Leo said.

"Well?"

"Well—nothing. It's too soon to talk about it."

"Leo?" Abby tugged warningly at his hand. "Why the defensive tone? Mia was just asking."

"I said it's too soon. Hell, can't we forget this? We came out here because it's time for dinner, not to discuss the missing twins."

"Mia didn't mean to upset you, darling."

"I'm not upset. You were the one who said it's a holiday. So let's just forget it."

"Fine," Abby whispered, even as a chill went through her.

Those were almost the last words Leo spoke that day. Whenever anyone asked him a question during dinner, he answered with a yes or a no but didn't elaborate. He remained withdrawn on the flight back to San Antonio, barely speaking to Abby. The next morning, he got up early, even though it was Saturday, and drove to his office.

Hours later, after she'd put up their Christmas tree and decorated the house all by herself, she began to wonder if he'd be home for dinner, so she called him on his cell.

"When are you coming home?"

"When I'm done here."

"Can't you bring your work home?"

"Look—"

"Leo, is there something wrong? Something you're not telling me about?"

"I've got a lot to do, that's all. Of course, I'd rather be with you," he said.

"That's all?"

"That's all."

"Why don't I believe you?"

"I don't know. Why don't you?"

"You always get upset about the Kemble twins…."

"I get upset about a lot of other things at work, too. You just don't see me here."

"You're sure that you're not upset about anything that has to do with us?"

He hesitated a beat too long. "No, dammit. Look, I'm sorry," he whispered, sounding worried. "The last thing I want to do is upset you. I'll be home before supper. Hell, I'll be home as fast as I can get there. It's you I want, though…not supper."

When he'd showed up an hour later, he'd swept her off her feet and carried her into the bedroom, where they'd made love for hours. Later, she'd awakened in the middle of the night and had found him at the window, staring outside, his hands clenched.

Something was wrong. She knew it. But until he told her, there was nothing she could do about it.

When she tiptoed across the room and laid her hand upon his arm, he jumped.

"Problems at work?" she whispered.

"Sometimes my thoughts won't stop."

He pulled her close and kissed her hair, her lips. But even though he held her and kissed her as she lay in his arms, she felt the coiled tension in his every muscle.

"Leo?"

"I love you," he said.

Then why, oh, why, did his bleak tone communicate such despair?

The baby was due around Christmas Day, and as Christmas approached she was so huge that Leo didn't want her on the road alone. So Abby put Kel in charge and quit driving into Austin to work. Abby handled what she could for In the Pink! by phone, fax and e-mail. In her spare time she busied herself decorating the nursery and buying presents for Leo and the baby.

She and Leo had chosen not to be told the baby's sex, so she lived in a constant state of excitement wondering whether they'd have a dark-haired boy like Leo or a beautiful little girl with shining black curls. Never once did she imagine her child looking like her.

Caught up in happy thoughts about the baby, she stopped dwelling so much on her absent father or Becky or even Leo's tension. Surely whatever was bothering Leo at work would soon resolve itself.

Lizzy and Mia e-mailed her constantly, mostly concerning the baby. With every e-mail and photo of her belly that she sent them, Abby's friendship deepened with the Kemble sisters.

Leo loved her. Abby loved him. They were joyously expecting a baby.

What could possibly go wrong?

Eleven

Connor held a photograph of girl with dark golden hair closer to his webcam.

"I've got a lead on Becky. I think maybe I've found her in Albuquerque, New Mexico."

The image on Leo's screen wavered. Connor wasn't holding the picture all that steady, but from what Leo could make out, except for the shorter hair, she looked almost exactly like Abby.

His throat tightened with alarm.

"You want me to fly out there?" Connor demanded eagerly. "Or do you want me to hold off until you gut up enough to have a conversation with your wife?"

"Go!"

"Leo, if this is our girl, you're going to have to tell her."

Leo knew that already. That didn't mean he was in

the mood for brotherly wisdom, spirituality, empathy, sympathy or whatever combination Connor chose to attack him with, so he said a curt goodbye and hung up. Then he picked up the folder on his desk labeled *Caesar's daughters: Abigail, Rebecca.*

For a long time he sat at his desk, thumbing through adoption records and Connor's reports on Abby and Becky. Feeling utterly disgusted with himself, he closed the folder and pitched it back onto his desk. Then he leaned forward on his elbows, steepled his fingers and stared into space for long minutes.

He had to tell her! His hands were shaking badly. His stomach twisted. He hadn't felt this coldly afraid in years. Not since Nancy had told him she was pregnant and Old Man Ransom had thrown him off the ranch and left him penniless and helpless. Not since Cal had called him dirt and had married his girl.

Hell, he was dirt now. He should have told Abby the truth a long time ago.

He was both in love with his wife and in lust with her. He'd never thought he could be this wildly happy with any woman. Or this miserable.

On one corner of his desk sat a tiny red jewelry box with a silver ribbon. Inside was a pricey gold horse pendant encrusted with diamonds along with a gold, choker necklace that he'd bought for Abby. He'd seen the miniature horse in a shop window and had thought of Abby the first time he'd seen her riding Coco. She'd looked slim and vibrant with her dark gold hair streaming behind her. He'd known instantly that he'd had to buy the horse for Abby for Christmas.

Not that the gift gave him any joy. If he didn't tell

her that he'd known who she was, that he'd bedded her knowing it, he stood to lose everything.

But when he told her, she might turn on him again as she had after that first night. As Nancy had.

"Why can't you understand why I had to marry Cal?"

He knew too well what it was like to be out in the cold.

He cursed. How many times had he rehearsed a speech and driven home to Abby, only to decide he didn't know what to say to her. He would see Nancy's shining eyes right before all hell had broken loose. Love was not an emotion he trusted.

Damn.

He had to tell Abby. First thing, as soon as he saw her. Tonight.

When the elevator opened, Miriam glanced up, her eager smile genuine and radiant. "Hello, Mrs. Storm. You're looking…"

"Big."

"But beautiful. How do you feel?"

Abby patted her belly. "Big. Really big. Really ready."

"I'll buzz Mr. Storm and let him know you're here. He'll be so happy to see you."

"No. I want to surprise him. I thought I'd invite him to lunch. If he's busy, I'll just go shopping until he has time."

"Well, you know where his office is."

Abby was smiling as she headed down the hall.

Kel had a meeting with one of In the Pink!'s clients this afternoon in San Antonio. Abby was glad that she'd asked Kel to stop by and give her a lift to Leo's office.

"You're sickeningly in love," Kel had teased as

she'd dropped her off in front of Leo's building. "Didn't I tell you?"

"It's rude to say I told you so every single time we talk."

"But didn't I tell you so?"

"Okay. Okay. You were right about happily ever after."

Abby was still smiling as she opened the doors to Leo's private office and found herself staring across the office at his empty black leather chair. "Leo?"

He didn't answer, so she shut the doors and then went over to his gleaming desk. She couldn't help but admire how neat his desk was compared to hers. A red Christmas present with a silver ribbon and a single file folder were the only items on top of the immense expanse of polished cherry that was his desk.

After reading the tag on the gift and realizing it was for her, she picked it up and shook it. Pleased that he'd taken the time to shop for her, she set it back down. She wished it was Christmas now so that she could open it and watch him open all his presents from her. But she had to wait. The elements of surprise and loving expectancy were part of the fun of Christmas that she'd always missed. Only this year, she would have what she'd always longed for: Leo and their baby and presents, lots and lots of carefully chosen presents. As soon as the baby was born and they could travel, they'd go down to the Golden Spurs to see Lizzy and Mia.

Vaguely Abby was aware of water running in Leo's bathroom as she leaned across his desk and lifted the folder. When she saw her name on the label, she started. Curious, she was about to open the file and read it when a door opened behind her.

"Darling, I'm so glad—"

She turned and smiled at him, but instead of running into his arms, she turned back because of what she'd just read on that label.

Caesar's daughters: Abigail, Rebecca.

When her eyes met his again, he froze. He was darkly flushed, guilt staining his cheeks.

As if in a daze, Abby flipped the folder open so violently adoption papers flew out onto his desk and floor. So did several all-too-familiar photographs of herself and Becky. She picked up a picture of Becky in braids and jeans and had to fight tears because her own memories flew at her like birds of prey.

Scattered among the photographs and adoption papers were several stapled reports from Connor's security agency about the missing twins. There was a DNA report that had to do with several beer bottles Abby had drunk out of that night Leo had picked her up in the bar.

With a little cry, Abby flipped pages in one of the reports about Rebecca Collins.

She began to shake. As she read, the awful feeling dislodged from the pit of her stomach and began to slowly crawl upward until it constricted her throat and cut off her breath.

Connor had been all over Texas and Mexico looking for Becky, but Abby knew that already.

Because she'd hired him.

What she hadn't known was that Becky and she were the missing Kemble twins.

How Connor and Leo must have laughed when she'd hired Connor. Like a fool, she'd played into their hands.

"Abby…"

At the sound of Leo's voice, directly behind her now, the fist around her throat tightened. Then the sadness and horror enveloping her turned into a roaring pain ripping her heart in two. Barely able to breathe, she sagged against the desk.

Leo said, "Darling, I can explain."

Darling. How she hated him calling her that now.

He was always so cocksure and confident, he probably thought he could talk his way out of this. He probably saw her as easy and needy and malleable.

To hell with him!

His tanned face began to spin, and suddenly it wasn't his face, it was Becky's.

Wait! Wait for me!

No! Come on!

Abby was shutting her eyes against the vision of Becky when Leo said, "If you'd just listen…."

Becky vanished, and Leo's tanned face came into sharp focus, his hair as shiny and black as wet ink, his stormy, pain-filled eyes flashing as he yanked his glasses off. He was outrageously handsome.

"You don't need to. I understand everything. Just leave me alone."

Intent on escaping him, she shoved herself away from his desk and stumbled toward the tall doors. But her legs were shaky, her gait uncertain, and since he was standing only a short distance from her, he got there much faster.

When he grabbed her arms and pulled her toward the leather sofa, she was too weak to fight him.

"I was going to tell you," he said.

"Sure you were."

"Connor told me to tell you right from the first."

"Then why didn't you?"

"Because I just didn't know how."

"And when did you first know the truth?" she demanded.

"Abby…"

"When?" she said through gritted teeth. "You've got to tell me."

"A few weeks maybe…before that night in the bar."

The fist strangling her throat, her heart, her soul squeezed tighter.

"Not that I was one hundred percent sure," he said.

"Why didn't you tell me then?"

"I had to make sure."

"By screwing me?"

"I took DNA samples."

"Right. The beer bottles," she mused, more to herself than to him. "You're nothing if not efficient. Why didn't you just do your job and take the damn bottles? Why the hell did you sleep with me?"

"Be fair. Why do you think? That was as much your idea as mine! You're the one who climbed on my table and started taking off your clothes!"

"No! You be fair! You've lied to me all along! About everything! I'll bet our entire life together is a lie! You don't love me. You just wanted to marry a Kemble."

"That's not true! I do love you!"

"You want to know something—I don't believe you! I was right about you in the beginning. CEOs like you are a despicable breed. I should know because I work with them every day. You're as ruthless and ambitious as the worst of them."

"Abby, I love—"

"Shut up! You didn't like being an outsider at the Golden Spurs, did you? Somebody they could hire and fire? You wanted to be an insider, and you saw me as your ticket. You wanted it so badly that you used my pregnancy to further your career by insisting on marriage. That's the real reason you married me!"

"No."

"I can't believe how touched I was when you pretended to be so understanding about Becky."

"I'm sorry."

"I'll never believe anything you say again! Never! Did you see me weak and vulnerable and so in need of your love that you could dupe me into believing what I'd always secretly wanted to believe, that there was somebody out there who could love me?"

"No! Hell, no!"

"You knew I'd thrown myself at Shanghai, didn't you? And that he'd dumped me for Mia? You thought I was vulnerable and easy—"

"No."

"Well, we may be having a baby together, but this marriage is over! I want you and your things out of my house tonight! I'll change the locks first thing tomorrow."

"You're upset. You don't know what you're saying. I'll drive you home."

"I'm upset? Who wouldn't be? But I know exactly what I'm saying. And I mean every word of it. I'm calling Kel. She'll drive me home. Not you! And, Leo, if you're smart, you won't tell the Kembles. They're my family. Not yours. I'll tell them who I am—when I'm good and ready. I don't mean this as a threat, but you'd better be prepared for the worst. You probably won't like my version of events."

Connor's blond head filled Leo's computer screen. "You look like shit."

"Thanks."

Not sleeping, not eating and drinking half the night took their toll in a helluva hurry. Leo didn't need Connor to tell him he had to get a grip.

"So what are you going to do now?" There was no trace of any I-told-you-so superiority edging Connor's voice. He was concerned and worried.

Leo finger-combed his black hair wearily. Last night when he'd gone over to try to deliver Abby's Christmas gifts, she'd forgotten to pull her kitchen shade. He'd caught a glimpse of her through her kitchen window when she'd come to see who was on her porch.

She'd been as big as a house in her white bathrobe, but beautiful—oh, so heart-stoppingly beautiful. And sad. He'd broken her heart.

For a long moment their eyes had met and held. His breath had caught in his throat. So had hers. His pulse had raced. Then she'd snapped the shade shut, and he'd felt lost and lonely—truly horrible. Was she going to hate him forever?

He'd knocked and knocked, pounded, yelled. In the end he'd had to leave her gifts on the porch.

His life was a mess. He was a mess.

He felt sick at heart, exhausted. It had been a long, dismal week since Abby had kicked him out and changed her locks. Even if his nights were hell, he'd been trying to work during the days. Connor and he had just finished discussing Connor's report on his trip to Albuquerque. Connor hadn't found Becky after all, but he thought it wouldn't be long.

"What can I do to get Abby back?" Leo muttered. He felt lonely and pathetic. "The only way she'll communicate with me is through Kel or through her closed door. So I talk to Kel every day and yell through her door." He didn't add that he'd drunk half a fifth of scotch after he'd gone home and was still feeling the effects from the hangover.

"Keep trying. I'll pray. What about the Kembles? How are they taking the news?"

"They haven't said anything, so I don't think she's told them. But frankly, I don't care what she tells them."

"Well, that's a switch."

"All I want is Abby."

"Tell her that."

"I would…if she'd open her door or answer her damn phone."

"You dug yourself a mighty deep hole."

"I just hope to hell it isn't my grave."

"Look, I don't like the fact that you're going through this alone, but I've got too much going on to get down to the ranch anytime soon. So if you end up with nowhere to go on Christmas, you're always welcome in Houston."

Nowhere to go….

"Thanks. But I want to be near Abby, just in case. And Kel's sworn she'll let me know when Abby goes into labor."

"Okay. I've gotta go. I'd wish you a Merry Christmas. But since that doesn't seem appropriate, I'll just pray it gets merrier real fast."

"You do that."

Abby sat sipping milk in her living room. Christmas Day was dark and gray but no darker than her sorrowful mood. She kept seeing Leo's face framed by her kitchen window. He'd looked so sad and apologetic… and handsome, too. She'd wanted to touch him. To feel his body against her own.

He was a rat. An ambitious, lying, scheming rat. Determined not to think about him, she shut her eyes. Her stomach felt tight, but that was probably only because she was so big. The baby was due any day, and she felt increasingly anxious out here on her own. She was huge and unwieldy, and it wasn't easy to get up and down off the low sofa without Leo around to help her.

To hell with Leo. The last thing she needed was a man who only wanted her because she was aligned with the rich family he worked for. At least she wouldn't have to spend Christmas alone. She'd be sharing Christmas dinner with Kel's family, and Kel would be coming over later to drive her there. But that was hours away, so she had the morning all to herself.

When she finished her milk, her stomach tightened again. Gasping, she remained on the couch. She needed to wash some clothes and towels and do a few dishes, but she lacked the energy to attack the mundane chores. With her stomach muscles knotting, she felt increasingly uncomfortable, so she just sat, listening to her own breathing as the walls seemed to close in on her.

She thought about her father and then made herself

push those attachments aside. Trying not to feel sorry for herself, she bit her lower lip and stared at the mountain of gifts Leo had left for her last night and that she'd placed under their tree.

Under *her* tree.

She'd never before had so many beautifully wrapped presents, and they were all from Leo. She shouldn't have brought them in. She shouldn't have put them under her tree, but she'd never had so many presents. She hadn't been able to resist keeping them. She was especially fascinated by the small red box with the silver ribbon that she'd seen on his desk that horrible day when her fantasy world had blown up in her face. She knew it had been the last he'd purchased and couldn't help wondering what it was.

His gifts shouldn't mean anything, not now. Not when she knew the truth. His marriage had been a career move. Period.

She'd hated him that day in his office when she'd read about Becky and he'd confessed about the DNA samples. She'd vowed to hate him forever, but he'd been so sweet and attentive for so many months. And those memories haunted her. Even now he kept up his act—calling her, dropping by, sending her notes. Not that she'd answered her phone or the door. And she'd shredded all his notes without reading them. But only after clutching them to heart and nearly dying of curiosity. And yes, she was such a sap, the bits and pieces were in her lingerie drawer. The guy deserved an Oscar. He really did.

He'd made sure Coco was taken care of, and he'd ordered her to stay away from the barn until after the baby was born.

She knew his interest had to do with his ambition. No doubt he was scared as hell she'd say something to the Kembles to destroy his career. And maybe she would. It would serve him right. But every time she picked up the phone to call Lizzy and tell her what a rat Leo was, she hesitated. She couldn't forget lying in his arms after they'd made love even if she wanted to.

She closed her eyes. If only her father would call. The stillness of the house was driving her crazy. Didn't he know it was Christmas Day and that he should call?

She picked up her phone and dialed her father's cell. He didn't answer, of course, so she left another message.

"Daddy, I…I want to wish you a Merry Christmas. I sent you a gift, and I keep wondering if you got it. Where are you? Did you get any of my messages asking whether Becky and I are adopted? It's really, really important that you get back to me on that. I…I'd like to hear from you. I miss you so much. And, Daddy, I'm going to have the baby any day now. I wish…I wish that you could be here…because, Daddy, I—I left Leo…and I'm all alone. Daddy, I…I need you so much."

A robotic male voice that wasn't even a recording of her father's voice said she had thirty seconds left, so she hung up without telling him she loved him.

Daddy, why can't you be here for me…just this once?

Never had Abby felt so alone, and it was all Leo's fault. For a few brief months when he'd been with her, she'd had the illusion she was loved. He'd made her feel so complete when he'd walked in the door at night and kissed her hello and pretended he was glad to see her. Even when he'd helped her load the dishwasher, or when he'd gone to the barn to help with Coco, she'd felt he'd done those things because he'd loved her.

All of it, every precious kiss and glance and thoughtful act, even the Christmas gifts that mesmerized her, had been part of a big, calculated lie to serve Leo Storm's ruthless ambition.

He was a heartless CEO to the core.

She'd been a vulnerable, stupid, naive fool.

Well, never again!

Twelve

Abby heard Kel's knock on her front door. She was rushing to answer it, when her stomach tightened. This time the pain was so excruciating she doubled over and took several deep breaths. In the next instant, she felt something wet trickling down her leg.

Her water had broken.

Oh my God. The baby is coming.

Her first thought was of Leo. Then she hated herself for wanting him so much.

Slowly she moved toward the door, but when she opened it, Leo was actually there.

"Don't slam it," he whispered, wedging his boot inside.

He looked thinner. Last night she hadn't noticed the lines of suffering etched beneath his eyes and beside his mouth. He hadn't bothered to shave or wash his hair, and there were circles under his eyes. His T-shirt and normally creased jeans were dirt-stained and limp with sweat. He certainly didn't look like the self-confident CEO she'd married, and if he were any other human being, she would have felt compassion.

"Where's Kel?" She tried to stand up straight. She was determined to feel nothing for him even though some part of her—that weak, naive, stupid, fatherless little girl that longed to be loved—was joyously glad he was here.

"Outside," he said. "In her car. She's waiting to pick you up."

"She knows what you did and how I feel. I can't believe that she would—"

"Abby, don't be mad at her. It's Christmas. I had to see you, to make sure you're okay. She felt sorry for me and let me knock on your door."

"Well, you've seen me. I'm okay. I want you to go. Get Kel. I need—"

Her stomach tightened, and the awful pain made her squint to hold back her tears. Even so, she grabbed her belly.

"What is it?" He stepped forward, his voice rough with concern.

"Nothing," she said, but she was gasping. And he wasn't stupid.

Understanding dawned and his tanned face tensed. "It's the baby," he said softly. "How far along are the pains?"

"They're not exactly pains."

"Contractions then?"

"I haven't been timing them, but I've been having them all morning. And I think my water just broke."

"Why the hell didn't you call me?"

"You are the last person—"

"Right." Pain flashed in his eyes and was gone. "Save it," he muttered fiercely. "Do you have a bag packed?"

She nodded, suddenly glad in spite of herself that he was here and taking charge.

She'd missed him. She'd missed him so much. And she needed him.

"Abby, I know you don't believe me, but I love you. Not because you're a Kemble heiress, but because you're you. After losing Nancy and Julie, I never thought I'd get a second chance, and that makes you and the baby doubly precious."

He would have said more, but her stomach tightened painfully again. Then Kel came up behind him.

Torn, Abby bit her lips in pain.

Instantly, Leo was all business. He told Abby to get changed and ordered Kel to find fresh towels for Abby to sit on in the truck. He grabbed Abby's suitcase and something from under the tree. Then he went out and drove his truck right up to the back door.

He was an ambitious, lying rat. She'd been trying to convince herself she loathed him all week. Still, it was hard to throw a man out when he was making himself so useful.

Before she knew what was happening, he lifted her into his arms and carried her down the steps.

"I...I want Kel," she said as he opened his door and helped her climb into the cab. Not that she really wanted Kel. His arms about her felt too good.

"I'll be right behind you," Kel said, taking Abby's hand reassuringly. "Besides, I'm so nervous I might have a wreck. He's a good man," she added. "And he loves you. He's told me that every single day, and I for one believe him." She leaned closer. "Nobody's perfect,

Abby. You should know that. You've never gone out with anybody who comes close to this guy. If it was me, I'd forgive him in a heartbeat and never look back. The fact that you're a Kemble is a plus. Who knows, the guy will probably find your sister for you."

Abby didn't say anything. To his credit, once they were both buckled inside his truck, Leo simply drove. Not once did he try to defend himself again or apologize. He simply kept his eyes glued to the road and concentrated on getting them safely to Austin. Her stomach kept tightening, and every contraction hurt more than the last.

Did he love her? Maybe he wasn't perfect. But if he loved her, wouldn't that be enough? Did he have to be as perfect as some ideal husband like the guys she read about in women's magazines? Did guys who did every single thing right even exist?

The next contraction had her panting.

Vaguely she was aware of Leo's foot on the gas pedal. The pastures and houses on the outskirts of Austin whipped by. He was passing every vehicle on the road now.

She would figure it all out later. Right now they were having a baby.

Their baby.

Tucked into crisp white sheets with her black-haired son making gurgling sounds as he sucked her nipple and Leo standing proudly beside her, Abby felt serene, if a little tired.

Very tired.

Surely the happiest days are when babies are born. As long as she lived, Abby would never forget the explosion of her son's little cry or how warm and loving

Leo's dark eyes had been above his blue surgical mask. She'd felt like a queen giving birth to a prince...and like a beloved wife, as well.

To have a healthy, normal son with a man she loved. A man who loved her. Did life get much better?

"Will you ever forgive me?" Leo asked.

His eyes blazed, but his countenance was suddenly as pale as a man facing a firing squad.

"I already have. Come here, my darling."

When he moved closer, she took his big, tanned hand in hers and turned it over. Then she brought it to her cheek and held it there, needing his warmth, his strength. "I already have. I want our son to know his father."

"What about you?" he demanded huskily.

The dark pain that lingered in his voice made her heart throb.

"I never stopped loving you. I tried, but I can't. You made my life too beautiful, and I missed you too much. When I went into labor, the only thing I wanted was you with me. You make feel safe. I've never felt that way before. Not with anybody. Not even before Becky ran away."

"You damn sure had me fooled."

"I had me fooled, too."

His fingertip traced her mouth lovingly. "Oh, Abby..."

"Do you think you'll ever find my sister?"

"I'll find her...or die trying. As you know, I can be pretty ruthless when I want something. Sometimes that's a good trait. And speaking along those lines..."

When he stopped talking, she met his eyes again, only this time they were sparkling.

"Guess who's outside," he said.

"I can't imagine."

"Your father. I had Connor track him down and haul him here bodily. He was in a South American jungle in a terrorist camp, writing the story of a lifetime. But he can't wait to see you and his grandson."

"First…kiss me and hold me, Leo, my precious darling."

Leo didn't make her beg.

Very gently he leaned over the bed, careful not to mash her IV or their son. Their lips met tentatively, first in love and forgiveness and then with eagerness and desire. A long time later, he kissed the top of their son's dark head.

Then he said, "I'll get your father."

"Merry Christmas," her father said as soon as he walked into her hospital room, carrying an armload of presents.

She imagined Leo had bought the presents for him because her father had never bought a present in his life, or at least not that she knew of. But that was okay. Her father was here.

When he leaned down to kiss her cheek, he reeked of cigarettes and leather and jungle scents. His face was rough against her cheek—he needed a shave, but she didn't care. He was here at last. And all because of Leo.

"Merry Christmas, darling," Leo said as she met his gaze over her father's shoulder.

"Merry Christmas," she replied. "The first of many together…I hope."

"I promise you a lifetime of Merry Christmases," Leo said.

And she believed him.

"I can't wait to get home and open that red box with the silver ribbon," she whispered.

"You don't have to wait. I have it right here." Grinning, he pulled it out of his pocket.

When he handed it to her, she pounced on the silver ribbon with the greediness of a child who'd waited a lifetime for a real Christmas.

Her father laughed, but she cried when she saw the exquisite, diamond-studded horse.

"Coco?"

"I think I fell in love with you the first time I saw you riding her," Leo said.

Circling his neck with one arm as she cradled their son in the other, she pulled him down, and he kissed her for a very long time.

Epilogue

A throng of Kembles pressed close to Leo and his golden wife, who was standing proudly beside him as she held little Caesar Kemble Storm in her arms outside the Golden Spurs Ranch chapel. Everybody wanted a closer glimpse of the baby. Even Joanne, who'd been less than pleased when Abby's true identity had been announced.

The February day was bright and warm. Not that that was the least bit unusual in South Texas.

"Well, I guess this makes you family now," Joanne said to Leo with a slight edge in her tone.

"I guess," he replied lazily.

Mia and Lizzy had been thrilled to learn who Abby really was. While not as pleased, Joanne had not seemed surprised when Abby and Leo had gone down to the Golden Spurs for a weekend right after baby Caesar had been born to tell Lizzy and Mia who Abby really was.

But Joanne had grudgingly accepted Abby as if her presence in their family was inevitable, and she'd even congratulated Leo several times. Then, strangely, as she had at the wedding, Joanne had asked Abby about her father and hung on every word as Abby had told her about his most recent visit.

"Did he ever tell you that you were adopted?"

"Not until I asked him during his last visit. He said he'd always intended to when Becky and I were grown, but that when Becky disappeared, he couldn't face it."

"He always seemed so unafraid to me. I was the one—" She broke off.

Again Abby wondered about Joanne's intense fascination with her father.

"How did you know my father?"

"We were friends, briefly," was all Joanne had said. Abby imagined her father must have neglected her because of his work.

Now Lizzy jingled a pair of tiny spurs in front of baby Caesar's plump hands, causing Abby to forget her earlier conversation with Joanne.

"I thought baby Caesar held up pretty well for the service," Lizzy said with a big smile. "These are his, and when you all leave, I'm definitely hanging them on the Spur Tree. Right beside Daddy's."

Abby felt happier every time she was with her admiring new family and their friends. The chapel and the Big House along with all the other buildings had been freshly painted since the fire. It had rained a lot in January, and there hadn't been a freeze, so lush green grass covered most of the earth that had been black last summer.

"Baby Caesar, you were way, way better than my

Vanilla during the service," Mia said. "She's over there sulking by the barbeque pit because I am here bragging on you." Not that Mia's voice was harsh as she told stories about her lively daughter while tugging at the baby's big toe.

Baby Caesar squirmed and bit his fist as if he were drawing on the last of his reserves to be patient.

"I'm afraid I need to feed him," Abby said right before he let out an anxious little cry.

Bunching his fingers, he jammed them frantically into his mouth. When that didn't soothe him, he began to kick. Then he let out another cry.

Smoke from portable barbeque pits drifted lazily against a cloudless blue sky. Immense white tents had been put up on the back lawn to accommodate the guests, who had been invited to celebrate three new members being brought into the family.

While Mia and Lizzy had been wild to welcome Abby, the baby and Leo into the family, it was Joanne who'd suggested that baby Caesar be christened on the ranch where all family members were always christened. Of course, a christening called for a real celebration, and since they were ranchers in South Texas, a celebration called for barbeque, beer and mariachis. The musicians were setting up near the Big House.

No sooner had Abby agreed than Lizzy had overnighted Caesar Kemble's original yellowed christening gown with a note that said baby Caesar *had* to wear the founder's gown.

So here Abby was, standing by her husband as she held their wriggling baby, and surrounded by her family, too.

Finally, after everybody had gotten to pinch the baby's

toes and arms and talk baby talk to him, Leo took Abby's hand to lead her to a private parlor in the Big House where she could feed the baby before they ate lunch.

When they were alone with their baby suckling at her breast, Leo leaned down and kissed Abby long and deeply. Like all his kisses, this one promised her forever.

Without thinking, she touched the exquisite little horse with the diamond bridle at her throat that Leo had given her for Christmas. Then her hand fell to the dark, downy curls on her baby's head.

Her father was back in Argentina, and she hadn't heard from him since he'd left. Still, on the morning of his departure he'd told her how he and Electra had selected an adoption agency to arrange the adoption.

"Electra was an old friend of mine. We'd collaborated on several books. She came to me when she was pregnant, and I told her how much your mother and I wanted children. And your mother and I were so happy…for a little while—before Becky disappeared and everything went wrong."

"Yes. We were happy."

"If only…." He'd paused. "I drive myself to write, you know, so I won't think about it. I've become something of an adrenaline junkie."

"Maybe you should reach out to someone new."

"I tried that once, not so long ago. And got my heart busted up all over again. No thanks."

"I'm sorry, Daddy."

"It's okay."

Abby wasn't going to think about her father or worry about Becky right now. She had too many blessings to count. In fact, she'd never been happier as she sat in a rocking chair with her blouse unbuttoned and Caesar pressed close, her husband smiling lovingly down at her.

She couldn't have imagined such happiness. Not ever. Not in her wildest dreams.

Maybe, soon, Leo would find Becky for her and her daddy.

If any man could, Leo would.

* * * * *

Turn the page for a sneak preview of
The CEO's Christmas Proposition
by Merline Lovelace
This glamorous Christmas story is available
from Mills & Boon® Desire™ in December 2009.

The CEO's Christmas Proposition
by
Merline Lovelace

Shoulders hunched against the icy sleet pounding Germany's Dresden International Airport, Devon McShay grimaced at the Christmas carols belting from the outdoor loudspeakers.

"Okay," she muttered under her breath. "Call me Mrs. Scrooge. Call me the Grinchette. Call me the ultimate Krank. I hate this time of year."

Well, that wasn't totally true. The hopeless idealist in her still wanted to believe people might someday actually heed the messages of joy and peace the season signified. *If* they could get past the crass commercialization, that is. Not to mention the hole they dug for themselves every year by splurging on gifts they couldn't afford.

Her parents' increasingly bitter arguments over finances had always peaked this time of year and led eventually to an even more bitter divorce. Christmases after that had become a battleground, with each parent trying to outdo the other to win a daughter's love.

Devon's own holiday track record was just as dismal. As she sloshed through ankle-deep slush toward the terminal, she shook her head at her incredible idiocy in falling for a too-handsome, too-cocky newscaster at Dallas's Channel Six. Silly her, she'd actually thought she'd broken the Christmas curse when Blake caught her under the mistletoe and slipped a diamond on her finger. Exactly one year later, she'd walked into the station to find her husband with his hand under the miniskirt of a female Santa and his tongue halfway down her throat.

Devon had put her jerk of an ex out of her life, but even now, three years later, she couldn't work up any enthusiasm for colored lights or eggnog. That's why she'd jumped at the chance to avoid yet another season of forced Christmas cheer when her friend and business partner came down with the flu yesterday, mere hours before she was supposed to leave for Germany.

Devon, Sabrina Russo and Caroline Walters had been friends before they became business partners. They'd met while spending their junior year at the University of Salzburg. Filled with the dreams and enthusiasm of youth, the three coeds had formed a fast friendship.

They'd maintained that friendship long-distance in the years that followed. Until last May, when they'd met for a minireunion. After acknowledging that their lives so far hadn't lived up to their dreams, they'd decided to pool resources, educational backgrounds and interests. Two months later, they'd quit their respective jobs, relocated to Virginia and launched European Business Services, Incorporated. EBS for short. Specializing in arranging transportation, hotels, conference facilities and translation services for busy executives.

The venture was still at the risky stage. The three friends had sunk most of their savings into start-up costs. EBS now had an office, a small staff and a slew of international advertising. They'd landed a few jobs, but nothing big until the call from Cal Logan's executive assistant.

Turns out Logan had played football in college with one of Sabrina's old boyfriends. Said boyfriend had tipped his pal to EBS when Logan mentioned his people were scrambling to lay on a short-notice trip to Germany. Sabrina had worked twenty hours straight on the prep work and had been all set to hop a plane yesterday afternoon when the bug hit.

So here Devon was, her chin buried in a hot pink pashmina shawl, her toes frozen inside her stacked heel boots and her ears assaulted by a booming rendition of "O Tannenbaum," on her way to meet their first major client.

Again.

He'd been scheduled to arrive earlier this morning, but his assistant had called to say his corporate jet had been grounded due to icing. After considerable effort, she'd gotten him on the last commercial flight out before JFK shut down completely.

Ah, the joys of traveling this time of year! Conditions here in Dresden weren't much better. Sleet had been coming down all day. Praying her client's plane made it in before this airport closed, too, Devon hurried into the terminal.

Her breath whistled out in a sigh of relief when Logan exited Customs. She recognized him right away from the newspaper and magazine articles Sabrina had found on the Internet during her frantic prep work.

Caleb John Logan, Jr. Thirty-one. Six-two. With jet-black hair, laser blue eyes and a linebacker's shoulders under his charcoal-gray cashmere overcoat. His jaw-dropping good looks didn't score him any points with Devon, however. She'd learned the hard way not to trust handsome heartbreakers like Cal Logan.

But he was a client. An important one. And she was willing to give someone who'd served a hitch in the Marines before earning a B.S. from the University of Oregon, an MBA from Stanford and his first million at the ripe old age of twenty-six the benefit of the doubt.

Right up until he spotted the hot pink pashmina, that is.

Sabrina had indicated she'd be wearing it, and the

flash of color was certainly more visible than the sign Devon held up with his name on it. So she wasn't surprised when Logan picked her out of the crowd and cut in her direction. She'd just plastered on her best EBS smile when he whipped an arm around her waist. The next moment, she was sprawled against his cashmere-covered chest.

"Hello, Brown Eyes."

Swooping down, he covered her mouth with his.

Sheer astonishment kept Devon rooted to the spot for a few seconds while her mind whirled chaotically. Her first thought was that her client had downed a few too many drinks during the long flight. Her second, that he'd seriously mistaken the kind of escort and consulting services EBS provided. Her third shoved everything else out of her head.

Whoa, mama! The man could kiss!

His mouth moved over hers with a skill that ignited sparks at a half-dozen flash points throughout her body. Devon hadn't experienced that kind of spontaneous combustion in a while. A *long* while.

The sparks were still popping when she pushed off his chest, only now they fueled a flush of anger.

"Do you always greet women you don't know with a lip-lock, Mr. Logan?"

A smile crinkled the skin at the corners of his eyes. "As a matter of fact, I don't. That was from Don."

"Huh?"

"He said he owed you one from New Year's Eve two years ago and made me promise to deliver it."

She stared up at him in total incomprehension. Logan hooked a brow and attempted to prompt a nonexistent memory.

"He abandoned you at the Waldorf. Five minutes before midnight. To deliver twins."

"I don't have a clue who or what you're—"

Understanding burst like a water balloon.

"Wait a sec. Are you talking about Sabrina's old boyfriend? Your buddy, who's now an ob-gyn doc?"

It was Logan's turn to look startled. He recovered faster than Devon had, though. His smile widened into a rueful grin.

"I take it you're not Sabrina Russo."

"No, Mr. Logan, I am not. And if you'd listened to any of the voice mails we left on your cell phone in the past twenty-four hours," Devon added acidly, "you'd know Sabrina came down with the flu and couldn't make the trip."

"Sorry. I've been in the air for twenty-three of those twenty-four hours. I had to make a quick trip to the West Coast before turning right around and heading for Germany."

She knew that. Still, that was no excuse for his behavior. Or…what was worse…her reaction to it.

"My cell-phone battery crashed somewhere over Pennsylvania," he said, his smile holding an apology now. "I crashed somewhere over the Atlantic. Any chance we can erase what just happened and start again?"

Oh, sure. As soon as her lips stopped tingling and

her nerves snapping. Reminding herself that he was a client, Devon forced a stiff nod.

"Good." He shifted his briefcase to his left hand and held out his right. "I'm Cal Logan. And you are?"

"Devon McShay. One of Sabrina's partners."

"The history professor."

So he'd done some checking on the small firm he'd hired to work the details of his five-day, three-city swing through Germany.

"Former history professor," she corrected as she led the way toward the baggage-claim area. "I quit teaching to join forces with Sabrina and Caroline at EBS."

"Quite a career shift."

"Yes, it was."

She left it at that. No need to detail her restlessness after her divorce. Or her ex's very public, very mortifying attempt at reconciliation on the six o'clock news. Dallas hadn't been big enough for both of them after that.

That was when she'd quit her job and joined forces with her two friends. Now Devon the history prof, Sabrina the one-time party girl and Caroline the shy, quiet librarian were hard-nosed businesswomen. With pretty much the future of their fledgling enterprise hanging on how well Devon handled Cal Logan's trip.

After this rocky start, she thought grimly, things weren't looking real good.

© Merline Lovelace 2008

2 FREE BOOKS
AND A SURPRISE GIFT

We would like to take this opportunity to thank you for reading this Mills & Boon® book by offering you the chance to take TWO more specially selected books from the Desire™ 2-in-1 series absolutely FREE! We're also making this offer to introduce you to the benefits of the Mills & Boon® Book Club™—

- **FREE home delivery**
- **FREE gifts and competitions**
- **FREE monthly Newsletter**
- **Exclusive Mills & Boon Book Club offers**
- **Books available before they're in the shops**

Accepting these FREE books and gift places you under no obligation to buy, you may cancel at any time, even after receiving your free books. Simply complete your details below and return the entire page to the address below. You don't even need a stamp!

YES Please send me 2 free Desire stories in a 2-in-1 volume and a surprise gift. I understand that unless you hear from me, I will receive 2 superb new 2-in-1 books every month for just £5.25 each, postage and packing free. I am under no obligation to purchase any books and may cancel my subscription at any time. The free books and gift will be mine to keep in any case.

Ms/Mrs/Miss/Mr_____ Initials _____

Surname _____
Address _____
_____ Postcode _____

Send this whole page to: Mills & Boon Book Club, Free Book Offer, FREEPOST NAT 10298, Richmond, TW9 1BR